BARNEY

A NOVEL

(ABOUT A GUY CALLED BARNEY)

GUY SIGLEY

Book Layout ©2013 BookDesignTemplates.com

Barney—A novel (about a guy called Barney) / Guy Sigley -- 1st ed.
ISBN (print) 978-0-9945483-1-3

For my wife, Anna, who makes everything better

ONE

You're not supposed to get fired from the public service.

It's supposed to be a job for life. A reliable paycheck until the day you retire. Or drop dead. But I'm still very much alive—it's clear from the anxiety pains crushing my chest—and yet no longer serving the public. Instead, I'm sitting at my kitchen table watching my flatmate Lucien disregard all adherence to law and order. He's pouring a half-empty box of fruit muesli into the plain muesli container, which is still one-quarter full.

Why? you ask.

Because he has no respect.

No respect for me. No respect for muesli. No respect for civilization.

"You all right, Barney, mate?" Lucien asks. "You look like a rabid dog with reflux."

I ignore my burning esophagus. "I'm fine. I just don't know why you can't keep the fruit and plain muesli separate."

"What difference does it make? It all tastes like cardboard. I only eat it for the guns." Lucien cocks his right arm and flexes his biceps, which expand like a water balloon against his tight, three-hundred-dollar business shirt. He chews with his mouth open, grins, and gives me a wink. "It's all for the ladies, baby."

I'm not sure what's more disturbing: comparing Lucien's biceps to my own, which have never developed beyond functional competence; his use of the word *baby*; or the resentment I feel toward the man who has shared a home with me for the past year. But without his weekly rent, I would have defaulted on my mortgage quicker than you can say "loser in his thirties who doesn't own any property."

That, and I've been hoping to meet a girlfriend through one of his many female "companions." So far, he's introduced me to his mother and great-aunt. Not exactly a great return on investment.

"So what's on for today, Barney?" Lucien asks. "Another seven hours and thirty-six minutes of wasting taxpayers' money?" This is his favorite joke. To belittle my chosen profession. I think the ribbing is meant to invoke camaraderie.

But the joke's on *him* because I haven't wasted any taxpayers' money for the past three weeks. Not since they fired me.

"Actually, mate, I've got a pretty busy day of campaign planning ahead of me. And I'm chairing a recruitment panel for a new communications adviser."

"The next breed of slacker, eh?"

Lucien chucks his bowl into the sink. It still contains half-eaten muesli, and milk splashes onto the backsplash (a name that encourages, in my opinion, just this kind of reckless behavior). He strides into the bathroom, only three strides away thanks to me buying an apartment so small that I'm scared I'll roll over in the night and end up in Lucien's bed. A terrifying thought given that I know *exactly* how often he washes his sheets.

I get up from the table, rinse out my bowl, and put it in the dishwasher. Lucien's atrocity waits defiantly in front of me. Try as I might, I can't stand the sight of it. My mind conjures up the various bacteria and other life-threatening organisms that will migrate to the leftovers, colonize, and breed generations of disease over the course of the day.

My arms tingle at the imagined microscopic filth frolicking along my skin.

I hear my mother's voice: "You need to teach people how to treat you, Barney." Or was that Oprah? Or Dr. Phil? They all sound the same in my head. Despite their advice, I cave. Again.

After decontaminating the bowl, my physical condition improves, but my resentment toward my handsome and muscular cash cow increases. Someone really needs to teach him a lesson. For his own good, of course. You know, teach a man to buy a fish kind of thing.

The beautiful bovine emerges from the bathroom like he's just walked onstage at Wembley Stadium.

I resist the urge to cheer.

"I'm leaving in three minutes if you want a lift," Lucien says.

"Nah, I'm right, thanks. I'll jump on the tram."

"Why? You hate trams. All those people touching you and flicking their hair in your face. Not to mention having to steady yourself on a handrail that's still warm from the last person who held it. I mean, who knows where *their* hands have been?"

He's mocking me, of course, but everything he says is true.

"Come on, I rarely leave this late. Take advantage. You know chicks dig my car."

Which is so irrelevant, I don't even know how to object. "All right, but let me brush my teeth first."

The bathroom looks like it just stepped out of a washing machine. Lucien has strewn wet towels everywhere—why anyone would need that many towels, I'll never know—and he's not only used my toothpaste, but also left the cap off so that a little fluoride worm has escaped out the top. Disgusting.

As I'm cleaning my teeth, I open the medicine cabinet in search of a cotton bud—clean ears are an indicator of long life—and immediately regret my lapse in judgment. In front of me is a line of lipstick caps. All different shades. All different brands. Even different sizes. Not the lipsticks themselves, just the caps. These are Lucien's mementos of girlfriends past. Seriously, the guy can't put the top back on a tube of toothpaste, but he somehow manages to steal a lipstick lid from every girl reckless enough to fall into his toned arms.

It's creepy and, for at least the fifth time this morning, I wish I could afford to throw him out. Instead, I pick up his wet towels, put them in the washing machine, and head out the door for another day of pretending I have a job.

* * *

You might be wondering why I bother pretending I have a job. Why don't I just tell Lucien the truth? Well, let me ask you this: have you ever had a highly successful flatmate and *not* had a job? It's humiliating. Lucien already thinks I'm a hack because he works in the private sector and makes twice as much money as I do. He only lives with me because he's involved in some sort of tax rort that means he can't move into his investment property before a set time has elapsed. Confessing that I lost my job would surrender the upper hand I have gained in owning this apartment, even if said upper hand is only a perception. But you know what they say: perception is nine-tenths of the law.

So I let Lucien drop me off where I used to work, and smile and wave at him like a little boy on his first day of school. He ignores me and speeds off in his black convertible. Then my pocket vibrates and I hear his phone ring. Which is odd given that he just sped off in his black convertible.

I take the phone out and realize that, because we have the same model, I've accidentally picked his up. I check the screen; private number. Better answer in case one of his parents died or something.

"Hello, Lucien's phone."

"Hello, Lucien's phone, it's Lucia."

I wonder if this is a joke. On account of her more or less sharing his name.

"Is this a joke?"

Lucia laughs, and it sounds like a bottle of red wine being poured over chocolate cake. "You're not playing hard to get are you, Lucien?" Her accent, from what I can tell, is Italian. It makes me want to order a pizza.

And it makes me outraged at the injustice of it all!

Lucien just drove away in a sports car that cost more than my annual salary, while I stand in front of the organization that just canceled my annual salary and talk to a woman who, were it not for this case of mistaken identity, would never talk to me *because* of my annual salary.

Another beguiling creature is going to fall into his trap, have her lipstick cap stolen, and then be discarded. I can't bear it.

"Of course I'm not playing hard to get, Lucia. That would make me a madman."

"*Molto bene*, Lucien. But what's happened to your voice? We only met once, but it sounds higher than I remember."

I hold my nose. "Blocked sinuses."

"Are you all right?"

"Nothing a spray of salt water won't fix!"

"Whatever you say. So where are we having dinner tonight?"

Here we go. Barney to the rescue.

"I'm so sorry, but I have to cancel. My flatmate is performing at a sellout stand-up comedy show tonight and I promised him I'd be there."

There's a pause. "Really? The public service loser you told me about?"

What? Is that what Lucien thinks of me?

"Did I really say he's a loser?"

"You told me he's a single guy in his thirties who works for the government and doesn't own a car."

"Well, you've got a pretty liberal definition of loser if that's all you're working with."

"Okaaay."

"Anyway, it's sold out, so you can't come."

"Lucien, what's going on? Have I done something wrong?"

"No, but I have. So it's best if you don't call me anymore." I hang up, which is a bit harsh, I know, but I've done her a favor.

The phone rings again and the caller ID displays *Barney Conroy*. Given that I'm performing to an imaginary sellout comedy crowd tonight, I go for hilarious. "Hello, Barney!"

There's a confused response: "Who is this?"

"Who is *this*?"

"If you don't tell me who you are right now, I'm going to track you down, and I'm going to gut you."

Mild overreaction.

"Lucien, it's Barney."

"Barney? What are you doing with my phone?"

"The same thing you're doing with mine."

"All right, well I'm at the office but I'm going to come back and get it. Can you meet me downstairs in ten minutes?"

If only he knew.

"Sure."

Nine minutes later, Lucien is marching toward me like he's Chris Hemsworth playing Thor. All big and scary and terribly attractive. "Thanks, mate," he says, tearing his phone out of my hand like it's his enchanted hammer. "I *really* need my phone today. I'm waiting on a call from the hottest woman on the planet. We're going out tonight, and I'm in the market for some new lipstick."

Now is my time to stand against the forces of evil in the nine realms, Thor-style. "Actually, if it's Lucia, she just called to say she can't make it. Her mother died."

Lucien looks devastated and I'm struck by a small pang of guilt. Perhaps he knew her mother well. "What am I going to do with the reservation?" he asks.

"You'll be all right," I say, placing my very *upper* hand on his shoulder. "I'm sure a night at home with me won't do you any harm."

* * *

That night, I'm home alone. Not in the hilarious, Macaulay Culkin hijinks–style home alone, just in the Lucien can find a replacement date any night of the week and I haven't had dinner with a woman in six months–style home alone. And I still don't have a job. And there's no ice cream left. Lucien ate it all.

After Lucien collected his phone, I went out for an orange juice, which I managed to stretch into an early lunch, which got me through to mid-afternoon before the crushing realization that my life has no purpose again descended on me. So I came home and spent two hours searching online for my perfect job. And by "perfect," I mean one that pays at least the $98,000 a year I earned before they fired me.

Jessie J. might think it ain't about the money, but Barney C. thinks that's exactly what it's about when you've got my mortgage. Would I prefer not to work in corporate communications and pursue, instead, my dream of being a stand-up comedian? Of course. But my stand-up comedy career has, to date, netted me precisely zero dollars. Plan B, a career in the public service, on the other hand, has allowed me to borrow so much money from the bank that it gives me night terrors.

To be honest, it was actually a pretty good gig. I had a steady job that I enjoyed enough to keep going back, it paid well, and people seemed to think I was okay at it.

But that's all history now. After what happened, I can't get another job with the government. I have to turn to the dark side of the private sector, a place I've never worked and know very little about that I didn't learn from watching *Suits*. So I really have no idea what kind of job I'm looking for, and I don't even understand most of the job titles: "Lead generation manager" sounds like the head of a hipster cult. Of the few job descriptions I could understand, they all required significant commercial experience. How can I get experience if I can't get a job? Am I the chicken or the egg in this scenario? It was too much for me, so I decided to pack it in and watch half a season of *Downton Abbey*. At least I'm doing better than those guys.

It's late now, well after nine thirty. I'm about to call it a night when the door opens and Lucien fills the room with his perfect hair and visible cheekbones.

I try not to be too obvious about my joy at his uncharacteristic failure. "You're home early. Didn't go as well as you'd hoped?"

"Barney, my dear friend. It went beyond even my wildest of hopes. I just stopped by to pick up my clothes before I move into Gisele's hotel room for a few weeks."

"Who's Gisele?"

"My date. Every cloud has a silver lining, right?" He shakes his head at the wonder of this profound truth. "I thought when Lucia's mum died that my evening had been ruined. I never thought I'd end up falling for a fingernail model."

Fingernail model?

"You're joking, right?"

"Not at all. They're amazing. They look fake but they're totally real."

"You can't just move into a hotel room with a woman you barely know."

"I know all I need to, Barney." Lucien's face switches from philosophical to concerned. He places his hands on my shoulders and squeezes so tight I feel pain in my toes. "It's all right, mate. I'll stay in touch. I'll check in on you." Then he pinches my cheek like I'm a three-year-old. "You'll be all right."

His pity collapses my soul.

As much as I have resented Lucien's proficiency at being more successful than me in every aspect of his life—from work, to women, to not obviously sweating on days above mildly warm—I've still thought of us as friends. "When will you be back?"

Uh-oh, he's smiling now like Bruce Willis in *Armageddon* when he knows he's never coming back.

"I'm never coming back."

"What are you talking about?"

"The restriction on living in my investment property expires at the end of the month. I'll be with Gisele until then. You're on your own now, pardner."

With a cowboy wink and click of his tongue, Lucien disappears into the bathroom so I can clean up after him one last time.

I'm left standing alone in an apartment I can't afford. An apartment that's going to destroy me. More than ever, I need a job. A real job. A high-paying job.

A job in the private sector.

TWO

I miss Lucien.

It's been nearly a week since he moved into Gisele's luxury hotel room, and the apartment is quiet and perfectly ordered without him. All cereals are appropriately segregated, towels are hung according to policy, and dirty crockery is swiftly quarantined.

And I'm terribly, achingly lonely.

Which is why I'm still dressing for work and heading into the city each day, despite being unemployed for the past month. I have no interest in physical contact with strangers, but just being around people makes me feel like there might be a bit of hope left in my otherwise hopeless existence. I do have moments when I doubt this philosophy, of course. Take right now, for instance. I'm crammed into the back of an over-capacity tram next to the hippest-looking hipster in all of Melbourne. He is the archetype, the Adam of bearded, fair trade coffee–drinking tweed wearers. And his tweed and his beard and his fair trade coffee breath are only millimeters away from a serious personal space violation.

I mold myself against the tram wall and jutting handrail in an attempt to avoid his encroaching facial hair. He's taller than me so his beard is right up at my face level. I try to shoot him a warning glance that says *back off, bearded one* but he deflects my threat with ironically vacant eyes.

My phone rings. Calls before nine o'clock are very rare for me, so this is exciting. I reach into my pocket, twisting my spine, and expertly maneuvering my arm to avoid contact with the tweed.

I turn to the window to try to make this a private conversation on a tram of eighty closely packed passengers. The bearded one's reflection stares back at me from the glass. He looks like the devil.

"Hello, Barney speaking," I half-say, half-whisper.

"Barney, it's Ed Middleton. How are you?"

Why is my old schoolmate Ed Middleton ringing me? I see him about once a year.

"I'm well, thanks, Ed. How are you?"

"I'm good. Listen, I heard you're in the job hunt."

"Who told you that?"

"Mike. I ran into him at a conference yesterday."

Why is my best mate, Mike, using my downfall as small talk at conferences?

"Anyway, my mum's got a friend whose husband's firm is looking for a communications adviser. That's your field, isn't it?"

I go for funny. I've always been able to make Ed laugh. "Well I'm not sure I can quite claim the field as my own, but, yes, I do work in comms."

The bearded one snorts. I narrow my eyes at his reflection.

"Right, whatever," Ed says. "So I know it's short notice, but they've had a candidate pull out and want to interview you today."

"What? How do they know about me?"

"I put in a good word for you, but you'll need to get them your CV by ten o'clock. The interview's at eleven. Can you do it?"

Can I? Is he serious?

I try to keep the desperation out of my voice. "Yeah, look, I'll need to move a few things around but it sounds good. Thanks, Ed."

"No worries, Barney. I'll text you the details. I told them you're a good guy, so don't make a liar of me, okay? I've got to go. Good luck."

It's always been a bit unclear to me how the universe works exactly, but I've had the distinct impression over recent times that the universe has been categorically positioned *against* me. When Lucien left, I felt the case was closed. In the great struggle of *Barney v. the Universe*, the universe had triumphed.

Now, though, I feel the tide turning. So either the universe has switched sides and is now working for me, or I'm starting to get the coveted upper hand. Either way, it's enough to fill me with a bit of hope that I'm going to make it out of my financial quagmire and employment-related identity crisis.

I look to my friendly hipster's reflection. We're in this together against the forces that would conform, contain, and control us. I give his reflection a nod. An understated, though fierce indicator that we're going to win this thing.

He sneezes into the back of my head.

* * *

All right, so here's my current status.

I'm riding an elevator to the forty-eighth floor of a Melbourne skyscraper to interview for a private sector job I know nothing about with a company

I've never heard of. Despite never having worked a day outside the public service, I'm staying positive about my shift to the big leagues. The private sector has to be better, right? Private sector workers are wealthier, smarter, and more fragrant. I know how this works, and I'm ready to work ridiculously long hours for a ridiculously large salary to buy ridiculously expensive cologne.

The elevator doors open. I take a deep breath to fill my senses with the sweet smell of moneymaking—something between floor cleaner and bug spray at this stage—and turn left. I push open the glass doors to commercial paradise and am greeted by a smiling young woman more radiant than anyone the government would ever employ. I maintain my cool, though, trying not to stare at her impossibly blonde hair.

"Good morning," she says.

And I believe her.

This is my first opportunity to prove I'm worthy of a role in a bottom-line-driven organization. I search for an appropriately eloquent greeting.

"Hi."

"Do you have an appointment?"

"Yes." I've stopped staring at her hair but now can't take my eyes off her teeth. So straight, so white, such a picture of natural health!

"Mind telling me who it's with?"

"I'm here for..." I think about saying "job interview" but decide against it; I don't want to sound desperate. "...a meeting with Archibald Rogerson."

"Oh, right, you're Archie's job interview. Take a seat over there; he won't be long." She waves her hand at an exquisite, L-shaped cream couch, the kind you'd expect to find Robbie Williams kicking back on with Kylie Minogue.

I start to ask her name—building rapport with the receptionist is always a good idea—but she turns away from me to talk to the other woman at the desk, so I just make a phlegmy, endearing sound in my throat.

"Barney?" a woman asks from behind me, questioning both whether I *am* Barney and whether my name actually *is* Barney.

"I'm Barney." I turn to greet her, again trying not to stare, but nobody told me working in the private sector would be like hanging out on the set of *Charlie's Angels*. She leaves the receptionist looking like a statutory authority short-term contractor.

The woman has dark hair pulled back so tight it shines, and her blue eyes search me for answers I don't know the questions to. We're the same height, unless she's in stilettos, but I dare not check in case it gives the impression I'm looking her up and down—never a good start to an interview. It's a war now between my eyes and my career prospects because my peripheral vision, straining so hard it's making my brain ache, is feeding back *look at this vision of beauty now before you mess this up and she throws you out of the office* signals. I resist the primal optical urge and maintain eye contact. Her features are sharp but not harsh, and she has a light sprinkling of freckles across her nose, a glimpse of the child she once was.

"I'm Gloria. It's nice to meet you, and thanks for coming in at such short notice." Her tone is friendly and polite as she extends her hand.

Shaking a woman's hand is an absolute minefield, so I employ my technique for ensuring I neither linger creepily, nor pull away so fast I rip her arm out of its socket. I start to count: one MC Hammer...two MC Hammer...release! I time it perfectly and wonder if perhaps being sacked wasn't the best thing that ever happened to me.

I am enthralled by the professional, yet welcoming, look in Gloria's eyes; the firm, yet kind, handshake; and, most importantly, the absolute absurdity of her name. Gloria—can you believe it? This is a great boon in a so far boon-free relationship, and a perfect opportunity to build rapport, which is critical when interviewing for a job. Always look for common ground. I'm about to remark on her "intriguing" name but lose my chance as Gloria turns and walks away without another word, her appetite for rapport clearly sated. Not surprising, really. This is the private sector, after all. I'm sure she's already had thousands of riveting conversations this morning about art and culture and philosophy with colleagues so sophisticated they learned about the Louvre by actually *visiting* it and not just reading *The Da Vinci Code*. Once. And then watching the movie. Twice.

So I tuck my rapport-builder away, skip to catch up to Gloria, and then walk in comradely silence alongside her. She smells like a bouquet of flowers sprayed with butterscotch.

The corridor tiles are an inspiring white and I follow Gloria through large, open double doors. The room we enter is enormous—a real boardroom, not just a poorly ventilated meeting room you can book through Lotus Notes—with a long, dark table right down the middle that must be made from actual wood. It's flanked by the kind of leather recliner chairs Sir Richard Branson sits in to eat breakfast. There are floor-to-ceiling windows running the length of the room and, from this forty-eighth floor, the city spreads out below us as a world we can own and command and obliterate. I am mesmerized and walk to the windows, staring out at the people and the buildings below, ready to control and order them like God Himself. The private sector—heaven, indeed!

An archangel coughs. Then I remember this is a job interview and I need to pull myself together.

"Sorry, sorry," I say, looking for the source of the cough. "It's quite a view."

"Indeed." God speaks and my eyes are drawn inextricably to his glory. He's as tall and magnificent as I had imagined. Striking in a dark suit and slicked-back, pure white hair.

God strides toward me, mountains tumbling at his feet. "Archibald Rogerson," he booms. "Welcome." When he extends his hand, my strategy is not to cry as though he just broke my fingers. Which he may have. He nods with what I assume is respect, and then gestures to a seat designated for me by the lone glass of water and lack of paperwork. They sit me facing the window, as if to tantalize me with the promise of what will lie at my feet if I get this job, and Archibald and Gloria sit side by side across the table.

My nerves are beginning to rally in attack formation so I send them a blistering salvo of selection criteria responses to steady their charge, to rally my own forces the way Russell Crowe does at the beginning of *Gladiator*: "What we do in life echoes in eternity!" he said. I settle for: "My well-developed communications skills are demonstrated by..." And then the phrases start spilling forth in my head. I have no idea what the job description is, no idea what the key selection criteria are, not even the desirable qualifications. But in ten years of serving the public, I've done so many interviews and been on enough recruitment panels that I've got a selection criterion example for every occasion. Like the presence of a trusted friend, simply having them by my side calms my nerves.

Archibald smiles and picks up my résumé. "Barney Elvis Conroy," he says, holding each word in his mouth for a little longer than is necessary, as though he's afraid to swallow in case they taste as bad as they sound.

"Yes." I nod, encouraging him to move on. But there's something in his facial expression, which is somewhere between incredulity and disgust, that makes me think he is thinking what everybody thinks when they first hear my name. That it's the most ridiculous name they've ever heard. Thankfully no one ever says that, and I'm ready for Archibald to start with a warm-up question.

"That's the most ridiculous name I've ever heard."

"I'm ready to take the next step in my career."

"I beg your pardon?"

Oh no.

I realize too late that he didn't go for the warm-up. He went for the great unspoken. And he spoke it!

I'm not prepared for this. "Um, yes. It's quite unique."

Archibald leans forward, compassion furrowing his brow. "Why would your parents give you the middle name Elvis?"

A little piece of my heart perishes as I start to explain, maintaining a courteous, respectful smile. "I was born on the anniversary of Elvis Presley's death."

Archibald flinches. I can tell by the proprietary look in his eyes that he's a fan. "August 16?" he says.

I knew it!

"Actually, I was born on August 17. My mum figured that because of the time difference, Elvis died on the seventeenth in Australia."

"Extraordinary," he whispers, with more than a small trace of admiration. "She must be one of his greatest fans."

I have never heard an Elvis Presley song played, quoted, or otherwise referenced in my house. "Oh, yes, absolutely. I grew up on 'Hound Dog.'" I'm finding some rhythm now as the rapport builds.

"You what?"

"The song 'Hound Dog.' I grew up on it."

"I don't understand. What do you mean you grew up on it?"

He's on to me!

I have to get us out of this line of conversation. "I'm really grateful for this interview." I can hear the strain in my voice.

Gloria throws me a lifeline by moving on from the topic of ridiculous names, perhaps because she has one herself and feels empathy for me. "Tell us, Barney, why do you want to leave the Department of Healthy Living?"

That's not a selection criterion!

I am prepared for this, though, and have devised a way to avoid lying about no longer working there, without actually telling the whole interview-ending truth, either. *I'm desperate to land a job before word gets out that I was sacked for a gross breach of the Public Service Code of Conduct* isn't exactly your world-beating icebreaker, so I've worked up some suitable rhetoric to keep everyone happy and move us on to the next question.

"I've worked in the public service for over a decade now, Gloria, and I'm ready to take the next step in my career. I'm keen to transition into the private sector in a role where I am both challenged and can provide a significant contribution." I finish with a *we're all in this together* smile.

"It says here on your résumé that you're the Corporate Communications Manager at the Department of Healthy Living. Is that still correct?"

I recognize this question. It's standard practice to confirm the applicant's current role. I've got an answer. "Corporate Communications Manager. My most recent departmental position." I realize this is an awkward, English-is-my-fifth-language response, but it'll do the job. And now I move them on. "So is this a new position or did it recently become vacant?"

Gloria's looking at me through narrowed eyes. "You're still working at the department, right?"

I start to sweat and head to the safe territory of my rapport-builder. "You've got quite an unusual name yourself. Did your parents like the Laura Branigan song?"

You know the expression "like a deer in the headlights"? Well, Gloria doesn't look anything like that. She looks more like someone recovering from the shock of being asked whether they're carrying any infectious diseases. I don't think I've quite established the rapport I was going for, but I have changed the topic.

Since the discussion about my name, Archibald has been staring at me like he wants to punch me in the face. Now, though, he shows some interest beyond pulverizing me. "What song?" he asks.

I forge ahead, hoping he calls the shots given that we're now getting on quite nicely. "You know, the big eighties hit." Then I do that thing when you try to sing a song to someone without actually singing it because you know if you attempt to actually sing, their ears will start bleeding. "Gloria...Gloria...Gloria," I chant, my voice so flat you could roll a coin on it from here to eternity.

"Sing it to me," Archibald says.

Gloria leans back, crosses her arms, and shoots me a bemused smile and raised eyebrow.

In interviews, you do everything you can to please the panel, especially when you're as desperate as I am, so I reach into the vast catalog of useless information that is my brain and retrieve the lyrics. I begin singing as though I don't want anybody to hear me but it's such a classic tune that I can't help bobbing my head and moving from side to side in my chair.

Archibald starts to feel it as well and he nods his head in time with my butchering of a platinum-

certified hit. Then disaster strikes and I can't remember the rest of the words. I don't think I've got
the job yet, though, so I can't stop now. I fall back
to the safety of the backup singers' part. Though a
touch repetitious, it keeps me in the hunt. "Gloria!"
I sing.

Archibald is as moved by the magic as I am.
"Gloria!" he yells.

Then me: "Gloria."

Archibald (clapping now): "Gloria!"

Me: "Gloria."

Archibald: "Gloria!"

Both of us: "Gloria!"

At the end of our glorious crescendo, Gloria
claps three times, her bemused look now more
sympathetic, like she's patting your three-legged
dog.

Archibald sits back in his chair and folds his
arms, chuckling. "You remind me of my second
wife."

What does that *mean?*

I wait for something more before responding.
He gives me nothing, so I just make a noncommittal kind of mewing sound, a bit like a dying cat
might make, and I sweeten it with a putrid half-
smile that says: "Yeah, I get that all the time."

Archibald's phone rings. He picks it up and leans as far back in his chair as he can while extending his long arm out in front of his face so there's about eight meters between his eyes and the caller ID. He stands up and strides out of the room, answering the call before he's through the door. Then he slams it shut.

Gloria tilts her head at me and holds her hands together on the table, fingertips touching. "Is this your first interview for a while, Barney?" She looks like she's on the verge of laughing—ordinarily, a cause for celebration, right now, a potential catastrophe.

It's time for the charm offensive. "Well, to be honest, Gloria, I'm normally the one asking the questions."

She leans forward and raises her hands, fingers intertwined, elbows resting on the table. "Is that right?" she says. "And what would you ask me?"

Time to strike!

"I like to rely on my powers of observation. So I can see from your wedding finger that you're not married, and I'd guess that you're about thirty years old, maybe thirty-two. What that tells me is you're career focused and you don't let your personal life get in the way of your ambition." In my head, this was a compliment. In reality, it hangs in the air like a guillotine. One nod from Gloria and my head's on the floor.

But she doesn't nod. She doesn't move at all. Except for another narrowing of her eyes and a slight parting of her mouth for a moment before she speaks. "You've worked in the public service for ten years and you have no idea that you just breached multiple human rights and equal opportunity laws with that performance?"

What's she talking about?

I raise my hands in confusion. "But this is the private sector. I thought anything goes."

Gloria laughs, revealing large white teeth. "You're kidding me, right?"

I feel the panic start to rise in my chest. It's filling up my eyeballs like ink poured into a fishbowl.

Gloria sees it, stops laughing, and smiles at me again like I'm that three-legged dog. "When Archie comes back, we'll ask you a bit about your experience, but I don't think it'll take long."

Breathing becomes a very deliberate act. "You've ruled me out already?"

"We need to make sure the cultural fit is right. For both of us." Gloria remains civil, but the warmth in her eyes has gone cold. She has adopted the classic recruitment technique of "professional detachment."

Archibald bursts back into the room. "I've just made an extraordinary discovery!" he says, one hand on each of the double doors like he's holding up the Red Sea. "Barney's mother is Audrey Conroy!"

And there it is. My blessing and my curse.

"Who's Audrey Conroy?" Gloria asks.

Archibald looks like he's just been slapped. "Who's Audrey Conroy?" he yells, his face twisted with the insult. "Just the greatest Australian actress of our generation!"

Gloria spreads her hands in a mock apology. "I'm not of your generation, so I wouldn't know."

"Ahh yes, as you never tire of reminding me, my young protégée."

Gloria shrugs. "I know you're a stickler for the truth."

"Well, if you were of my generation, you wouldn't be so ignorant about the great talent of Barney's mother." Archibald flicks his thumb in my direction.

My reflexes kick in. "Actually, she's still on television, so she's of *both* our generations. She celebrated forty years in the industry last month." I hear myself rolling out by rote the kind of phrases I've been using since I could speak. It's less a deliberate act and more an involuntary reflex. Like gagging.

"I don't watch much television," Gloria says. "We didn't have one growing up."

What kind of barbarians were her parents?

"And I'm sure your mother is a lovely person, Barney, but I don't really buy into the culture of celebrity worship. I think there are many other far more worthy people whose achievements we should be celebrating."

"Wash your mouth out!" Archibald roars. "Audrey Conroy is the most enchanting, elegant, electrifying actress this country has ever seen."

I know what's coming next. Archibald will ask me what it's like being the son of a celebrity. Then he'll talk to me as though he's a personal friend of my mother. Then he'll just stare at me for a while as though *I'm* the celebrity. He sits down next to me. Here it comes.

"So what was it like growing up with Audrey Conroy as your mum?"

"Oh, you know, pretty normal, I guess. I didn't know any different, and she was always just Mum to me. Still is, of course!" I sneak a quick peek at Gloria. She's looking at me like I'm a grotesque museum exhibit, fascinating and yet repulsive at the same time.

Archibald is salivating. "You must have met all the stars. Were they always coming around to your house for dinner?"

"Oh, no, Mum was just like everyone else. Her friends were our next door neighbors and the parents of kids at school. She wanted us to live as normal a life as possible." Gloria dry retches; I'm pretty sure I hear it. Fair enough, too. I'm speaking complete rubbish. There was absolutely *nothing* normal about growing up with a celebrity mother, but I'm sticking resolutely to the family brand.

"I don't believe that for a moment," Archibald says, winking at me as though we're the only two people who know the truth. Then his eyes open wide. He lowers his voice, almost to a whisper. "What about Hugh Jackman?" he asks. "Have you ever met Hugh Jackman?"

Gloria groans and throws her head back. The skin of her throat is smooth and pale.

I put on my best demure expression. "Well, actually, yes. Mum was appearing on a TV variety show and Hugh was performing a song from his debut musical, *Beauty and the Beast*. We got to listen to him rehearse." I call him "Hugh" because it makes it sound like we're old mates. I make myself want to vomit sometimes, too. But my career is on the line here so I can't stop now. "He came over to

34

catch up with my mum before the show. He was a huge fan of hers."

Archibald shakes his head in reverent awe. I'm half expecting him to get down on one knee or something, as though he's speaking to a prophet of the Almighty God. God being Hugh Jackman, me being the prophet who never actually spoke to him because I was in the toilet when he came to say hello to my mum. "What was he like?" Archibald asks.

"Lovely bloke. You wouldn't even know he was famous."

Archibald's eyebrows begin to twitch. "I knew it! I knew he'd be an ordinary bloke—you can just tell by watching him in interviews!" He suddenly stops talking, breathing, and salivating, as though frozen solid, iced over by the opportunity of a lifetime. He lowers his voice again. "Do you think you could get Hugh involved in one of our campaigns?" he whispers, as though speaking it might break the spell I can no doubt cast to get one of Australia's most successful international performers on board at Rogerson Communications.

Okay, so this is going a bit far. Archibald has perhaps not quite grasped the nuance of me once meeting Hugh Jackman, though not actually meeting him, as a teenager back in the nineties. It's pretty unlikely he'd remember me, especially given I was in the bathroom at the time.

Gloria rescues me. "Archie. We've talked about this. Hugh Jackman is not the public relations silver bullet."

Archibald chuckles and smiles. "Hugh Jackman and Audrey Conroy in the same room, hey. How about that?" He looks at me as though I am both Hugh Jackman and Audrey Conroy. I smile back as though I am both Hugh Jackman and Audrey Conroy.

Gloria packs up her papers and stands up. "Thanks for coming in, Barney. We'll call you later this week with our decision."

Archibald slaps his hand down on the table. "No need! Barney here's our man."

There's a choking sound and I'm not sure whether it's me or Gloria. She looks as stunned as anyone who just saw a fascinating, yet repulsive, museum exhibit come to life and walk right out of its box.

Archibald continues. "We want someone who understands the public service and also knows what it's like to generate publicity. If Audrey Conroy's son can't do that, nobody can." He stands up and heads to the door, but turns back and waves a finger at me. "We'll give you a six-week contract

as a trial. If you're any good, I'll offer you a permanent job. What were they paying you over at the
department?"

Oh man, this is it. This is the moment I find out
how expensive the cologne will be. "Pay grade 6.4."
My stomach churns, my mind races, and, in an unrelated response brought on by a large caramel
milk shake before the interview, my bladder starts
to ache.

Archibald looks like he wants to punch me
again.

"Sorry, $98,436 a year," I say.

"Right, you can start here on $75,000."

*What? That's not how it works. This is the private sec-
tor. You guys invented inflated salaries!*

"See you tomorrow morning."

What?

"Yes, sir. Thank you, Archibald."

And then he's gone. At least for about one and a
half seconds before he sticks his silvery head back
into the room, his body obscured behind the door
frame so his head hangs suspended six feet above
the ground. "Audrey Conroy, hey?" he says. He
shakes his head and smiles. "If I'd had my way as a
young man, Barney, I would have married her in a
heartbeat." Then he puckers his lips like he just ate

a packet of sour Warheads. "Which, I guess, would make you my son." He looks disappointed.

Rightly so.

* * *

Archibald's second departure leaves something of a conversational vacuum. Gloria's clearly still in shock. Her eyes are wide and vacant. Her mouth slightly open. Her fingers tapping on the table as she stands staring at the wall. Given the failure, so far, of my usually watertight rapport-builders, I remain silent. I settle, instead, for imagining what it might be like to kiss Gloria.

Just as I consider proposing, Gloria shakes her head once, the way cats do when flicking away an annoying distraction. "Archie's approach to recruitment isn't always very orthodox."

She speaks without emotion, so I can't get a read on whether this is a good or bad approach. Who knows, maybe she got her job the same way. I use a classic conversational technique to try to draw out some more information, the open statement that invites opinion. "You know what they say, I guess. It's not always what you know..."

Gloria looks at me without responding, and I notice she's wearing lip gloss. The silence starts to get uncomfortable, for me at least, so I decide it

might be time to find out what I'll be doing, exactly. What this company does, exactly.

"So your website describes you as a full-service,
traditional communications agency for the new
millennium. What does that mean, exactly?"

"It's supposed to mean we're a mix of the old
school with Archie and the new breed with me and
Chad, our other consultant." She pauses for a moment before adding: "And now you as well, I
guess."

A little alarm bell goes off in my head as I wonder how big this full-service communications agency can actually be if Gloria, Archie, and some guy
called Chad are the sum total of its old and new
experience. And why are they describing it as built
for the new millennium? The year 2000 is so long
ago that I've had enough time to forge the average
man's lifetime of regrets since then.

"What have you done in the social media
space?" Gloria asks, in what sounds dangerously
like an interview question.

Social interaction isn't my forte, real life or
online. I have seen *The Social Network*, though, so
I'm not totally clueless. I've got a Facebook page
myself, but I no longer use it because a whole
bunch of people I don't know/remember/am-
trying-to-forget wanted to be friends with me. I

also started a Twitter account to try out a few of my yet-to-be-publicly aired stand-up comedy lines. Unfortunately, the only genuine follower I could muster was the guy who sat next to me at work. And I think that was a charity follow, anyway, because he never retweeted a single one of my gags, despite describing every one of them as "absolutely, unequivocally brilliant." So I settle for an answer to Gloria's question that will give an accurate representation of my experience.

"Heaps."

She does that interviewer trick where she nods but doesn't say anything, and then keeps staring at me, the candidate, to try to get the candidate to elaborate on their answer. Except I'm not a candidate, I've got the job, a fact that seems to have escaped her.

"Well, I've got to go. Great to meet you." I stand up as I speak, leaving her trapped in the silent, interviewer-probe vortex. I'm out the door before she can say "please elaborate," but I steal Archibald's trick and stick my head in for a last hurrah.

"Thanks for your time, Gloria. I'm really looking forward to working with you." Then I throw her a wink to give her the heads-up that I'm just a little bit of a cheeky, roguish vagabond, despite my professional appearance. It's tremendously endearing.

She stares at me for a moment, then picks up her phone and turns away.

THREE

Day one and I'm out to make a big impression.

And the best way to impress people is to turn up early to work. It doesn't matter what you're doing, as long as you're in early, people get the impression you're a bit of a workaholic, burning the candle at both ends and all that. Until they fire you, of course.

So I woke up super early this morning and now I'm striding through the city, confident I'm going to be at Rogerson Communications early enough to knock their patterned socks off. I check my watch; 8:42. I'll be there before 9:00, easy.

"Morning, sir," an overly cheerful man says to me. He's wearing some sort of leather apron and one of those little hats you expect to see on leprechauns, bookmakers, and young men who have lost their way.

"Morning," I say with a smile, but without breaking stride.

"In need of a shoe shine, sir?" he asks, a little boldly in my opinion.

"No, thanks." I'm still smiling but he's blocked my path now and I can feel the benefits of my early arrival ticking away by the second.

"Okay, sir. Have a nice day, sir."

This "sir" business is making me uncomfortable. I take a few steps away from him when my eyes, traitors that they are, drop to my shoes. I've only had this pair for about three years, but they look like they've just spent ten in the French Foreign Legion. I can't remember the last time I shined them and wonder, with a fair measure of doubt, whether I even own shoe polish. I remember using it on my school shoes back in the nineties, but things get a little hazy after that. I turn back to see the leprechaun smiling at me. "How long will it take?" I ask.

"Only a few minutes, sir. Make 'em look as good as new."

Okay, I can spare a few minutes to make a good impression. In fact, I *have* to spare a few minutes to make a good impression. It's what we in the private sector call a "calculated risk."

The shoe shiner seats me inside a little glass box before guiding my foot onto a stool. I avoid eye contact with every single person walking past because I feel like the most pretentious person in Melbourne sitting here having my sixty-dollar shoes shined by a bloke who refuses to address me as anything other than the lordly "sir." I fear that if he doesn't do a good job, I'm basically compelled to slaughter him on the spot, Middle Ages–style.

But I'm not in a particularly murderous mood this morning, just a bit of a rush, so I'm very pleased to see that he's doing remarkable work on my loafers. The right one is looking very promising as he buffs away. I feel a small thrill of satisfaction at calculating my first risk in the private sector and triumphing.

"Barney?"

Cease peasant! Away from my feet!

"What are you doing?"

This is both a reasonable and redundant question. I think it's pretty obvious *what* I'm doing. What is less clear, perhaps, is why. And that's what Gloria is asking me.

I look up and her searching blue eyes are trained on me. She has her head tilted to one side and is wearing a bemused expression, again. Not the *wow, you're amazing the way you support the work-*

ing class kind of bemused. More the *why are you sitting there like some obnoxious millionaire while some poor sap breaks his back shining your shoes* kind of bemused.

I stand up abruptly, knocking my serf down in the process.

"Wait," he says in panic. "I'm only half done."

Irrelevant. I can't sit here a moment longer while Gloria is staring at me. She already believes the only reason I got the job is because my mum is famous and I once met Hugh Jackman (sort of). Even though this is the first time I've ever paid for a shoe shine, I'm sure she's judging me as a cultural elitist who trades daily on his cultural elitism to exploit the cultural non-elite. This isn't true, of course; my cultural standing couldn't even get me a free burger at Maccas. But perception is everything in life, so I wave a ten-dollar note at the shoe shiner to signal that I'm ready to move away from the scene of my bourgeoisie crime.

"Sir, I haven't finished. I can't take your money."

I lean down and whisper to try to avoid an unpleasant scene. "Yeah, yeah, right. Don't worry about it. I've got to go. How much is it?"

"Well a shoe shine is seven dollars, but that's for two shoes. So it'll be three-fifty, even though I hate for you to walk away like that." He points at my shoes, which look like they've been separated by the Iron Curtain.

I shove the ten-dollar note at him.

"You're my first job, I haven't got any change."

I reach into my pocket, feeling Gloria's eyes all over me. I start to sweat, pulling my wallet out and fumbling around inside it for coins. I imagine what this looks like as I'm handing over twenty-cent pieces, clearly too cheap just to give the guy the tenner and be done with it. I finally get there, though, and he gives me a reluctant thanks.

I take a breath to calm myself and put on a smile so fake my cheeks hurt. I stay positive as I walk to Gloria; at least this means we'll be able to go into work together. That'll be a lot easier than showing up on my own. She hasn't moved since I first spotted her watching me, other than to cross her arms. She raises an eyebrow as I approach.

"Morning!"

"Soft start to the new job?"

I don't know what this means, but assume it has something to do with the shoe shine. I'm not exactly sure how to respond, so I go for beneficent, lordly nonchalance. "The shoe shine? No, that's nothing." I wave my hand at my charge. "I just had some time up my sleeve and thought he could use the work."

"Why?"

"Why what?"

"Why did you think he could use the work?"

Tread carefully, Barney.

"Well, because the guy is shining shoes so, you know, he could probably do with the work." I lower my eyebrows to pass on my coded message of "hey, just because we're rich and good-looking doesn't mean everybody is, so show a little discretion around the poor people, will you?"

"You're assuming he's poor because he doesn't wear a suit and work in an office?"

"I assume he's poor because he's shining shoes for a living."

"Maybe he likes shining shoes for a living. Some people actually enjoy hard work."

I laugh, and then regret laughing lest it indicate I don't enjoy hard work. Although, frankly, manual labor has never really been my thing.

"Well, carry on, Mother Teresa. I don't want to hold up your good works, and I've got a meeting to get to," Gloria says.

Alarm bell. "You mean you're not going to the office?"

"I've been at the office for an hour."

An hour!

I think my heart *actually* stops. I look at my watch: 8:55. There's only one possible explanation for Gloria's behavior. "Are you leaving early today?"

She stares at me.

"You know, is that why you started so early? Because you've got an appointment this afternoon?"

"This isn't the public service, Barney. We don't keep school hours here." By the time I work out what "school hours" means, Gloria has turned on her heel and is marching up the street in the opposite direction to our office.

I breathe out as I watch her go, reliving the moment when she looked at me with a bemused expression.

"C'mon, mate," my serf says, appearing alongside me. "You look like you need to sit down. And I've got to finish that other shoe."

He walks me back to the chair and I forget to calculate the risk. I stare after Gloria as I feel the brush run over my toes. When the job is done, I rummage around for some more change.

"No, sir," my poor, working class shoe shiner says. "You've got to get to work. That one's on the house."

I throw him a lordly wink that lets him know he can keep his wretched life.

Here I go. I'm ready to make my big impression.

It's 9:01.

* * *

I arrive in the building lobby sweating, panting, and trying very hard to maintain consciousness.

I spent the last four years of my public service career at the Department of Healthy Living, but I think it's fair to say I wasn't exactly the department's greatest brand ambassador. I went through a three-week period back in the mid-noughties when I did push-ups twice a week but, other than that burst of activity, I've pretty well steered clear of exercise.

There's a fair bit of activity in the lobby, which I find reassuring because it means perhaps I'm not so late after all. There's a section for lifts running from the ground to the twentieth floor and then another for the more important floors above. I feel a surge of pride at working on the forty-eighth floor, only two floors from the top of the building. I wonder who's on the fiftieth floor. Probably God. Or Google.

A bell sounds and a light illuminates above one of the lifts, directing workers to the less important floors. I pity them as they cram into the elevator like nineteenth-century miners heading to another long day of darkness, fear, and drudgery.

I smile at the three other guys who are left, each of us waiting to travel the stairway to Heaven, kind of. None of them smiles back. One takes a step away from me. When the lift does arrive, I suffer a little chill thanks to the drought-breaking amount of sweat that has now soaked through the back of my shirt. Thankfully, I'm wearing a navy suit, so as long as I leave the jacket on, no one will uncover my shame.

I'm the last one in the lift by the time it gets to forty-eight, which makes me a little teary. I might be later than I'd hoped, but I have arrived.

"Hi," I say to the receptionist with the impossibly blonde hair. I'm sure she'll recognize Rogerson's gun new recruit—the whole building probably knows about me by now!—so I let my charismatic smile do the rest of the talking.

"Hello."

A moment long enough for a fresh bead of sweat to roll down my back passes before I realize she may be waiting for a bit more.

"I'm Barney Conroy. I start with Rogerson Communications today."

"Good for you," she says, before turning her attention to the computer screen in front of her.

"Well, should I just go through, then?"

"Through what?"

Blondes!

"Through to my office." To encourage her, I point toward the boardroom where I had my interview.

"Oh, right. Sorry, yes. You had an interview here yesterday." Her face lights up. "Is it really true that Audrey Conroy's your mum?"

The phone rings and the receptionist presses a button on the computer—computers that answer phones; how very private sector!—and speaks into the tiny headpiece attached to her ear. "Good morning. Gartner Fine Jewelry. How can I help you?"

What?

What's Gartner Fine Jewelry and why is she helping anyone trying to find it?

"Hold the line, please...Avi, I've got a Liam Henty for you, shall I put him through...Transferring you now, Mr. Henty." She turns to me but the phone rings again and she holds up a finger to stop me from talking. "Good morning. Tildensky Accountants. How can I help you?"

I stare at her as she talks. I hear her words, but they make no sense at all, like she's a parrot that's swallowed a thesaurus.

She ends the call. "Rogerson's on level six," she says, without looking up at me. "You'll have to go back to the ground floor and take the other lift well."

I feel a bit like crying again, this time in the soul-crushed, devastated, *I don't work two floors from God* kind of way. "But the interview was up here..."

She looks up. "Archie always hires the board-room for interviews and big meetings. Impress the clients, con the candidates." I think a tear actually wells in my left eye. She takes pity on me. Tries to buck me up a bit. "You know what it's like in this game," she says, eyes wide with suggestion.

I don't, of course. I don't know what it's like at all. I don't even know what the game is. "Why are you answering other people's phones?"

"This is a serviced office. I cover reception for four different companies."

"But you work for Rogerson?"

"No. I don't work for any of them. Small busi-nesses that can't afford or don't need a full-time receptionist sign up to a shared services agreement, and I work for the company that provides the shared service."

This is incomprehensible. How could Rogerson, a full-service communications agency for the new millennium, not need a full-time receptionist? I begin sweating again.

Impossibly Blonde Hair dismisses me. "When you get off at level six, take a left, then a right, then the third door on the left. There are signs, I think, but I've never actually been down there."

* * *

The lift ride back down reflects my plummeting spirits. It's now 9:17 and my first day in the private sector still hasn't started.

I can't even find the private sector!

But it's a job, I have a job. Yesterday, I had no job, and no prospects. Today, I have a lower-paying, poorly defined, difficult to locate job. But I have one, nonetheless.

I get off at six with my head bowed in case somebody I know sees me. There's no reception, nobody around. Just a sign on the opposite wall with five company listings and arrows pointing left and right. I find the Rogerson name. It's misspelled "Roggersons."

I push the doors open, turn right and walk down an empty corridor to the third door on the left. It's closed and has no sign on it, so I do what any confident professional would do in this situation.

I walk straight past, pretending I'm looking for something else.

But then I realize this is inconsistent with my new private sector attitude, so I turn on my heel and stride back to the aforementioned third door on the left like I'm Emilio Estevez in the 1980s. I raise my fist to knock, but remember that I work here and perhaps knocking would show a lack of corporate bravado. So I decide to just burst in, boldly announcing my arrival as the new hotshot on the block.

I turn the handle and push. Somebody pulls from the other side, throwing me off balance, and I fall into the arms of a woman who smells like my grandmother's soap. I disentangle myself from her saving embrace before this gets awkward. She's about fifty, a touch portly, and has the kind of face you like your friends' mums to have.

"You always introduce yourself with a bear hug?" she asks.

"Love to make an impression!"

She gives me a broad, welcoming smile. "You must be Barney," she says, extending her hand. I take it and notice how dry it is compared to the sodden disaster that has become my own.

"You nervous, darling?"

"Just a little."

"Well, don't be, we're all very friendly here. Isn't that right, Achal?"

She looks into the room, which is filled by an arrangement of seven workstations. There is one, enormous desk at the far end of the room, with a window behind it. Parallel to it, and leading back toward the doorway, are two rows of three inter-connected desks down either side, joined by a mass of cords in the middle that reminds me of that snake pit in the first *Indiana Jones* movie. The whole setup looks quite a lot like a classroom. Full of blue snakes.

There's only one other person in the room; Achal, no doubt. He's Indian by the look of it—but don't quote me, I'm not great with minorities—and he gives me a less than friendly glance from under dark, furrowed brows before returning his gaze to the two monitors on his desk.

"Don't mind him," the woman says. "They're all a bit like that before they get to know you."

"Who? Indians?"

Her eyes open wide. She leans in and whispers. "No, IT people." That's all she says, but I'm also sure she's thinking "you racist, scum."

"I'm Diana," she says. "Let's get you settled." Diana walks me through the classroom and sits me down at a desk on the left-hand side of the room, two deep from the principal's chair. There's a lap-top sitting in a docking station, which Diana turns on. The desk on my right is clearly empty—no personal effects, no files, no lunch scraps—but the one on my left is occupied by a magnificent woman. At least that's what I'm hoping. It's also devoid of personal effects, but there are files and stationery arranged with a level of precision no mediocre man could muster.

The computer boots up to a log-in screen. "Achal," Diana says. "Have you got Barney's log-in details?"

Achal takes off his enormous headphones—the ones that are supposed to make you look like a serious music lover but just make you look, well, ridiculous, really; at least if you're white and you're a corporate suit. Achal is wearing a black hoody, and we've already confirmed his heritage, so he actually looks okay in the headphones, despite them being metallic red.

"Why would I have log-in details?" he asks.

I love the Indian accent, the way it dances through the air to your ears. Like all of life is a scene from a Bollywood movie. Achal's voice makes me smile, until I see the hostility in his eyes, which makes me realize he hates my guts for no other reason than that I'm a sweaty, white racist. But he couldn't possibly know that yet, could he? Except the sweaty, white part, I guess.

"Because he starts today, and you set up new users." Diana is explaining this like she's talking to a child, and it's clear from her exasperation that this is not the first run-in she's had with the IT department.

"Nobody logged a job," Achal says, folding his arms over his chest.

"I heard Gloria tell you about it yesterday morning. Before lunch!"

"Would you like to see my in-box? I will show you that nobody logged a job."

"Achal, I *heard* her ask you. I heard *you* say yes."

"I said if she logged a job I would happily set up a new user. And if I had received an e-mail to the IT requests account, I would have added it to the live jobs list." He points to a whiteboard in the corner behind him with the title "Live Jobs List." There's nothing on it. "It's not on the live jobs list."

"So what exactly *are* you working on Achal?"

"I don't report to you." He puts his headphones back on.

"Achal!"

"Send me an e-mail," he yells before ducking below his computer screens.

Diana exhales like she's trying to blow out a ninety-year-old's birthday candles. "Sorry about that, sweetheart," she says. "Here, I'll log you in.

The folders won't mean anything to you but at least you'll be able to read the paper online."

I look away from the keyboard as she types in her password; I don't want to get stung for a privacy breach this early in the piece.

"My log in is 'dianac,' all lowercase, and my password's 'worstjobever.' All one word."

"Thanks."

"No problem, sweetie. I'm going to get a coffee. You want one?"

Please don't leave me with the maniac in the headphones.

"No, thanks."

"All right, love, you're all logged in with full Internet access. Just keep the dating sites to a minimum on your first day, all right?" She elbows me in the back of the head, which I think was meant to be comradely, but really just hurt; she has very bony joints for an otherwise well-cushioned woman.

Then it's just me and Achal. I fire up a news website and try to find some sort of article that makes me look professional. There's something with the word *finance* in the title so I go with that. But I have no intention of reading it. It's just for show if somebody suddenly barges in or checks my usage.

I begin to stake out Achal, strategizing about how to get him on my side. It's very important to give your coworkers a good first impression, and your ability to get the IT department in your corner will make or break your career.

Achal takes off his headphones and I seize my chance. "You worked here long?" I call out across the snake pit that divides our desks. A little run-of-the-mill, but never fails.

"Far too long, mate. Coming up to six months. How about you?"

Achal has devastated my charm offensive with an incomprehensible question. Not wanting to appear rude, I move my jaws up and down and make a kind of gurgling, noncommittal sound so he doesn't think I'm ignoring him.

Achal slams his palm down on his desk and laughs like an exploding firework. "C'mon, mate! I'm only joking. Haven't you got a sense of humor?" He skirts around the snake pit and sits in the magnificent woman's chair next to me. "I'm Achal."

"Barney."

"What?"

"Barney."

"Is that a real name?"

"Yes."

"Okay, pleased to meet you, Bernie."

"Barney."

"What?"

"Never mind."

We shake hands. "Bernie, man, you're sweating like a beggar in a heat wave. Take off your jacket."

My drenched shirt is not fit for public display. "No, thanks. I'm all right."

"Suit yourself, Bernie. Listen, I've got to go out for a while, but I'll set you up with a log-in when I get back."

"You're going to leave me here on my own?"

"You'll be fine."

"What if somebody turns up?"

"Nobody's going to turn up, mate. We don't have any clients!"

Achal heads toward the door with his headphones hooked around his neck.

"Okay, I'll see you soon," I say. I hope Achal recognizes my very obvious plea not to leave me alone for too long.

"Maybe."

"What do you mean?"

"Maybe you'll see me again, maybe you won't. Life is uncertain, Bernie. Either of us could be dead before I get back."

He's a madman.

Achal walks out, leaving me with the sinking feeling, not that I am going to die, but that this company is not a full-service communications agency for the new millennium. It feels, at the moment, more like something I might have set up myself.

* * *

I used to hold public service orientation procedures in a kind of fond contempt. Like an artistic brother, you were more or less compelled to love them, even though they took up way too much of your time and didn't appear to serve any valuable purpose. I long now for that estranged brother of mine. I long for the comfortable disdain of a check-the-box procedure dreamed up by someone in HR who has never actually *seen* a new employee, let alone had to induct one.

I long for orientation because I've now been working at Rogerson for more than an hour and I have no idea how to use the phones, make a coffee, or request leave (which is a little premature, of course, but I would have known by minute sixteen down at the department). Instead, I'm staring at an article about the financial ramifications of an unexpected sell-off of a major investments company by one of its largest hedge fund shareholders. I don't even know what a hedge fund shareholder is, let alone what the ramifications of a sell-off are. And I don't care. I just want to know how to find the stationery closet!

A phone rings, shocking me out of my eyes-wide-open coma. The sound is coming from the other side of the room. I stare at the offender, which also has a flashing red light to indict itself. I wait for it to ring out—five repetitions if it runs to government standards—but, instead, the phone next to me springs to life as the original perpetrator goes silent.

A warm, nostalgic feeling spreads through my chest. I smile at the phone, which is a mere pawn in what used to be one of my favorite tricks: the call-forward routine. Voice-mail is probably mankind's greatest invention, with call-forwarding undoubtedly the crowning achievement of the Enlightenment. Not only do you not have to deal with the intruder immediately, you don't have to deal with them at all because the sap gets shunted to someone else's voice-mail and can't leave you a message. Genius!

Then something unthinkable happens. The phone next to me goes silent, but the red light doesn't stay on to indicate a message is being recorded. Instead, the original phone lights up again and recommences its shrill call of damnation.

It's the eternal call-forward loop!

Despite my new private sector attitude, which hasn't really had a good chance to flex its growing muscles, my overly developed public service instincts kick in. They call it the public *service* for a reason, and the code of conduct by which we live and breathe and get fired does not tolerate a call-forward loop.

Although I haven't moved for an hour, I leap into action, darting around the principal's desk as the ring continues on the other side of the room. I grab the phone off the handle but the rush of blood forces me to my knees.

I almost answer with "Department of Healthy Living, Barney speaking," and only just stop myself as the words well up in my throat. I race through my head for an appropriately hip greeting for a full-service communications agency for the new millennium. Something polite, but not too formal. Helpful, but not stuffy.

"Hello."

It's not me speaking. I'm taking so long to generate the perfect private sector greeting that the woman on the other end of the line beats me to it. But I'm not licked yet.

"Howdy."

"I beg your pardon?"

Try again: "Um, hello. Yeah, hello, how can I help you?"

"May I speak with Chad Sylvester, please?"

Something's not right. It's the voice on the other end of the phone. It sounds familiar. But how...

"Um, sorry, Chad's not here at the moment. Can I take a message?" I start sweating again. My sweat glands work like the Sydney Harbour Bridge painters; just when you think I've sweated out and all dried up, they turn around and do it all over again.

There's a pause. "Sorry, who am I talking to?"

I panic inside, but stay cool outside. "Ahh, no one, no one. Ahh, Chad's not here."

"Your voice sounds very familiar."

I drop it an octave and tuck my chin to my chest to generate a kind of deeper, manlier version of myself. "Really. That's strange, I just started working here."

"What's wrong with your voice?"

"Nothing, just had a tickle before. This is how I talk."

"Are you putting on a fake voice?"

"No."

"What's your name?"

I've almost got a fix on the caller. I'm nearly certain I know who she is, and if I'm on the right track, I *cannot* let her know it's me. So I seize the opportunity to christen myself, albeit temporarily, with a more run-of-the-mill fake name. "Marmaduke," I say.

A pause. Then: "Seriously?"

"Yes," I say deeply, like a man.

"Okay, well can you please ask Chad to call me? It's Margaret from the Department of Healthy Living."

I knew it! I don't hear her recite the number because I've stopped listening and started palpitating again, but I know it by poorly functioning heart so I promise to pass on the message. Then I hang up and exhale with my eyes shut tight. That was far too close.

"Who's been sitting in my chair?" asks a man with an American accent.

I open my eyes to see that Gloria has returned. Beside her is a man in a suit who may or may not be a male model. He's at least six foot, looks like he works out three times a day, and has windswept blonde hair that gives you the impression he's been surfing all morning.

"Hey, man, you must be Barney," he drawls, like he just stepped off the set of *Beverly Hills 90210* (original series). I stand as he walks over. "Good to meet you. I'm Chad." We shake hands. His is warm and smooth. Calm and assured from spending so much time with Luke Perry. Mine is clammy and limp; not enough time with Priestly. I do that thing where you don't quite grip the other's guy's palm and if he closes properly, you end up like a microwaved Twinkie in a gorilla's fist.

"Didn't quite get there," he says, letting my hand go. "Let's try again." He's giving me a second chance at the handshake, and there's no hint of gamesmanship. I don't trust him—he's American and he's with Gloria—but his green eyes are quite mesmerizing, his voice is like honey and his handshake is a general anaesthetic for all your deepest fears. He is as slick, well-produced, and intimidating as a high-end cologne advertisement.

Of course he is, you fool. He's an American! Don't fall for it!

I don't like the way Gloria is looking at him; too familiarly, too admiringly, too much like I want her to look at me. She might be under his spell now, but I'll rescue her, and I'm not falling for his charm in the meantime. Although I've never actually been to America, I've seen enough episodes of *How I Met Your Mother* to know how to get under his skin.

"Good to meet you, too," I say. "What part of Canada is that accent from?"

Bang! Take that, Yankee Doodle Dandy!

Chad takes it in his stride, although there is a flicker of annoyance in his eyes, which I claim as a resounding victory. "It's actually a little further south. Southern California."

"Never heard of it."

"Right...Well, welcome aboard, Barn dog. It's good to have you on the team."

Did he just call me Barn dog?

"Is this for me?" Chad picks up the Post-it note I've scribbled Margaret's name and number on.

I nod, playing his words back in my head. Did he really call me Barn dog? And is that a term of endearment or an insult? What kind of dog lives in a barn?

I don't get a chance to pursue this further because Chad starts punching the number into his phone. Then his honeyed tones are traveling a couple of blocks down the road to the department. "Hi, Margaret, it's Chad Sylvester from Rogerson Communications. How are you?"

A pause at this end.

Then: "I'm great, thanks for asking. Archie told me you'd be getting in touch, so I appreciate your call."

I'm standing about a meter from Chad, but he pays me no attention during this initial exchange.

Then a look of confusion creeps over his beautiful face.

"Ahh, no. There's no one here called Marmaduke." He raises a hand as if to ask me "what's the deal here, homey?" but I'm not sticking around to answer any poorly constructed American questions.

I blind turn and scurry to the safe refuge of my desk, a full three meters away, with the snake pit in between us.

Chad is deflecting Margaret with the sheer force of his charisma. "Might have been someone new on reception. Anyway, tell me more about this project. It sounds very exciting."

Gloria's sitting next to me, my hope of a magnificent woman at my side now realized, and the scent of her perfume is making it difficult for me to eavesdrop on Chad. When she speaks, Chad is obliterated. "We've got a staff meeting this morning. They're on every Tuesday and it'll start when Archie gets here. You won't have to say much today. Just introduce yourself, watch how it works."

This is the closest thing I've had to corporate induction. I choke up with gratitude.

"Why don't you take your jacket off? The air-conditioning really struggles in here on hot days," Gloria says to me.

I shake my head to regain some composure. These will be my first official words to Gloria as her Rogerson colleague. I'd like to make them count. "Nah. I'm fine, thanks."

"Suit yourself."

I spend the next few minutes pretending to read about the hedge fund thing, while actually staking out Chad. He's off the phone and hasn't dropped his eyes from his computer screen since I started spying. I don't know the guy, but he looks excited.

The door opens and Diana walks in ahead of Achal. A moment later, it opens again and Archibald barrels into the room. He's even taller and more commanding than I remember, his white hair making him like a snowcapped Everest among us suburban hills. But his powerful aura is slightly compromised by his chosen attire: cargo shorts and a blue Hawaiian shirt.

Now I saw some pretty shocking atrocities across ten years of public service casual Fridays—pants above the belly button, jeans rolled up at the ankles with light denim facing out (hasn't been acceptable since Wham! broke up), and, in more recent times, a plethora of men older than thirty wearing polo shirts with upturned collars.

But never in all that time did I see a man in cargo shorts and a blue Hawaiian shirt. On a Tuesday.

Archibald strides through the snake pit and I start to stand. Gloria shoots me a glance. I sense the warning, sit back down, and whisper: "I thought we were going to a staff meeting."

"We are. It's here."

I wasn't expecting us to be back in the boardroom after the comments from Impossibly Blonde Hair, but I had at least expected a meeting room. This just seems to me to be a little too, well, *amateur* for the private sector.

Archibald sits down at his desk. "Welcome, everybody. Thanks for coming," he says as though this is a meeting of the United Nations Security Council. "Let's get straight into it."

"There's an agenda on your desk, Archie," Gloria says, slipping one across to me at the same time.

This is more like it. Six items, clearly categorized with accountable persons next to each, actions arising from the last meeting, general business. Very impressive. I love a woman who knows her way around an agenda.

"Right, so there is." Archie looks down at the agenda, his eyes moving back and forth, his mouth puckered as though he's just eaten a spoonful of kitty litter. "Okay. But first, the big announcement." This is not item one. Item one is the annual training calendar. "Chad, over to you."

Chad stares at Archie. He looks like he really wants to say something, but the big announcement appears to have eluded him for the moment.

"C'mon, lad," Archie says. "Give us the good news about our new client!"

There's a collective intake of breath. I steal a look at Gloria. She's sitting forward in her chair, her eyes are sparkling, and her lips are just slightly parted. I think she may be holding her breath, and I decide that I will personally secure a million clients a week for this company if it makes Gloria react like this.

"New client?" Chad says, *really* wanting to be part of this news.

"The phone call, Chad. The phone call you received this morning. You *were* here when they rang, weren't you?"

Chad and I seem to realize what Archie's talking about at the very same moment. Our eyes lock. He speaks, without dropping my gaze. "Well, no. Not when they first rang. But Barney spoke to them and took a message, and I called straight back."

"Aha!" Archibald slams his fist down. "I knew we'd hired the right man for the job. First thing you do if you want to invade a foreign country is recruit a few former nationals."

What?

Chad continues: "They just sent me the brief, which I've had a quick look over, and they want us to pitch next week. It's a short turnaround, but I think we're in a really strong position to win the job. I wouldn't go as far as calling them our client just yet, but I'll talk to Gloria and Achal after the meeting and we'll start working on our pitch straightaway."

"Nonsense. Barney's leading this one. Mandela's coming home."

What? And what?

The collective excitement turns to collective shock. Gloria speaks the obvious. "But, Archie, Barney has only worked here for a few hours. Chad and I have been building our pitches for months."

"Barney," Archibald says. "How long did you work at the Department of Healthy Living?"

"Four years."

"And how long did you work in the public service?"

"Ten."

"Right. Well, I think that settles it. Moving on, then, do we have any other business?"

Nobody speaks. They're all looking at me. Gloria's expression is pure bewilderment. Chad's is grave insult, Achal's is mischievous, and Diana's, well, actually, she's not looking at me at all, but appears to be playing sudoku.

"Meeting closed," Archibald announces, six minutes after it began, without a single agenda item covered.

"Wait, wait," Chad says. "There's something else we need to do." He turns to me and there are fifty-one states of menace in his seductive eyes. "Since Barney's new, maybe he should tell us a bit about himself. So we can get to know him a little better before we start working together."

"Great idea," Archibald says. "Barney, tell us about your mum."

"Who's your mum?" Diana asks.

"Audrey Conroy," Archie says.

"Oh, I love her! She's so sophisticated."

"Actually, I'd like to hear a bit about you, Barney," Chad says.

Archibald looks like he might throttle Chad, but relents. "Well, all right," he says. "But keep it quick."

You can count on it.

I clear my throat and smile. "First of all, it's great to be here at Rogerson Communications." Lie number one. "I'm really happy to be part of the team." Lie number two. "I've always wanted to work in a dynamic communications business." Lie number three. What I really want is my ergonomically perfect desk at the department. This one is too high, and reaching for the mouse to scroll up and down that same finance article for an hour has jinked my neck. I can feel a headache coming on and I don't have any accumulated sick leave.

But I battle on. "I worked in communications at the Department of Healthy Living for four years, and spent six before that in various public sector organizations. I graduated with a bachelor of communications..." Pause to build anticipation. "...as a bachelor who could work on his communications!" I hope the inclusion of this self-deprecating joke will impress Gloria. I steal a glance her way. She's examining a fingernail.

Tough crowd!

"But what about outside of work, Barney? What gets you excited away from the desk?" Chad asks this question in polite, interested tones, but I can sense the hostility beneath his sugary words. There's a challenging curl at the corners of his lips that betrays him.

Now, I know I'm not the world's *most* interesting guy—Benedict Cumberbatch has that title well and truly sewn up—but I'm no sap, either, and I don't have anything to prove to these people. From where I'm sitting they still have to prove to me that this is an *actual* workplace. So I go for intriguing with just a hint of flirtatious charm. For Gloria's benefit. Not Chad's. "I don't want to give everything away on the first date," I say, casting an impish smile around the room.

"Right, well, just so you can get to know us a little better..." Chad's talking to me but he's looking at Archibald, who's picking at a loose thread on his Hawaiian shirt. "...I'll tell you a bit about me. I'm president of the Victorian chapter of the Public Relations Professionals Association, I'm an alumni and regular guest speaker at the Australian Public Affairs Institute and I'm currently studying for my postgraduate degree in communications management and stakeholder relations for the new millennium."

"Like the website," I say.

Gloria snorts.

Another win to me.

Chad smiles while his eyes damn me to an eternity of watching M*A*S*H reruns. "So if you ever want to do any professional development, or just want to broaden your horizons, let me know, and I'll help you out."

Archibald looks up from his shirt. "Barney!" he yells, as though I'm a misbehaving dog. He waves his finger at me. "Why didn't you follow in your mother's footsteps?"

I've been asked this question a million times. It's incomprehensible to many people that the son of a TV star could not also want to be a TV star. "It's not really my thing."

"What exactly is your thing, Barney?" Chad asks, looking at me like I'm a cardboard cutout of a man. Or Flat Stanley.

Everybody stares at me. I haven't had a crowd this captivated for more than a decade. It spurs me on. "Comedy," I say. "Comedy is my thing."

Chad flinches. "Stand-up comedy?"

"You're a comedian?" Gloria asks, leaning forward in her chair.

Jackpot!

"I knew it!" Archibald says. "Dogs don't make cats, Barney..." He's waving his finger again. "...and I know a dog when I see one." He winks like we're involved in a grand conspiracy to conceal the fact that I am, in fact, a dog. Whatever that means.

"Well, yeah. I mean, I'm not Jerry Seinfeld or anything, but I do a bit of stand-up around town." This is stretching the truth, but it's pretty safe unless they grill me on whether "around town" means in your kitchen to a goldfish who died the next day. Unrelated to my routine, I might add.

"Where's your next gig?" Chad says.

Okay, now it's getting dangerous, but for the first time since we met, Gloria looks mildly interested in me. I can't back down now. "Richmond Tavern, this Friday." The Richmond Tavern has had open-mic Friday nights for the past two years. I've never performed at one, but I check once a month to see if they're still running in case I wake up one morning with the ability to overcome the ghosts of comedy routines past.

Chad smiles like a deranged hyena. Sweat works its way past the elastic band of my imitation Calvin Klein trunks. I have a premonition of dread.

"Awesome," Chad says. "Our monthly social event is this Friday night."

I saw this on the agenda—item five—and I turn back to it now. The action column is filled with the words "This week—suggestions?" Everybody groans, including Archibald, and I feel a surge of hope.

Gloria: "Seriously, Chad, I think it's pretty clear no one really wants a monthly social night."

"No way, Gloria. That's just because we've never had any decent suggestions before. Going to Barney's stand-up routine will be perfect."

"We're doing it," Archibald announces, ending any further debate. "Barney, invite your mother.

I've got to go. Meeting closed. Roger that!" He rises from behind his desk and strides back out through the snake pit. He stops in front of me and nods. "I like a man who wears his suit jacket no matter the temperature. Very professional. Very Lawrence of Arabia."

My underpants are wet through.

FOUR

Mike and I have been best mates since we were six years old. Our friendship has survived the rough-and-tumble school years, the university years, and that time in 1999 when I had blond tips put in my hair.

If you had to map the trajectory of our lives, it would look something like the graphs they give you after strengths test in your high school sports class. The blue line, sailing high and free, indicates above-average performance. The red line, shamefully tracking the bottom of the graph, illustrates your paltry attempts to haul yourself up a rope on arms so thin other kids start climbing up on you.

Needless to say, Mike is the blue line, his chart characterized by roaring success, mine by devastating mediocrity. That's why he's got a three-bedroom apartment in Port Melbourne with city and bay vistas, and I've got a two-bedroom only a block away with no vista at all. Just a view. Of a brick wall.

"Hello, mate. Come in," Mike says when he opens his front door. "I've just started cooking dinner." He shakes my hand and then scurries into the kitchen. I follow him over and lean up against the breakfast bar that separates the food preparation area from the open-plan food consumption area. I love modern architecture.

At just over six foot, Mike's a little taller than me. With dark hair, thick eyebrows, and a big forehead just to show off the size of his brain, he looks like a professor who plays professional football in his spare time. His stubble after only one day is impressive and enviably masculine. Like a man. He's wearing a pink apron over his suit pants and shirt, without tie, and has kicked off his shoes to reveal luxurious woolen socks that cost more than my entire wardrobe.

He grins at me over a steaming pot of browning mince. "So how was it, mate? What are they like?"

Before I get a chance to respond, a dangerous, menacing creature enters the room. "Aaaarrgghhhhh," it yells to announce its naked, dripping wet arrival.

"Oliver, get back here now!" Mike's wife, Beth, calls from the bathroom.

I freeze, caught between playing the friendly Uncle Barney and not wanting to be implicated in any pre-bedtime criminal activity. In truth, I'd really rather drop the friendly uncle act. I find interacting with children, anybody's children, even those of my best friends, incredibly daunting. All those wide eyes and honest appraisals. Those piercing questions and looks of justified contempt. So I stand and watch for Oliver's next move. He starts dancing and, as the hissing from the browning meat dissipates, I hear a tinny broadcast of Diddy's "Coming Home" from the *Last Train to Paris* album.

Oliver is working it in the middle of the room with Beth's phone in hand, rather than returning to his mother as suggested. I doubt the two-year-old Oliver is quite Diddy's target demographic, but he's clearly connecting with Diddy's Harlem roots.

"Dance, Unca Barney?" Oliver says, holding his hands out to me.

"Oh, no, mate. You dance, I'll watch."

"Pleaaassseeee."

Mike is smiling at his out-of-control son like a proud criminal patriarch. "Go on, Barney, have a dance with him. I've got to keep this dinner moving."

I walk toward Oliver and begin swaying my hips in time with my boy Diddy. The music loosens me up a little and I experiment with a flick of my hands and a shrug of my shoulders, J-Lo-style.

Oliver copies me, wiggling his hips and shrugging his shoulders as water drips down his beaming face from the thick mop of dark hair plastered to his head. "Pick me up! Pick me up!" he yells as the chorus begins.

I'm into it now. Music has that effect on me. Energizing. Hypnotizing. Even if my dance partner terrifies me. I lift Oliver's slippery body in my hands and hold him at arm's length, whirling him around in a circle. He throws his head back in gleeful abandon. I do the same. The miracle of a child's innocent joy transports us out of the streets of Port Melbourne and into the badlands of Diddy's Harlem. The rising smell of packet-made fajitas adds another layer of texture to our Peter Pan–style journey. It's all laughter and sunshine, shooting stars and lullabies.

Until Oliver urinates on me.

It's a direct hit on my chest. Warm, sticky, and tangy in my nostrils. I start to gag, but manage to get the kid onto the floor and aiming away from me before I go under.

"Barney!" Beth yells, running toward us. "What are you doing?"

What am I doing? What are you doing? What's your kid doing?!

"Mike, tea towel!" Beth says.

Mike tosses a tea towel to Beth like we're on the set of *Grey's Anatomy*. Beth drops to her knees, catches the remaining stream in the towel, and then mops up the rest before it sinks into the rug. The woman's a machine. She should be in the military. Beth takes the phone out of Oliver's hand and, with the swipe of her thumb, Diddy is gone, never making it home.

Beth rests her hands on her knees and breathes out a long sigh, like she's just spent the better part of twelve hours taking care of a volatile, unpredictable maniac. She gifts me a warm, compassionate smile that mirrors the kindness and fatigue in her dark brown eyes. Her straight black hair falls down past her shoulders, more disheveled now than in her corporate acquisition days.

I should mention, just so you get a better picture of Beth and not because I am into racial profiling and/or stereotyping, that she is Asian. Malaysian to be precise. Well, her parents are Malaysian, she was born in Queensland. Despite the fact her Australian accent is thicker than mine, I'm still intimidated by Beth's exotic mystique. She's smarter, better-looking, and more Asian than I will ever be.

She's wearing tracksuit pants and a loose white shirt, sleeves rolled up to her elbows, her forearms still speckled with bubbles from Oliver's bath. She reaches over and guides her son onto her lap. He sits back against her, molding into her body, his wet hair on her chest, his legs resting on her thighs like she was custom-made for him.

I am struck by an unexpected, irrational pang of primal longing at this intimate family moment.

"Hello, Barney."

"Hi, Beth." I look down at my wet shirt.

"Don't worry about that. It's just a bit of wee."

I don't know at what point in one's life the abjectly degrading experience of having another human being urinate on you becomes "just a bit of wee," but I do know that I've yet to arrive at that point. Possibly because I don't have children. Or perhaps because I'm deeply immature. At any rate, Mike lends me a shirt and Beth tosses mine into the washing machine with, no doubt, a whole lot of other clothing that Oliver has soiled throughout the day. Fabulous.

Once Oliver is packed off to bed and Mike has finished preparing his Mexican masterpiece, we all sit down at the table and slump into our chairs.

"Congratulations on getting through your first day, Barney," Mike says, raising a glass of wine. "Now, tell us all about it."

"Well..." I search for the right words. I've known Mike all my post-toddler life, and Beth for the past fifteen years. They are the only two people in the world I don't need to pretend to. "...it was an absolute shambles."

"What do you mean?" Beth asks, sitting up straight and leaning in toward me.

"I don't know how to describe it, Beth. I mean, you worked in the private sector right up until Olly was born, and I always imagined you and Mike rocking up every day to these amazing offices with secretaries and city views and free coffee."

They both stare at me, their blank expressions confirming my suspicions that this is *exactly* what they rocked up to. What Mike still rocks up to.

"But this joint might as well be running out of my mum's garage. It's the most amateur outfit I've ever seen. And the boss is completely nuts. He wore a Hawaiian shirt today!"

They both nod and laugh, and I can hear the mixture of mirth and sympathy, like it's something everybody has to experience before making it to the big time.

"So what's the role? What have they actually got you doing?" Mike asks through a mouthful of fajita.

"Nothing. But it doesn't matter because I've decided to quit."

"What? It took you a month to find a job and you've only worked there one day. You can't quit!"

"I have to."

"Why?"

"Because they want me to work on a campaign for the department."

"Okay," Beth says. "That could be awkward, but I can't see why it's a reason to quit."

"But don't you see, Beth? The only reason I got the job is because I worked at the department. If they find out what happened, they'll fire me on the spot."

"Mike said you got the job because the boss wanted to marry your mum."

"That's what I thought, but then today he started talking about Nelson Mandela."

"What's he got to do with it?"

"I'm not really sure, but there's some link between Mandela liberating South Africa from apartheid and me securing a communications contract with the Department of Healthy Living. I thought this was going to be my great escape, my triumphant re-entry into the workforce. Instead of that, there wasn't even anyone there to greet me at reception. There is no reception!"

They start up again with the sympathetic nodding.

"This is probably the most unprofessional organization in Melbourne and I'm still way out of my league. They've got me working with this guy Chad. He's an American and a complete PR fanboy, but he's very good at his job. We had a brainstorming session this afternoon and he wiped the floor with me. He and Gloria acted like I wasn't even there."

"Gloria?" Mike says. "From the interview?"

"Wait, there's a Gloria?" Beth says. "Mike, why didn't you tell me there's a Gloria?"

"Because Barney said he's in love with her and if I told you about every person Barney says he's in love with, all we'd ever talk about is British girl bands."

"Two words, Mike: Posh Spice."

"Get real, mate. Baby Spice every day of the week."

"Okay, so if we could just step back from your teenage fantasies for a moment," Beth says, "maybe you could tell me about this real person, Gloria."

"Don't be cruel, Beth. The Spice Girls are real people, too," Mike says. "And they've stuck by Barney for a lot longer than the three girlfriends he's had since we've known him."

Beth ignores Mike's distressing, though accurate, summation of my love life and looks at me like I'm on the stand.

"Gloria was on the interview panel," I say. And then I'm a bit lost for words. How do you describe perfection? "She has a tiny scar on the right side of her chin."

Mike groans.

Beth grabs my hands. "Barney Conroy, you really have fallen for her!"

I smile at being found out, and then I remember my insurmountable conundrum. I stop smiling. "It's pointless, Beth. I have to resign. I can't work on a campaign for the department. You know I can't."

"Rubbish," Mike says. "You *have* to go back. Show those fools exactly what they gave up."

Beth: "You didn't do anything wrong, Barney. They're the ones who should be ashamed of themselves. You can hold your head high."

"There is something else," I say in the same tone I had to use when I told Mike I was going to see P!nk in concert. For the third time.

"Oh, Barney. What did you do?" Mike asks, sensing I've got myself into trouble by being a clown, again. He knows me well.

"I told them I'm a stand-up comedian and that I'm performing at an open-mic night this Friday. They've decided to make it the venue for the monthly work social event."

There's a moment of silence. Then Beth's cheeks balloon out from the air she's trying to hold in her mouth. But the pressure is too much and she does one of those laughs when you try to stop yourself but you can't and the result is an explosive raspberry. Mike follows suit with silent convulsions of his shoulders as tears well in his eyes.

"Thanks, guys," I say. And then I start laughing, too. How can I help it? If somebody told me the story of my life, I'd want to laugh at them as well. With great relief, in fact, in a *thank God that's not my wretched existence you're describing* kind of way.

Three days later, when the laughter dies down, Mike wipes the tears from his eyes. "What were you thinking?"

"I was trying to impress Gloria."

"Mate, this Gloria must be *extraordinary* for you to commit to an open-mic night."

"Not extraordinary, Mike. Unrivaled. But I can't do it. Just the thought of standing on that stage scares me half to death."

Beth finishes the last of her fajita and sits back in her chair. She folds her arms and creases her brow like she's a prophet. "You know what you need, Barney?"

"What?"

"A spinal cord."

She's on to me!

But I play it cool. "I have a spinal cord, Beth."

"Yes, but it doesn't seem to be working. You're an educated, experienced, highly intelligent man. But for some reason, you've got no self-confidence. And you've got no spine. You remember our university days?"

I nod.

"You were the funniest guy I'd ever met. Seriously, you made Mike look like a concrete slab."

"Turn it up!" Mike says.

Aside from the no spine part, Beth's words fill me with a warm, unfamiliar sensation. A sense of being appreciated, worthwhile, *valuable* even.

Then my best mate Mike speaks. "Beth's right, Barney. Oliver's spinal fortitude puts you to shame and he wears Elmo underpants *by choice.*"

"Not funny."

"Not meant to be. Meant to be inspirational."

"Seriously, Barney," Beth says. "You need to work on this campaign for the department. You need to own this job, and you need to do that comeback stand-up routine you've been dreaming about for years."

"You both know I can't do that."

"Why not?" Beth says, getting all Tom Cruise up in Jack Nicholson's face on me. "You had one bad routine. Everybody has off nights."

"What was the headline, Mike?" I ask.

He sucks in a breath through his teeth like it's going to hurt him to speak the words. He screws his face up. "Barney Unfarney."

"That's right," I say. "Barney Unfarney; the description of my routine in front of a thousand people at the end-of-year university ball. I rest my case, Your Honor."

"It was one review," Beth says. "And it wasn't that bad."

"That's like describing the battle of Armageddon as a minor skirmish. The review mourned the death of comedy. And it was printed in the university yearbook, which thousands of people still have on their bookshelves."

"They do not. And, anyway, who cares about them?" This doesn't strike me as a particularly compelling argument, but Beth ploughs on with the attack. "You need to find that funny guy we all loved at university. Bring him back onto the stage."

"I don't know if he still exists. That was a long time ago and now's not the right time for a comeback. I think I might be having a midlife crisis."

"Barney, you're thirty-four," Mike says. "You're not eligible for a midlife crisis for another ten years."

"Two times thirty-four is sixty-eight, and by the time you're sixty-eight, you might as well be dead. So this is my midlife."

"I'm just going to ignore that," Mike says. "And I'm going to tell you, Barney, that we've talked about your comedy a million times. You need to forget about what you *think* people want to hear, and start focusing on what makes you laugh. That's when you're actually funny."

He's about to mention the book.

"And get rid of that stupid book."

"What book?" Beth asks.

"It's a how to write comedy book that Barney bought after the Unfarney incident. I blame it for the disintegration of his stand-up career."

"Get rid of the book, Barney," Beth says.

The book was supposed to teach me how to write a routine that was guaranteed to make people laugh. I once tried its formula on Mike. I didn't get the guaranteed laugh; instead, he looked like he'd come face-to-face with the Angel of Death.

They both stare at me, waiting for my decision. I may not be midlife, but I'm definitely in the throes of a crisis. I never planned to be a public servant. I never even planned to have a real job. I was going to tour the world making people laugh. Instead, my fallback option became my career and the farthest I've traveled is Far North Queensland. Maybe this is my chance. Maybe this is my time to reclaim my life before it's too late. I still need a reliable income, but I don't want to die without giving my dream one more shot.

I ball my hands into fists. "Okay. I'll get rid of the book. I'll smash this routine to pieces. And I'll nail the job with the department."

"My oath, you will," Mike says, slapping his knee.

"Good for you, Barney," Beth says.

"All right, thanks, guys. I really appreciate it. All I have to do now is come up with the greatest idea for a communications campaign the Department of Healthy Living has ever seen. Then I can concentrate on my routine."

"Well, what are you waiting for?" Mike says. "Get out of here. Go home and begin the magic."

I hesitate. "Can I just check one thing first?"

"What?"

"What's for dessert?"

FIVE

I'm so early, I'm the first to arrive. This should be cause for celebration, but they forgot the part in the orientation when they give you a key to the locked door of the office. So I start by pacing up and down the hallway, rehearsing the presentation to accompany my slide deck (nobody in the private sector calls them PowerPoint presentations these days).

I stayed up all night but I'm not feeling the lack of sleep because I'm running on the buzz of a great idea. *The* great idea. The *greatest* idea I've ever had in my private sector career.

Thirty-six minutes later, I'm slumped on the floor. I'm in that half-world between sleep and consciousness. Not the delicious *Gloria's about to kiss me* half-world, but the excruciating *my blood has turned to cement* half-world. Accompanied by the drool I can feel, but can't stop, rolling down my chin.

I don't know how long I'm out before I hear the voice. "Barn dog. You okay, man?"

"Huh, ahh, yeah, what, yeah, cool, yeah, just stretching." I straighten my right leg and reach out to touch my toes, wiping the drool from my chin with the back of my left hand. "Cramp. Been running." I pump my arms as evidence that I know how to run.

"Right. Can you stand up?"

"Yeah, of course, man." But when I do try to stand up I realize that, while my right leg is functional, my left leg has, in fact, cramped up. I stand, and immediately fall over. Chad gives me his arm and drags me to my feet. I brace myself against the door as he walks through, sucking in some deep breaths to get the oxygen back into my legs.

I load my slide deck onto my computer and go through the presentation a few times in my head, waiting for Gloria to arrive. Yesterday afternoon, after Chad was finished mopping the floor with my ineptitude, we all decided in favor of Chad's communications campaign proposal. I'm at a bit of a loss to explain it, but I heard the phrases "online seeding," "strategic communications thread," "metaphoric hook," and "blogger outreach." It has something to do with uploading videos of yourself exercising to a campaign website that people can then comment and vote on. Most votes for best exercise routine equals winner. It has interaction, shareability, and online community engagement. It's the perfect campaign for the new millennium.

And the department will hate it.

If there's one thing I know, it's that the Department of Healthy Living is not interested in online community engagement. They don't want anyone going on a department-sponsored website, ignoring the purpose of the campaign and slagging off the government instead.

So I've come up with a campaign that is innovative, creative, and, most importantly, much safer. The only thing I can offer Rogerson is my experience, and I've distilled that down into one, awesome deck.

When Gloria finally arrives fourteen minutes into my rehearsal, I've been through my presentation about 42 million times. I spring to my feet like Usain Bolt off the blocks, and immediately cramp up again. Need more oxygen. I keep my feet and limp toward her. She looks at me the same way everyone with a job looks at the toothless, homeless guy walking toward you in the city mall at lunchtime. She actually moves her handbag away from me, so I try to tone down the desperation.

"Morning!" I yell.

Gloria takes a step backward as if something just exploded in front of her. She touches her ear. It's a quick, delicate gesture, but I can tell she's checking for blood from a ruptured eardrum.

"Morning, Barney."

"Morning!" I yell again. I need to come up with something more personable. "Can we book a meeting room?"

"What?"

"We need a meeting room."

"What for?"

"I've got another idea for the Healthy Living campaign."

Chad stands up from his desk, sensing the challenge. He's like a lion that can smell a threatening slide deck from five hundred yards. He prowls across the room, growling his words, Mufasa-style. "We've already settled on an idea, Barney."

Look at the stars, Simba. The great kings of the past look down on us from those stars.

Man, I need some sleep. Can't get James Earl Jones out of my head.

"We don't have time for new concepts," Gloria says. "We're going to have to work all weekend just to get Chad's campaign scoped and ready to present on Tuesday."

I channel the great kings of the past. "Okay, sure, I understand. But I promise this will only take fifteen minutes. If you don't like it, we move with Chad's campaign straightaway. I really think it's worth it, just to make sure we've covered all bases." And then I slip in the line that's going to win me Pride Rock. "I understand the way these guys think. I spent four years there, so I can get inside their heads."

I actually see the decision pass across Gloria's bright, intelligent eyes; my cramping body is failing, but getting no sleep has endowed me with powerful extrasensory perception. I get overconfident and stare at her like I'm Edward Cullen, trying to divine her true feelings for me. Trying to unearth her desire. Trying to unmask her passion.

"I'll call Martha."

"I love you, too."

"What?"

"My left shoe."

"What?"

"Nothing."

Change the subject!

"Who's Martha?"

"Receptionist on forty-eight."

What?

Impossibly Blonde Hair is called *Martha*. How ridiculous.

Martha tells Gloria we can have the boardroom for fifteen minutes only, "right now."

As we're walking out the door to the lifts, Archibald arrives. Thankfully, he's wearing a suit. "What's this?" he asks. "Early morning mutiny?"

"Barney wants to pitch a new idea for the Healthy Living campaign," Gloria says.

"Yesterday, you recommended Chad's idea. What's changed?"

"Good question," Chad says.

Archibald looks us over. Then he smiles, opens his eyes wide, and flares his nostrils. "I see what's going on here," he says. "It's a good old-fashioned pitch-off. Let's spill some blood!"

I'm concerned that he may be speaking literally, but we all follow him to the lift and then ride up to Heaven in silence. Now I really know how Russell Crowe felt before entering the Colosseum. There's a comic moment of tomfoolery when Gloria insists I go out of the lift first because I'm closest to the door and I insist that she go first—"age before beauty!" (doesn't go down well, by the way)—and then the doors close on us and we ride back down to thirty-two. By the time we get back to Nirvana on forty-eight, the boardroom is now ours for ten minutes only.

Achal calls to find out where we are and arrives in the boardroom just as the computer loads up and the projector hums to life. I now have six minutes to run through my deck. I hit the slide show button—the one that makes dreams come to life—and my presentation begins. The screen fills with a blank white screen. I click the mouse to make the first word appear (I go for the classic animation *appear* rather than the more ritzy *fly in* or *pinwheel*).

The word *Track* appears in big, black, bold, Arial font.

Another click.

Your

Last click.

Attack

I pause to let the magnificence sink in. Chad's squinting at the words like he can't see them properly, which is impossible, unless he's actually a badger in a human suit, given they're forty-four-point type on a two-meter-wide projection canvas. Gloria is staring as though she's waiting for more, Archibald is breathing with such gusto at the imagined scent of blood that it's threatening to put me off my game, and Achal is motionless.

"Track Your Attack," I say, channeling my old mate Hugh Jackman in *The Boy from Oz*, my arm arcing across the room, tracing the giant words on the screen.

"Detail," Gloria says, which is fair enough given we've got five minutes left.

"We ask people to sign up to the Track Your Attack campaign by setting targets for the amount of kilometers they aim to walk or run every week. It runs for two months with weekly prizes like healthy eating cookbooks and exercise equipment, and a grand prize of a family and friends healthy living pack. Six gym memberships for them and their family or friends. A weeklong retreat to a detox spa and, just to show we're in this for the long haul, a Fitbit each to encourage them to keep up the good work."

Gloria tilts her head to one side as though she's actually considering the idea.

"How will they track their kilometers?" Archibald asks. "What's the social element? How are we going to get share-ability? Why would people engage with this online?" This is an unforeseen development. I wasn't expecting Archibald to actually listen and I certainly wasn't expecting probing questions. It stuns me for a moment until Gloria comes to my rescue.

"We're running out of time, Barney. Take us through the rest of the slides."

Me: "That's it."

Gloria: "That's it?"

Me: "Yeah, that's it, no more slides. Just the idea."

Archie: "Pitch-offs aren't what they used to be."

James Earl Jones: "Everything the light touches is our kingdom."

To be honest, I haven't thought a lot past the broad idea. Details haven't really been my thing since I got my first job as a supervisor. That's what staff members are for. But this morning, with my extrasensory perception and Simba-before-his-uncle-kills-his-dad confidence, I start to create on the fly.

Track-ability: "We'll give everybody who signs up for the campaign a pair of shoes. And we'll put a tracking device in them that automatically maps their progress online. That's all the technology they'll need." I have no idea whether this is technically possible, but it sounds great.

Social element: "Entrants will each be given their own page on the master site, which displays on a map where they've walked or run that week. They'll be ranked on a leader board alongside others in their age and fitness categories, and against their personal goals." I have no idea whether this is technically possible, but it sounds great.

Share-ability: "And they can post their results to Facebook or any of their social networks. They can tweet about their progress or even just e-mail people with automatically generated text summarizing their performance for the week." I have no idea whether this is technically possible, but it sounds great.

I finish, a little breathless from my lack of sleep and professional career being on the line. There's a terrible moment of silence that feels like the eternity between asking a girl to go out with you and watching as her mind races to fabricate a reason to say no.

Then Gloria fills the room with her smile. "I like it. I think it could work."

Archibald leans back in his chair, crosses his arms, and nods his head.

Chad's not licked yet, though. "When exactly do you propose to invent a shoe that has inbuilt GPS capabilities that can be mapped on a website built in a government content management system that integrates with Google maps and Facebook?"

I hate Americans.

But then the sound of the subcontinent dances around my ears. "Easy, mate. We'll just fit each shoe with a tiny RFID and use some open-source plug-ins for the rest."

I love Indians.

We all turn to Achal. "RFID?" Gloria asks.

"Radio frequency identification," Achal says, as though he's just spelled out the universally known acronym YOLO.

Archibald continues. "It's basically a little barcode that you could stick in the shoe to see where it goes. It'll be perfect for Barney's campaign."

I *love* that he's named a campaign after me.

Achal gets up and starts to walk out of the room as though that's the end of it.

"Wait, where are you going?" Chad asks, unable to hide his desperation. "We haven't voted."

"Time to spill some blood!" Archibald yells. "Sit down, Achal. We'll go around the table. Barney and Chad have to abstain." He rubs his hands together. "All right, I'll strike the first blow...Track Your Attack!" He turns to Gloria.

She hesitates and looks at Achal. "Do you really think you could provide the technical support to make it happen? Have we got the resources?"

"Yes. And I can get extra contractors if we need them. My cousins are always harassing me for a job."

"Minimum wage," Archibald says.

Then Gloria turns to me. "You really think this could work, Barney? You think it's got a better chance than yesterday's idea?"

I'm thirty-four years old, but I've spent most of my life since I was fifteen feeling like I was fifteen. Sometimes fourteen. I've never felt like I belonged in the grown-up world. Even when I kept getting promotions at work, more responsibility, more staff members, I felt like I was just a kid playacting and waiting to be uncovered as a fifteen- or sometimes fourteen-year-old fraud.

But when Gloria looks at me like she values my opinion. When she looks at me like I'm about to say something meaningful that is meaningful because *I'm* saying it and not because I read it on Wikipedia, well, at that moment, I feel at least twenty-three.

"Yes. I think they'll like it."

"Okay, then. I vote for Track Your Attack."

"It's a massacre!" Archibald cries, and Chad, the poor bloke, actually looks like he's lost a lot of blood. His face is paler than the back of my knees and I'm pretty sure I hear his heart break.

The door swings open and some jaundiced, pot-bellied bald guy barges in. "We've got this room booked!"

Barney

The four of us are forced back out into reception, which then becomes the backdrop for the greatest moment of my twenty-three-year-old life. Gloria places a hand on my forearm. "Nice work, Barney," she says with a smile. Her touch is so gentle I can only just feel it through my suit jacket, yet it's strong enough to fill my whole body with what I believe Huey Lewis would call the power of love.

Such a magnificent moment requires me to play it confident, yet cool. Man of experience, yet still hip enough to be in touch with the latest trends.

"Hakuna matata," I say. And then I further ruin the moment by winking at her, which, from the look on her face, she interprets as a disturbed, leering gesture. So I try to smooth it over with a nonchalant click of my tongue as I enter the lift.

She takes the stairs.

SIX

On Mum's instruction, her driver pulls up three blocks away from the pub. She insisted on giving me a lift, convinced I'd be too nervous to drive. She was right. We're sitting in the backseat and I'm due on stage in fifteen minutes. I think Mum knew that if I arrived at the pub too early, there was a huge chance I'd flee the scene.

Mum is supposed to be at a charity gala right now, but as soon as she found out about my gig, she told the organizers she'd be late. She's wearing a long black dress that ties up around the back of her neck, leaving her arms and shoulders bare. It's accompanied by a thick silver belt that accentuates her still-taut waistline, and she's wearing a diamond necklace. Her dark hair is pulled back into a tight bun and her blue eyes flash at me beneath long lashes. She looks every bit the television royalty that she is, and she will be the most over-dressed person ever to set foot in the Richmond Tavern.

"Well, Barney. This is your time, my love." She smiles at me like she believes I'm going to do well.

"I'm terrified."

"I know you are. And I'm glad you are. If you weren't scared, it would mean you didn't care."

"I've never cared this much about anything, Mum."

"Excellent. That means you're ready to take the stage." She reaches across and holds my hand. "You're having a bit of a rough time, Barney. I know what it's like to have rough times. And I also know that the best way to cope with them is to get out there and do the thing you love."

"How do I know that I still love it?"

"I'll tell you how I know. When I'm in a scene, and I'm living out a character, when I'm inhabiting her and bringing her to life for people to see and know, that's when nothing else matters. That's when the rough times fade to nothing."

"I could do with a bit of that."

Mum places her hand on the side of my face like she used to when I was a little boy. "And that's how you know you've found your passion...when you're doing it, nothing else matters."

Oh, how I would love it if nothing else mattered.

"Do you mind if I go in on my own, Mum?"

"Wouldn't have it any other way. I'll slip in when the lights go down." Mum takes my hands and holds them up in front of us like we're making a pact. "Be brave. Be funny. Be yourself."

* * *

Comedy is built on two fundamental pillars: surprise and recognition. At least that's what the book tells me. The book Mike told me to throw away...which I didn't throw away. How could I? What it's saying makes sense. I know everybody wants me to be myself and all that, but I don't think bending myself around a bit of structure is such a crime. And despite getting all Pat Benatar about reclaiming my comedy with Mike and Beth the other night, they're not the ones who have to stand up here and invite public ridicule.

The book also says that when performing stand-up, you should build slowly by starting with a few funny, but not laugh-out-loud, jokes. A theme is a good idea because it's a great way to keep the routine flowing. So I've got a theme, and right up until about six seconds ago, I thought it was a really good one.

Now I just wish I was dead. Or perhaps simply on another planet. At the very least, not in the same hemisphere as this stage.

The back room of the pub is smaller than I had anticipated. I was hoping for some cavernous, great barn with nobody in it. Like an advertising industry ethics convention. Instead, I feel like the patrons are on stage *with* me. Like if I sneeze too enthusiastically, I'll knock somebody's beer glass onto their lap, which I'm also sitting in.

There are half a dozen tables scattered around the dimly lit room, and it smells like beer and sweat and abject terror. Or that could just be me. The crowd is fidgeting, there are still pockets of conversation going on in dark corners, and now is the time I need to own the stage.

I look at the Rogerson table, which also has Mike and Beth on it, and everybody, even Chad, smiles at me. Mike shakes an encouraging fist and Beth nods like I'm a sure thing. But it's Gloria's part-expectant, part-encouraging smile that propels me forward into my routine.

"Hi, everyone. I'm Barney."

An awed silence descends upon the room, which, frankly, catches me completely off guard. Could it really be that easy to tame a crowd? Just by telling them your name is Barney? There's some whispering, some movement in the semidarkness, and then I realize what has captivated the moderately inebriated (except for the guy at the front table who is unconscious) patrons of the Richmond Tavern. Australian television royalty has just entered the room.

I squint to see my mother gliding to the Rogerson table. She looks like a queen being revered by her subjects. A chair appears out of nowhere—that happens all the time when you're famous—and Mum wedges in between Mike and Beth. I lean around the beam of the retina-frying spotlight to get a proper look at her. She smiles and gives me a small wave.

I'm ready to go.

Introduce the theme: "So there's this new coffee shop down the road from me called the Literal Café."

Comedy is about surprise and recognition. It's also about pushing boundaries without offending the audience: "I went in for a coffee and ordered a short black."

Pause to build anticipation.

"They brought me a Kalahari bushman!"

Silence. Dead, murdering, heart-stopping silence.

But it's not racist. It's observational and boundary pushing. Kalahari bushmen are short and black. It's comedy!

Move on, move on! Gross them out a little but don't go too far, just enough to make them chuckle, but not vomit. "And then I made the mistake of using the slang term for a vanilla slice. 'One snot block, please.' And that's what they brought me, a big block of snot! So I gave it to the Kalahari bushman because he looked like he could use a feed!"

Silence. Dead, murdering, heart-stopping silence.

But it's not racist! There's nothing to eat in the desert!

Explain (desperately): "Because it's the Literal Café, you see!"

Nothing. Although I do think I hear somebody's appendix burst. I begin to wish again for my own death and waste precious seconds imagining the epitaph on my gravestone: *Barney Elvis Conroy. So unfunny he deserved to die.* I long for the sweet release of the overhead lighting tumbling down and cracking my head open. Or for somebody in the audience to spontaneously combust.

Neither happens and I am left stranded on stage. Gotta keep going. "I tell you one thing you don't want to get wrong at the Literal Café, and that's talking about eating a horse when you're ordering your breakfast. Nobody actually wants a horse on their plate; how would you swallow its shoes?"

The crowd is frozen. Extreme, collective shock is plastered across their faces. Nobody moves, or speaks, or breathes, until a soft voice breaks the trance. It's a familiar, subcontinental voice that repeats the same phrase over and over, growing in strength as the people cast off the shackles of witnessing the assassination of comedy. More voices sound. The chorus rises until the chant becomes a living, threatening, hilarious thing.

"You suck! You suck! You suck!" they cry as one.

And as I step off the stage, four and a half minutes before I was scheduled to wrap, the crowd erupts into applause. Wild, reckless applause as though this is the greatest night of their lives. "You suck! You suck! You suck!"

* * *

"You know Achal started the chant, don't you?" Gloria says as we stand at the bar waiting to order a drink.

"Yeah, I could tell from the accent. Why'd he do it?"

"Don't really know. He's unpredictable."

It's half an hour since my act finished. There were three other comedians after me and, although my routine was the shortest, it attracted the most laughs. Now I'm in the middle of the most engaging and longest-running conversation I've ever had with Gloria that isn't about work. I'm very keen to keep it going. "I thought I heard Archibald in there as well."

Gloria laughs. "Oh, yeah. Archie can't control himself around angry crowds. He took me to a football match last year and we were supposed to be in the corporate box together. But when Archie realized the bay in front of us was full of chanting larrikins, he opened the window, leaped out, and immediately joined in the fun. I spent the rest of the game watching him whip the crowd into a frenzy. They loved him. I drank champagne."

"I can't figure that guy out. The Hawaiian shirt made me think he was insane. Then I thought maybe he was a genius after the pitch-off. But now I think maybe he's insane again."

Gloria laughs. "He's not insane. He's charismatic. That's part of the reason I love working for him. He's one of those very smart guys who doesn't need to let everybody around him know just how smart he is. And he's got no shame, which makes him a lot of fun."

"So that explains the shirt."

"Not quite. Archie's the patron of a charity that raises money for children living with heart problems. Once a year, they hold a Hawaiian shirt day. You wear a shirt to the office and your coworkers donate to the cause."

"Wow, I had no idea. Were his kids sick or something? Is that how he got involved?"

"No, the charity just asked him to be a corporate sponsor. And he's a good guy."

"But he is a little odd, right? I'm not making that up."

"No, you're not making that up. But a little odd's not necessarily a bad thing, is it?"

Maybe it's the euphoria of being chanted off stage, but I wonder for a moment if Gloria is referring to me as being a little odd, which is *not necessarily a bad thing!* I haven't had this kind of positive reinforcement from a woman since Jessica Taylor told me she liked my *ALF* T-shirt back in the third grade.

"I think he might have proposed to your mum."

"How'd she take it?"

"Gracefully, but I'm pretty sure it was a no."

"Good, because I'm not ready to start calling him Dad just yet."

"She was nice."

"Even though there are many other far more worthy people whose achievements we should be celebrating?"

Gloria laughs. My first genuine laugh of the night. It's a rich, throaty sound that I could listen to for the rest of my life.

"What would you like?" the barman asks, interrupting the sound I could listen to for the rest of my life.

Your sudden, unexpected, and very welcome death.

"Two pots of draught, please, mate," Gloria says.

I get my wallet out.

"My shout, Barney," Gloria says. "A celebratory drink."

"What are we celebrating?"

"That you're still alive. There was a tense moment there after the Kalahari bushmen joke when it could have gone either way. You're lucky they went for the chant and not the guillotine."

"Which way were you leaning?"

"Well, it would have been fun to see you try to escape an on-stage beheading, but I need you for our meeting next week, so I helped bolster the 'you suck' chant with Achal and Archie." I love Gloria even more outside the office. She's relaxed, she's funny, she's talking to me without issuing instructions.

Mum walks over to us. "Well, that was a lot of fun, Barney. Did you enjoy yourself, Gloria?"

"I did, thank you, Mrs. Conroy."

"Please, it's Audrey. I'm only Mrs. Conroy in court."

"That sounds intriguing."

"Not really. Just defamation suits against trashy magazines mostly. They paid for Barney's education."

"Well, I can see from tonight that was money well spent."

Mum laughs. "You're funny."

Despite Gloria's bravado about famous people being just like the rest of us, she blushes.

Mum turns to me. "And you, Barney, were fantastic."

"Mum, they chanted me off stage. I think you may have lost your objectivity."

"Not at all. I joined in the chant. It was brilliant. You came here to make them laugh, and that's exactly what you did."

"Even if it wasn't deliberate?"

"Especially because it wasn't deliberate. It means you're a natural."

I get a bit carried away by all this praise and launch into a humble bow, channeling Jackman again. While I'm at ninety degrees and staring at

Gloria's very practical flats on very stained carpet, I wonder, too late, whether this is pushing it and I'm heading into annoying idiot territory. I straighten up, fearing the contempt in Gloria's eyes. But I'm met only by warmth and Gloria with her hair out. She's still wearing her work suit—no casual Friday for her—but she's taken out her ponytail, and her long dark hair is falling over her shoulders. I'd really like to reach out and stroke it, but I don't have the street cred of Robert Downey Jr. so I refrain.

"Well, children, I have to leave," Mum announces. "I'm due on stage myself in half an hour, so I'd better get moving."

"Thanks for coming, Mum. I really appreciate it."

She hugs me like I'm eight years old.

Gloria extends her hand. "It was lovely to meet you, Audrey." Mum ignores her hand and hugs Gloria the same way she just hugged me. Gloria stiffens, but then relaxes in Mum's arms. A shadow passes over her eyes, leaving the trace of tears in its wake.

What's that all about?

"Good-bye, Gloria. Don't let Barney stay out too late. He gets grumpy without enough sleep."

"Are you okay?" I ask Gloria when Mum has left.

She sniffs and dabs at her eye with a knuckle. "Yeah, of course. I just haven't been hugged like that for a while. Your mum really hugs like a mum."

There's guaranteed to be a subtext I'm missing, but I don't get to explore it because Gloria picks up our beers and heads back to our table. Only Mike and Beth are left.

"Where'd everybody go?"

"Chad and Archibald are playing pool in the next room," Mike says. "I'm not sure what happened to Achal."

"He went home in disgust after being served a flat lemonade," Beth says. "Is it just me or is that a bit of an extreme reaction?"

Gloria sits down beside Beth. "Achal takes his lemonade very seriously," she says.

I take the chair next to Mike.

He puts a hand on my shoulder. "Well, mate. We've decided your routine was officially the worst attempt at comedy this country has ever seen. But it was also the most fun I've had chanting 'you suck' in my life."

"Thanks, Mike. That means a lot."

"How many times in your life have you had to chant 'you suck'?" Gloria asks, in what I can only conclude is a thrilling defense of my dignity.

"You forget, Gloria, that Barney and I went to a private boys' school. At said private boys' school, we were forced to support our private boy colleagues in their many and varied manly sporting adventures. Support generally consisted of ruthlessly mocking the opposition with the universally known, and devastatingly effective, 'you suck' chant."

"And here I was thinking I didn't need the privilege of a private school education. I could not have been *more* wrong." Gloria shakes her head in mock despair. Mike and Beth laugh. I stare at Gloria, imagining, again, what it might be like to kiss her. Her phone rings. "Excuse me for a sec."

As soon as she's out of earshot, Beth begins a four-hour monologue entitled *Things Barney Already Knows*. "Barney, you *have* to ask her out. She's smart, she's funny, she's beautiful, *and* she's got great dress sense. She's perfect for you. Absolutely perfect. You could have children with that woman, Barney, I mean it!" Beth is leaning across the table with crazy, zealot eyes that both inspire and terrify me.

"Beth's right, Barney," Mike says. "And I reckon you might be in with a shot. I saw the way Gloria was looking at you during your routine."

I want to ask Mike how Gloria was looking at me during my routine, but Gloria herself turns up. So I fill in the blanks: admiringly, yearningly, I know I shouldn't fall for the unstable yet inspired genius of the stand-up comedian, but I just can't help myselfly.

"I have to go," she says.

My heart implodes.

"And so do you."

My heart replodes.

Beth's mouth drops open. Mike's eyes are wide in shock.

Thanks for the vote of confidence, guys.

But I must admit, I'm also unprepared for this development in our relationship. Gloria, the most stunningly intelligent and beautiful woman I have ever met, just told me we have to leave together. It's enough to make a grown man weep. I settle for choking on my beer. I cough and splutter in recovery while Mike whacks me hard enough on the back to convince my lungs it's not yet over. When I come to, Gloria is looking at us all with narrowed eyes, unconcerned about my near-death experience.

"So...I'm going home, then," she says, partly as a statement, partly questioning whether we all got that.

"Fabulous!" Beth cries.

"Terrific!" Mike says.

"Barney, have you got a minute?"

"He sure does!" Mike and Beth yell in that weird *we've been married too long and now we say the same thing at the same time* phenomenon.

Gloria leads me outside into the open air with the noise of the pub still ringing in my ears. We walk to the edge of the light, just far enough away from the bouncer to avoid a stray concussion if things get ugly with the boofheads in tight-fitting T-shirts who just rocked up.

Gloria stops and gives me a worried look. Then I get worried. About her. Then I feel guilty because I've been so busy thinking about whether to kiss her first or let her kiss me that I've ignored the fact that the phone call may have brought bad news.

"I have to go home tomorrow," she says.

"I thought you were going home tonight?"

"No, I mean *home* home. Back to the country to see my dad."

"You're from the country?" I did *not* see that coming. I thought country people were more or less barbarians. Like the guys on *Farmer Wants a Wife*.

"You got a problem with that?"

The natives are getting restless!

"No, not at all. You just seem so, you know, normal." It's clear from Gloria's facial expression—intermingled offense and blinding rage—that I'm

126

turning the kiss-or-wait-to-be-kissed conundrum into something of a moot point. So I deftly change topic. "What's your dad's problem?" This ends up sounding quite a bit more obnoxious than I had planned.

"He doesn't have a *problem,* Barney. But he's received a letter from the tax office telling him he's up for a massive fine if he doesn't get his BAS lodgment sorted out."

I have absolutely no idea what a BAS lodgment is, but I nod like I'm the head of the Treasury Department and make a worried sound to counteract my inadvertent obnoxiousness.

Gloria softens. "I hate to ask you this, Barney, but we really need to work on the pitch this weekend, so I was thinking that maybe..." And before she finishes, I catch a glimpse of Paradise as Gloria looks vulnerable. Or is it indecisive? She bites her bottom lip. "...maybe you could come with me. It's a long drive and I'll only need a few hours to sort Dad out, so we could work on the pitch on the way up and back, and for a good half day at the farm as well."

I think long and hard about how I should play this. Do I stretch it out, make her work for it? Do I act like this isn't the greatest offer I've ever had in my life? Do I pretend that it's going to be really tough for me because I've got lots of things on this weekend? I don't know exactly how long a nano-second is, but about two of them pass before I respond.

"I'm in." I try to say this with a deep and definitive voice, but my sudden turn of *amazing good fortune* has made it difficult for me to manage more than a strangled croak.

Gloria looks surprised, which makes me think maybe I should have held out for longer. But it doesn't bother me for long—four nanoseconds maybe—because the next thing I know, her hand is on my forearm again, but with real pressure this time.

"Thanks, Barney. It means a lot to me."

If it wasn't for the memory of her hand on my arm, I think I'd suspect that I was dead. No other part of my body appears to be responding to my brain's commands. But then again, my brain isn't giving any commands other than "Remember what that touch felt like! Remember what that touch felt like!"

"Text me your address and I'll pick you up in the morning. Is nine o'clock okay?"

Remember what that touch felt like! Remember what that touch felt like!

Nod. Smile. Offer to wait for a cab. Notice that cab carrying more tight-shirted boofheads has pulled up alongside curb. Make sure Gloria gets safely into her cab. React to her wave. Lift right hand. Wave back.

Remember what that touch felt like! Remember what that touch felt like!

Gloria calls to me from the window of the cab as it prepares to pull away. "Barney!" She's forcing a smile. "You're not a closet psychopath or anything, are you?"

"Depends who's asking!"

The cab speeds off.

Back in the pub, Mike and Beth have hit parenting Cinderella hour. I look at my watch: 10:03 p.m. They both look catatonic. Somebody snuck in and painted even darker circles under their eyes while I was outside. That same scoundrel propped invisible matchsticks between their lips so they could conserve energy by breathing without having to open and close their mouths.

"What happened?" Mike asks with the enthusiasm of a three-toed sloth.

"I'm going to her country house tomorrow. She has to help her dad with some tax problem so we're going to work on the pitch on the way up and back."

"Well done, Barney." Beth manages an opiated smile and looks at me with the animation of a giant tortoise on Valium. "You should ask her to marry you."

Not the worst idea in the world. I imagine being married to Gloria, which of course I've done before. Only now it seems a millionth part closer to a genuine possibility.

I imagine having Gloria in the same house as me *every day*. And then I wonder whether I could handle it. Her strength would expose and wipe away every weakness I've built my life upon, yet I would love her because she's funny and kind and beautiful. Perfection. I can think of no other word to describe what marriage to a magnificent woman must be. Pure, melodious perfection.

"Take me home, Mike," Beth says, interrupting my reverie. "I'm exhausted after washing the floors and cleaning out the bins this afternoon. Remember you're on nappy duty in the morning. Change it before you bring Olly into bed with us. I don't want to wake up smelling poo in my face again."

SEVEN

There are a lot of people you don't want to be stuck in a car with on a long drive. Genghis Khan, Vlad the Impaler, the guys who wrote "The Macarena." Up until today, I would have added my own name to that list. But for the past two hours, I've managed to sound intelligent, mature, and professional. It's basically a miracle.

We've sorted out a lot of the details for our pitch to the department and I've made copious notes for our PowerPoint presentation (Gloria told me if I called it a "deck" one more time, she'd throw me out of the car at 110 kph). We're still an hour away from Gloria's family home—it's seriously in the middle of nowhere—so we're pulling into a service station to stretch our legs.

My knees pop when I get out of the car. Gloria puts her hands in the small of her back and pushes her hips forward, arching her body in a functional, yet wholly exquisite maneuver. She catches me staring and smiles knowingly (though I'm not entirely sure *what* she knows and hope she doesn't know what I know I know).

As she fills up the car, I rummage through my overnight bag in search of my deodorant can. The combination of a hot day, close confinement with Gloria, and the relentless pressure of trying to be impressive has caused me to sweat up something of a rancid storm. However, in the kind of tragic situation Shakespeare would write about if he was still alive today, the can appeareth not. I didn't pack it!

I need to think quickly here. "Back in a minute!" I call out to Gloria over the sound of the pumping petrol, and then run into the shop without further ado about nothing.

When I find the toiletries aisle, Shakespeare reappears to continue his sabotage of my love life in iambic pentameter. Instead of the usual abundance of men's deodorants with ridiculous names and unrealizable promises, I am staring at two options only. The first is a can of Dry Life, but it's not alcohol-free so won't be suitable for my sensitive skin. The second is a roll on with the top only half on. Need I say more?

I'm left with no choice. There's one alcohol-free can in the women's section and it's called Summer Breeze. I grab the travel-sized can, which fits just neatly enough into my hand to conceal my shame from the other patrons. I rush to the counter. Just as I get there a mother with two kids cuts across my path.

"Petrol on three," she says, and then follows it up by screaming: "I said no, Dylan! You've already had enough chocolate today!"

The infamous Dylan, a ratty-looking kid aged somewhere between six and ten, screams back. "I hate you! I hate you! I hate you!"

His mother counters Dylan's attack. Instead of keying in her pin number, she crouches down and looks Dylan directly in the eyes. Then she screams in his face. "One more word out of you and you're walking to the campsite!" Dylan, to his credit, drops his eyes and scuffs his shoes. His younger brother, on the other side of his mum, clearly hasn't mastered the art of *noticing what's going on* because he then asks for a chocolate as well. Dylan's mum is pretty done in, by this stage. She puts both hands over her face and sighs like a woman who's got nothing left to give.

My heart is pounding and I've started to re-sweat, convinced that Gloria is only moments away from stumbling upon my unmanly plans. "Um, excuse me, do you mind? I'm in a bit of a hurry," I say to Dylan's mum.

She rises up from her crouching position the way Bruce Banner does when he's turning into Hulk. Dylan and brother-of-Dylan freeze.

I start praying.

Dylan's mum reaches her full height of five foot two, takes in a measured breath, and stares up at me with the wild-eyed look of a homicidal chimpanzee. Her voice is soft. "And just what is so important that it can't wait another second?"

Retreat! Retreat! Retreat!

"Um, nothing. Sorry, you go." I motion toward the service station attendant, hoping to encourage Dylan's mum to pay up and get out of here. She ignores him and focuses her assault on me.

"No, no. I wouldn't dream of holding you up a moment longer. Come on, tell us. What have you got there?" She looks down at my closed hand. I look down at my closed hand. I feel my face fill with hot, red embarrassment. Dylan's mum lashes out her arm like it's a frog's tongue. She grabs my wrist and turns my own hand over in a movement so fast and irresistible, I wonder if she's going to snap my arm in half, right there in front of Dylan and brother-of-Dylan.

She snatches the deodorant can out of my hand, pops off the rounded top with her thumb, and begins spraying me like we're in a hilariously playful romantic comedy. The psychotic, murderous designs have fallen from her eyes but a terrible, mocking cackle is rising from her throat.

"What are you doing?" I shout.

"Freshening you up, sweetheart."

"Cut it out!" I swipe for the can, but she ducks out of my way like a prizefighter. Then she raises her arm and sprays the deodorant into my eyes. The woman is a complete maniac.

"Aarrggghhhh!" I scream at the sting as I go down on one knee and lift an arm to try to shield myself from the onslaught. The sound of the Summer Breeze suddenly dies, and I'm left with the gentle sensation of soft deodorant particles falling like tiny snowflakes on my skin. I can't see what's going on around me, but it doesn't sound like anyone else in the service station is concerned for my welfare.

What has become of this people?

My vision returns and I see that Dylan's mum has vanished with Dylan and brother-of-Dylan. The deodorant can is sitting on the counter and the attendant looks down at me with blank eyes. "You have to pay for that," he says.

"Have you no compassion? I've just been as-saulted."

"You try it, you buy it." He points to a sign that says: "You try it, you buy it."

"I didn't try it."

"I can smell it on you."

"I was assaulted!"

"It's six ninety-five."

I surrender, hand over the money, and stick the can into my pocket.

"What are you up to?" Gloria asks over my shoulder. I jump. Not figuratively, but literally. Off the ground. "Whoa, sorry, I didn't mean to scare you," Gloria says with a laugh. "You're a bit jumpy there, mate." Then, with a level of concern that sends a thrill to the center of my feeble heart: "Are you okay? Your eyes look really red."

I'm pretty quick off the mark here. "Yeah, yeah, fine. Just got hay fever. I was grabbing a bite to eat." I reach out for the nearest thing that looks like food. Unfortunately, it's not actually food, but one of those honey seed bars that would cost you a cruelty to animals prosecution if you fed it to your pet canary—worst $2.80 I've ever spent.

I offer Gloria petrol money, which she declines, and then head back out into the world of cars, die-sel fumes, and Dylan's mum giving me the bird as she drives by. I pretend not to see her, and then erupt into a violent sneezing fit courtesy of the overpowering aroma of the sweet Summer Breeze.

* * *

The first mistake I make is switching the deodorant can from my front pocket to my back pocket because I think it'll be less obvious there. The second is being really obvious about the fact I can't sit down like a normal passenger because there's something in my back pocket. The third is responding with "piles" (as a joke!) when Gloria asks me why I'm sitting like that. She doesn't laugh.

I offer to drive the next stretch of the journey but she waves me away and mumbles something about wanting to get there alive. I take the high road and don't respond.

We drive in silence as I try to wriggle myself into a more comfortable position. I settle for mild discomfort that will most likely end in a hip replacement, and steal a look at Gloria. Her eyes seem distant so I decide to leave her in peace. I keep my own eyes on the road, trying to ignore the scent of my overpowering, womanly aroma.

Then I panic that she thinks I'm a weirdo because we stopped for petrol and I came out smelling like a Las Vegas dressing room. "Everything okay?" I ask with a forced smile.

Gloria blinks. "Yeah, sorry, Barney. It's just that the closer I get to home, the more I miss my mum. We drove this road a lot together after I moved to the city."

While I'm trying to think of a suitable response, Gloria overtakes a truck at high speed, which diverts all my mental faculties to the important task of *staying alive.* I grip the door handle until the danger has passed. "I'm glad you're at Rogerson, Barney," Gloria says. "Archie's a little unorthodox but he's very clever, and he cares about people. He's just got a unique way of showing it. I worked with him when I was fresh out of university and we were both at one of the top five agencies."

"Archie worked at a top five agency?"

"He was the managing director and he took me under his wing. He's never told me why, but I think it's because he's a country kid as well."

"You're kidding me?"

"I kid you not. He grew up on a sheep farm. You should ask him about it."

That's never going to happen.

"Anyway, I was going through a pretty rough patch career-wise, and Archie asked me to join him at Rogerson. I'd actually moved back home, but the idea of being part of a start-up with somebody I could trust made me excited again about my job.

He told me that he'd be going after government contracts and I thought it would bring rewarding work. Work I could be proud of. Work my mum would have been proud of."

Gloria's words hang between us and I remember her emotional response at the pub when my mum hugged her. I drop the forced smile. "What happened to your mum?"

"She died of cancer last year." Her voice is level, but I can hear the sorrow just below the surface.

"I'm sorry. I can't imagine life without my mum."

"I can't imagine life *with* your mum."

"Yeah, it is kind of weird. But when I was growing up, she was still the one who patched up my cuts, tucked me into bed, and told me that everything was going to be okay. After finishing photo shoots and signing autographs, of course."

Gloria smiles. "My mum used to sing me to sleep. There's something about the way your own mother sings that can never be replaced. Even now, when I'm lying in bed in the middle of the night worrying about something I can't possibly fix, Mum's voice comes to me."

"I just pick up the phone. Mum loves to do a bit of karaoke."

"Not funny."

"Then why are you smiling?"

"I just remembered a joke I heard the other day."

"Was it about the Literal Café?"

"Uh, no. That made my ears bleed."

"My mum liked it."

"She was lying."

"Never. She *actually* believes everything I do is a roaring success. Despite the evidence being over-whelmingly *not* in my favor, Mum still seems to think I'm going to turn out okay. I even think she might be a little bit proud of me."

"Well, that's misplaced emotion if ever I've seen it."

"Harsh!"

"But fair. So, anyway, back to *me* and *my* story."

I laugh. "You're actually pretty funny, yourself, you know."

Gloria rolls her eyes, which I'd prefer she didn't do while hurtling along at high speed. "Mate, I'm funnier than you when I'm not even trying. If I'd been doing the stand-up routine, they wouldn't have *let* me off the stage."

And now I know I'm in love with her. Seriously. When she's not being professional Gloria, she's quick-witted, bordering on brutal and mildly ob-noxious; everything I've ever wanted in a woman!

"So Mum used to take care of all the finances. That's why Dad needs me. Mum tried to teach my sisters before she died, but they're like Dad, practical people who don't have a lot of time for spreadsheets."

"Who has time for spreadsheets?"

Gloria chuckles and it fills me with warmth. I decide to take a chance. "You've got a beautiful laugh, Gloria. I could listen to it all day."

She doesn't look at me, but she smiles, as if to say *that one was okay, but don't push it, buster.* "Thank you, Barney."

"My pleasure," I say, feeling very satisfied with the way things are going.

"Barney, can I ask you a personal question?"

I brace myself. This never ends well.

"Are you wearing my deodorant?"

* * *

Half an hour after leaving the service station, we turn onto a single-lane road. We cruise along in silence until Gloria begins to slow down. I look ahead for a turnoff, or some sign of civilization. There's nothing; just endless rows of crop paddocks, intermittently decorated with the eternally stoic gum trees of rural Australia.

"Something's wrong," Gloria says. She starts tapping her foot on the accelerator, but we continue to lose speed. "I'll have to pull over." She parks the car well off the bitumen and opens the hood.

We both study the engine. In truth, I'm about as adept at mechanics as I am at open-heart surgery. Still, I squint my eyes and rub my chin as though I'm Dr. House.

Gloria reaches in, shakes something, hits something else, and grunts.

"Lupus?" I say.

"Cracked distributor cap."

"Thought so."

"Dad will have a spare. We're only half an hour from home, so I'll give him a call." Gloria takes out her phone, stares at the screen, and shakes her head like it just spat at her. "No reception. I'm going to walk to the top of that hill. You stay here in case somebody drives past. You never know, they might be able to help."

"You want me to stay here on my own?"

"Is that all right?"

"Yeah, yeah, of course." I try not to look petrified. "I'll just stand here all alone on a deserted road. Nothing could go wrong."

Gloria laughs and shakes her head. "You'll be okay, Barney. It's the country. We're all friendly." She gives me a pat on the shoulder, which makes the debilitating fear worthwhile. "And you'll be able to see me the whole time."

When Gloria is out of earshot, I think of Mum again, and the song we adopted as our own after she took me to see *Jesus Christ Superstar* in the seventh grade: 'Everything's Alright'. It became something of an anthem whenever one of us was going through hard times. I contemporized it with lyrics from East 17's classic tune 'It's alright' and, as always, singing it to myself now makes me feel a lot better.

With my spirits restored, I decide to take advantage of this rare trip to the bush with an artfully composed selfie. It would be cool to have me, the car, and the endless blue sky in the shot, so I cross the road. Stretching out my arm as far as it will go, I snap away. The pics look great so I text the best three to Lucien to put his mind at ease about how I'm coping without him. Because nothing says "I'm doing well" like a random picture from the middle of nowhere.

Looking back down the road, I see a black pickup truck approach. It slows down and, with Gloria's encouragement and the buzz of a triumphant selfie spurring me on, I decide to ask for help. The driver's side window is open but all I can see is a hat and a beard. I wave like I'm a local and put on my best *got meself a bit of engine trouble* smile.

"G'day, cobber," I call out, chewing an imaginary piece of hay. But my cobber doesn't respond. Instead, just as I reach the car, the driver's side window goes up. I hear the doors lock. Which seems like a strange thing to do when you're a friendly local stopping to help a man in need. The windows are tinted black, so I go to the front of the car to look through the windscreen. Maybe he didn't see me.

But then why did he stop?

In the driver's seat I see a man in a wide-brimmed hat with a long unkempt beard. His chin is resting on his chest and his hat is pulled low on his brow, as though he is sleeping.

"Hello," I say.

He doesn't respond.

Okay, this is getting weird. Scary, even.

An enormous black dog launches into the front seat like it just burst out of that guy's stomach in *Alien*. It barks at me like it wants to tear me to pieces, paws up on the dashboard, long nose banging against the windshield. I jump back from the car. The man stretches out his arm, placing his hand in front of the dog's mouth. The dog calms down and nuzzles his master's hand, chewing it like a baby's pacifier. The man opens the glove box, takes some-thing out, and rests it on his lap. Then the two of them sit motionless in the front seat, the dog's eyes staring at me, the man's hidden behind the brim of his hat.

My brain starts to send warning signals to the rest of my body. My stomach tightens, my heart rate increases, my muscles twitch. Backing away from the car, I look behind me to locate Gloria. She's almost at the top of the hill now. A warm gust of wind caresses me from head to toe, like one of the ancients preparing me for burial.

Turning back to the car, I peer at it through the heat haze. There's no movement. No sign of life. Then, without warning, the driver's side door be-gins to ease open. I hear the faint laugh of a kooka-burra somewhere in the distance. My twitching limbs go into overdrive as I prepare to run.

The car body shakes. A boot appears beneath the open door. Then, like Nessie out of the Loch, rises the most enormous human being I have ever seen. He straightens up to his full height and stands with one arm resting on the roof and the other on top of the open door. He's wearing jeans and a flannel shirt, apparently immune to the heat. His beard is a great wilderness, flowing untamed onto his colossal chest.

The dog starts barking again.

Bolting around Gloria's car, I close the hood and get in. The key turns and the motor comes to life. A manic, relief-filled screech escapes my throat. Then the engine dies. I turn the key again. The engine starts, hesitates, then dies. I turn the key. Nothing. I turn the key again. Nothing.

I look into the rearview mirror. He's gone. The door to his car is still ajar, but the man has vanished. In the distance, Gloria is on top of the hill. She's on her phone, pacing back and forth, not looking my way. I sound the horn to try to warn her, while turning the key hard. The motor makes a terrible grinding sound and Gloria continues to talk on her phone, oblivious to the danger.

Then the door flings open and he's upon me. He grabs my hand with a giant paw, tearing the keys out of the ignition. "Don't move." His voice is soft, his mouth millimeters from my ear. He reaches down into the car, filling it with only a fraction of his massive bulk. He pops the hood, goes to the engine and lifts the lid to make it look like he's helping. Gloria will walk right into the trap; I have to get to her first. After counting to ten, I take a deep breath, and launch. Grabbing the handle, I swing my legs up and kick the door open with both feet. I rock forward with the momentum and throw myself out of the car, bracing for the impact with the ground. But I never get there. He catches me in midair, tightens his fist on my shirt, and rams me back into my seat.

"I said don't move," he says, his voice still soft and light. He slams the door.

I look up to see Gloria hurrying down the hill. I have to warn her. The man is heading back to his own car. He needs to be distracted when I make my move, so I wait for him to get there. He opens the trunk. He's so tall that I can still see his head above the lid. He is rummaging, focused, searching.

Now is my chance. I fling open the car door and start running toward Gloria. My whole body tenses as I close the gap, waiting to be grabbed from behind by a gargantuan claw.

Gloria quickens her pace until she is running as well. "What's wrong, Barney?" she calls.

"Run, Gloria! Turn around and run!"

I chance a look back. The man has left his car. He's now marching toward us, his giant strides eating up the ground, his body tilted forward.

I turn back to Gloria and stumble. Though my life depends on me keeping my feet, I'm going too fast to stop the fall. The dust fills my mouth and my nostrils but I don't feel any pain. Scrambling back to my feet, I see that Gloria is still advancing toward the danger. She will be upon us in a few terrified heartbeats. There's nothing else for it. The time to run is over. I must stand and defend her.

I spin on my heel and charge at the giant. There's enough distance between us for me to reach maximum speed. I drop my shoulder just before we connect, aiming square at his rib cage.

Then there are stars, pain, and more dust. I'm left sprawling, cast aside by the still upright beast who is now upon the woman I love. He reaches out to grab her with arms as thick as tree trunks.

"Sebastian!" Gloria shouts, and she throws her own arms around him, unable to encircle his massive frame.

What? Why is she hugging him? And how does she know his name?

They do a little spin, and I see a joy-filled smile of dazzling white teeth crack open Sebastian's dark beard. His eyes are shut tight. As he lifts Gloria off the ground, she squeals with delight.

When the embrace ends, they come and stand over me. I'm laid out like I'm about to start making dust angels. The sun is blinding behind their heads, the sky a pale merciless blue. Sebastian reaches down and again grabs me by my shirt, twisting his hand to tighten the grip. He lifts me off the dust with no apparent effort, and plants me on my feet.

"Barney," Gloria says. "This is Sebastian. We went to school together."

A gentleman never lets a near-death experience get in the way of good manners. "Hello, Sebastian. Nice to meet you."

Sebastian nods and, in that voice that's as gentle as the breeze on long, dry grass, he says: "Hello, Barney."

Gloria is staring at me with an expression I don't recognize. Her lips are turned up in a smile, her eyes sparkling. It's thrilling, but I'm not sure why. "Sebastian's the local kindergarten teacher," she says.

"Obviously."

Sebastian returns to our engine and he and Gloria do a bit of work under the hood while I try to lower my heart rate with a stroll. They're finished by the time I get back and Sebastian bids us farewell with a tip of his hat.

Gloria turns the ignition and the car starts without a hitch. "Good as new," she says, still with that enchanting smile and glint in her eyes. We put on our seat belts, but Gloria doesn't pull onto the road yet. "Sebastian is sorry if he was a bit rough when he put you back in the car. He's wonderful with kids, but painfully shy around adults. He thought you might try to get out and start a conversation."

"I understand his concern."

"He's a big guy."

"I noticed."

"A lot bigger than you."

"Are you going somewhere with this?"

"You wouldn't stand a chance against him."

"Thanks, I got that."

"And yet you still threw yourself at him to protect me."

Now the source of Gloria's joy is revealed, and it makes me feel like a gladiator. I've got to play it cool, though, because women like a guy who can keep a lid on things, even if he *is* basically a hero. "I was protecting the car."

Gloria laughs and squeezes my hand. "Thank you, Barney."

As she pulls back out onto the road, I'm certain this is going to be the greatest weekend of my life.

* * *

I should have been born in the country. I don't say this out loud, of course, but by the time we're turning off the single-lane bitumen and onto a dirt road, I'm pretty convinced there's rural blood in my veins. There's no need for office politics, strategic maneuvers, and seven-dollar shoe shines out here. Yes, this is where I belong, breathing the simple clean air of the country, with the dirt under my feet and the distant blue sky over my head.

We pull into a driveway in front of a modest, well-kept house. Gloria is smiling like she's about to laugh, and I feel the corners of my own mouth rising in a merry grin. We're both home.

We open our car doors together and, as the hot air rushes over me, my instinct is to vomit. I want to slam the door and retreat back into the car, but I take only shallow breaths until it passes. Gloria is taking deep, delirious breaths, so this smell is not going to pass. I gag. The country may not be for me, after all.

"Are you all right?" Gloria asks at the sound of me trying to maintain airflow through my lungs.

I gasp. "Yeah, fine...it's just...what's that smell?"

"What smell?" She's immune to it. Like a superhero.

"You know, the smell. All around us."

"What does it smell like?"

Cow dung, I think. And tons of it.

"Nothing, nothing," I say, and then I'm rescued by the sound of an approaching car. It pulls up in a swirl of dust. Doors fling open, there's a lot of laughter, and from the cloud that has now enveloped us all I see two young women in overalls and an older, bearded man heading our way.

Gloria runs to meet her sisters and her dad. They wrap each other up in an all-embracing hug, creating another little dust cloud of their own. Once they're disentangled, the two young women head toward me like they're striding through a scene of *McLeod's Daughters*. "So you're Barney, then, are you?" the taller, younger, wavy-haired one says.

"Depends who's asking!"

She laughs. A real laugh. I just got a real laugh straight off the bat!

"What if I said the cops?" the shorter, older, straight-haired one asks.

"I'd plead the Fifth!"

She looks like she really wants to get the joke, for my sake rather than hers, but hasn't a clue what I'm talking about. Then I remember that they grew up without a television and have probably never seen an episode of *Law and Order*.

Gloria's dad steps into the picture. "The Fifth Amendment," he says. "Part of the United States Constitution, so technically not applicable here in Bungleton West." He's got a lopsided smile and the weathered skin of a man who works for a living. "Pleased to meet you, Barney. I'm Jeremiah Bell. You can call me JB."

"Pleased to meet you, Mr. Bell."

"JB."

"BC!"

"What?"

"Nothing!"

"These are my daughters, Rebekah and Grace."

"Nice to meet you, Barney," Grace says, shaking my hand. She's the wavy-haired one. I'm surprised at how soft her palm is, totally incongruent with her dirt-streaked face and filthy overalls. Her cheeks dimple just the tiniest bit when she smiles, exactly like Gloria's. Rebekah also shakes my hand, though her palms are a little rougher than her younger sister's. Like Gloria, her eyes are bright and challenging, confident and enticing. Their mother must have been formidable.

"You're just in time for lunch," JB says, slapping me so hard on the back it gives me a vertebral subluxation.

The house is neat and tidy, with a little bit of a grandmotherly feel about it—knitted rugs, sofa covers, black-and-white pictures on the walls. There's a bedroom with a foldout sofa bed assigned to me. Three large, overflowing bookshelves line the walls. You can tell a lot about people by the books they keep. And the Bells appear to be a far superior species than me—more educated, more intelligent, and more well-rounded. Not what I was expecting this close to Thunderdome.

Tucked away at the bottom of one of the shelves are two children's books: *Are You My Mother?*, by P. D. Eastman, which is dog-eared and battered, and *Oh, the Places You Will Go*, by Dr. Seuss, which, though well-read, is in better condition. I read Seuss as a kid. I don't remember this one, though, so I take it out for a closer look. There's a handwritten note on the inside cover: *To our darling Gloria as you graduate from school. May the places you go fill you with excitement and wonder all the days of your life. We are so proud of you and love you very much sweetheart. Mum and Dad.* I feel an unexpected little knot form in my throat, mixed with a touch of embarrassment that I have stumbled on such an intimate family moment.

"You like Dr. Seuss?"

Gloria's voice startles me. I feel as though I've been busted with her diary. "I remember reading them when I was a kid."

"You mean you don't anymore?"

"No, I don't know this one at all."

Gloria's eyes lose focus and she gazes somewhere beyond me, speaking in a wistful, enchanted, lyrical voice. It's the voice of a child, a voice full of wonder. "Oh the places you'll go," she says, before reciting a whole section of the book.

Then her eyes mist over and her voice drops to a whisper so soft I can barely hear it over the thudding of my heart. "Oh the places you'll go."

She stops. My throat dries up. The room is filled with silence as Gloria's eyes reflect a moment long passed. They fill with tears. She takes a deep breath and turns away. When she turns back, her eyes are red, but dry. She looks down and smiles. I really, really want to hold her in my arms.

"Mum gave that to me when I was seventeen, but it always makes me feel like a little girl again. I miss her so much."

"It must be hard coming back here."

"Yes and no. It's tough being home without her but, in a funny way, I still feel like she's here."

"It's the memories, right? Sometimes they grow more vivid as the years go by."

Gloria looks at me with wide eyes like she has no idea who I am. "That's exactly what it's like, Barney. How do you know that?"

I'm not ready to tell her all my secrets just yet, so I decide to offer up a half-smile that I catch in the mirror. While going for enigmatic, I've managed crazy orangutan. I put the book back on the shelf and the moment ends.

"If you want to put your bag away, you can use that closet," Gloria says, pointing to a wall of built-in cupboards. I start to open one of the doors. "Not that one!" she screams.

But it's too late. I can't unsee this. The cupboard is lined with shelves from floor to ceiling. They're about a foot apart and each shelf is occupied by miniature plastic horses. Thousands of them, in every color of the rainbow, plus some offensively fluorescent colors God hasn't invented yet. Their hairstyles are as varied and gaudy as my circa-1995 parachute pants collection. "Oh. My. Goodness."

Gloria tries to close the door but I jam my foot in the way. "I think a seven-year-old sociopath may be living in your father's house."

"Stop it!" she says, slapping me on my upper arm. (Man, I wish I had some discernible biceps.)

I open the cupboard doors wide, exposing the full extent of the madness. "This is serious, Gloria. There's somebody living here who needs professional help. We need to stage an intervention."

"That person does not need professional help," Gloria says. She's trying to act proud and defiant, folding her arms and looking down her nose at me. But her face is flushed red. It's the first time I've seen her embarrassed, and her vulnerability is so enchanting, I'm not going to give her an inch of mercy.

"I beg to differ. I'm even worried we might be too late."

"There's nothing wrong with My Little Pony."

"Arguable, but there's certainly something wrong with stealing the entire planet's supply and stashing them in your cupboard."

Gloria laughs. "It's only three years' worth from the late eighties."

"And your dad funded this madness? I'm disappointed. I had him pegged as a more responsible parent."

"What can I say? He's a loving father." Gloria smiles at me, her embarrassment now fading. She can tell I actually find this endearing, and I'm not going to make fun of her.

Well, maybe just a little. "What I don't get is why a girl who lives on a farm with real horses needed to have a billion plastic ones in her collection."

Gloria rolls her eyes and scoffs. "Have you ever actually played My Little Pony?"

Is that a serious question?

"It's about nurturing the plastic figurines, Barney. Do you think their synthetic hair would be so silky smooth without years of loving and patient attention? You can't do that with a real horse; they'll kick you in the face."

She's trying to throw me off the scent of personal discovery with a bit of self-deprecation. I know this tactic well and I'm not going anywhere. I'm on to her. "Were you just a *little bit* of a dork as a kid?"

She scoffs and tries to hide her smile. "You wish you could have known a dork like me when you were a kid."

I don't try to hide mine. "That I do."

She gives me her *easy, buster* eyes again, and then closes the cupboard doors. Much to my disappointment, serious Gloria returns. "Barney, there's something I need to talk to you about."

The deodorant. She found it, despite my emphatic denials. I don't know how but she found it. Run for it, Marty!

"Grace and Rebekah want to take you down to the dairy this afternoon. You know, give you a bit of the authentic country experience." Her voice is hesitant, which I interpret as doubt in my ability to handle said authentic country experience.

"Sounds like a great idea."

Gloria bites her bottom lip, which I'm very encouraged by, because you don't generally worry about people whose lives mean nothing to you. She screws her face up and sucks in a theatrical breath. "It's pretty dirty down there."

I stare at her. I don't know what that means. "I don't know what that means," I say.

"Well, it's just that, well..." She pauses and bites her bottom lip again.

I'm flattered. I know she needs me for the presentation. I know she doesn't want to work on it alone. "I know you don't want to work on the presentation alone," I say, annoyed at my new habit of saying, almost verbatim, every thought that pops into my head. "But you could work on the animation and tidy up the formatting while I'm gone. We might have some time now to update the content. When do they want to go?"

"I think you're too soft."

I look over my shoulder to check that she's not talking to someone else.

"I don't really think you'll be able to handle it," she says with a *but you've got a great personality* smile.

"Handle what?"

"The dairy. It's pretty rough-and-tumble, it doesn't smell great, and there are about forty-two billion flies down there at any one time, all of them moving rapidly from fresh cow dung to your face. I'm not sure it's really the place for a city boy like you."

A city boy like me? A city boy like me!

I make no attempt to hide my affront, puffing out my chest and planting my feet a little wider apart, country-style. "I don't know what you mean. What's so city boy about me that I can't handle the dairy?"

Gloria looks embarrassed about what she has to say next. I place my hands on my hips, again country-style. "Come on, Barney. I don't know you that well but I can tell you've never done a day's manual labor in your life. Your hands are softer than mine."

This allegation requires a strong defense. "Your sister's got soft hands!"

"She moisturizes every night because she *works* with them every day. Do you?"

I don't know whether she's asking me if I moisturize every night, which I refuse to answer on the grounds of breach of privacy, or whether I work with my hands every day. I maintain a dignified silence.

"I could hear you gagging when we first arrived. I love the country air because it *does* smell like the land and the animals and everything that comes with it. For me, it's the smell of home, but I thought it was going to make you throw up on your two-hundred-dollar sneakers."

Hang on a minute. This all seems a bit forced to me. Why does Gloria care whether I get roughed up at the dairy? If she was so concerned, she wouldn't have brought me here in the first place.

"What's going on?" I ask, raising my head in challenge. "Why don't you want me to go to the dairy?" And then it hits me. "It's your sisters, isn't it?" Gloria folds her arms and looks away. "What are they going to tell me that you're so worried about?"

She meets my eyes. "You're not as dumb as you look."

"That's the nicest thing you've ever said to me."

She chuckles and unfolds her arms. "Look, Barney, it's up to you. But don't say I didn't warn you, okay?"

"I can handle it. I'm a lot tougher than you think."

* * *

Imagine being asked to shuffle down a descending walkway into a pit. On either side of the pit, eighteen cows are lined up. Their bony buttocks are facing you at about two feet above eye level. Place at their heads a trough full of food to kick their digestive systems into action, thereby encouraging them to defecate enthusiastically on your head. Lock them in so they get a bit antsy, and then position yourself within striking distance of powerful, unpredictable legs, capped off by hooves the size of dinner plates.

This is my present hell. This is the way the Bell family carves out its living. It makes shoe shining look like the role of a lifetime.

I'm dressed in a set of rubber pants that include their own boots, like I'm on a fishing expedition. They're too big for me so there's a considerable gap between my stomach and the waistband, which means anything could get in there and contaminate my jeans. They have overall straps to hold them up, which are rubbing against my shoulders with such vigor that I fear for the future of my fitted T-shirt. It's stinking hot.

The milking machine is running on a generator so loud they can hear it in the center of Melbourne, and Gloria's estimate of 42 billion flies was conservative, at best. They are swarming so prodigiously, I wouldn't be surprised if Pharaoh walked in searching for Charlton Heston. Bovine feces and urine have turned the cement floor into a slippery, hazardous non–*Top Gun*–style danger zone. My quadriceps have never worked so hard at keeping me upright.

Rebekah and Grace move around the dairy with an elegance more suited to a ballroom dance floor.

They hum and sing as they go, cajoling the cows into their stalls, attaching teat-sucking machines, and ducking their heads at errant kicks. They make the whole horrifying procedure look effortless and dignified. As for me, I'm sweating so hard that if I dropped dead right now, there'd be no need for an embalmer.

My hopes of quizzing Gloria's sisters on her past were dashed the moment I realized I might die here today. I need all my mental faculties on high alert if I'm going to make it out alive, and I certainly don't have the capacity to build rapport and then ask subtle, yet probing, questions.

Rebekah shouts at me over the cacophony of the generator, the plague of flies, and my overworked sweat glands. She's got a businesslike air about her. I could imagine her sitting beside Gloria in a boardroom, terrifying anybody who dared to question the Bell sisters' judgment. "All right, Barney. Are you ready?"

I nod rather than speak to limit the risk of flies and/or fresh cow excrement entering my mouth. She's already shown me what to do. Now it's my turn. Grace has just finished getting the next lot of cows lined up, and Rebekah hands me what I can only really describe as a suction contraption. There is one at every cow stall and they each have four short leads with plastic suction cups about as long and thick as a decent beer glass extending out from the centerpiece.

"Remember to just line them up and drive them on. The machine will do the rest," Rebekah says.

I nod again. Here I go. I approach the cow. Oh man, it's big. Its enormous udder fills my vision like an overinflated pink sandpaper balloon. Four teats hang from the udder, stumpy bratwurst sausages dangling ready and poised to slip out of my grasp and humiliate me. I grab one of the cups on the suction contraption in my gloved hand. I take a deep breath. Bad idea, but I manage to suppress the gag. The cow's legs twitch as I approach. It's like it knows I'm there, daring me to steal its milk before it splits my skull in two.

Rebekah stands alongside me. "Go on, Barney, that's it." She smiles and places a hand on my back, giving me a little shove closer to the cow. I hold my breath and reach out. Just as I'm about to begin my upward thrust, the cow starts urinating. I jump back. Rebekah catches me. "Cool your jets, mate. A little bit of milk won't hurt you. Here, watch."

Milk? You've got to be kidding me. Of course it's milk, you city-bred ignoramus, it's coming out of a bratwurst sausage!

Rebekah grabs the teat and points it in my direction, spraying milk all over my T-shirt. She's smiling but it's in a *I just bought out your company and made you redundant* kind of way. I suppress a scream and make a mental note never to cross her, or invite her to a staff meeting.

Grace laughs at the shenanigans/hazing but remains true to her name. "Cut it out, Bek!" She takes my hand and guides it toward the cow. She's far gentler than her sister, and though she's pushing me forward, she hasn't broken eye contact with me. Her calm stare helps me to breathe again and she guides my hand toward the udder. The sucker attaches, and begins its sucking. Grace helps me onto the second and third teats. Then she gives me a nod. "You can do this," she says. She pats me on the arm and stands back.

To my great surprise, I grab the fourth cup and drive it onto the cow's final, neglected bratwurst. It takes! The cow is being milked! There's cheering from the ladies. A great bubble of pride wells up in my chest. Gloria doubted me, but I've done it. I've milked a cow!

* * *

"I milked a cow!" I announce to Gloria and her dad, hands on hips, chin held high.

Instead of jumping to their feet and bursting into spontaneous applause, they both flick their eyes up at me, then back to the papers they're poring over on the kitchen table. "That's great, Barney," Gloria says.

But I'm not perturbed. This is my grand triumph. I'm buoyed and energized by passing the test Gloria set for me. I'm living off the land now and I feel a special connection to the earth and all its inhabitants. I respect and revere nature and her many wonders. Now, when I breathe in the dirt and the dung and the diesel fumes, my lungs fill with the sweet scent of my spiritual home.

"You smell putrid, Barney. Why don't you take a shower and get changed?" Gloria doesn't look up, but points in the direction of the bathroom. "Leave the rubber pants outside. Dad'll take care of them."

I grab my towel, head to the bathroom, and strip off my working man's clothes. Actually, they're the same clothes I wore on the way up, and they come from Gap, but since I just milked a real cow in them, I think I've earned some descriptive liberty. I enter into a ten-minute battle with the showerhead. It alternates between blasting me with pinpricks of burning hot water and dribbling out a cold stream voluminous enough to wash one eyelid if I cup my hands under it for three days straight. I manage to clean up enough *not* to smell like a dung-encrusted cow, though, and it's at the moment I wrap the towel around my waist that I realize my error. No change of clothes.

We've already ascertained that I'm not the fittest bloke getting around. My metabolism, though, has done me a favor by keeping pace with my mental development. So, while I'm not what you'd call chiseled, I still retain a slimness usually ascribed to teenage boys. I'm not rapt about being seen with no shirt on—I certainly don't think it will make Gloria any *keener* to marry me—but if I move quickly enough through the kitchen, I should be able to effect an Axl Rose, waiflike sensuality that distracts the crowd from my muscular atrophy.

I secure the towel high and tight, clench my stomach muscles (not much to work with), grab my dirty clothes, and shimmy out of the bathroom into Paradise City. Except I'm welcomed to the jungle.

Grace is standing right in the middle of my exit path. She's taken off her rubber milking suit and is wearing old jeans and a white singlet, which has mud (I hope it's mud) streaked across it. Her wavy, dark-blonde hair is tied back and there's a smudge of dirt on her forehead. Rebekah is standing next to her. She's also in jeans but she's wearing a spotless navy T-shirt. She has a cap on now, which casts a shadow across her face, but I can tell from the way she's holding her chin up and looking down at me that I'm being appraised. If I have to win the Bell sisters over to secure Gloria's heart, it's clear Rebekah is going to be the tough nut to crack.

"Hey, Barney! Great work down at the dairy!" Grace says.

I'm forced to stop and smile. "Thanks," I say, as though I'm not standing in a towel in the kitchen of the father of the girl I want to marry with her two sisters looking on. I decide to keep playing it cool by swaying my hips in that rhythmic Axl Rose motion, hoping it might show off my abs (they must exist—something's holding me up!).

"Are you all right?" Gloria asks. "Is your back sore?"

"Didn't work you too hard, did we, Barney?" Rebekah says, knowing full well that they did.

"Nah, nah, not at all. Could've done that all day."

"Perfect. You can come back at six tomorrow morning."

I fake laugh to make it clear that I'm treating the invitation as a joke.

"What's that on your hip?" Gloria asks.

I look down to see a previously unnoticed red welt that is both unattractive and incongruent with my Guns N' Roses persona.

"It looks like a bite," Grace says. "Let me see it."

Before I can escape, Grace is crouched down in front of me, pulling my towel down over the front of my hip to get a better look at my affliction. I grip the folds of the towel extra tight.

"Definitely a spider," Grace says. "Not sure what sort, though. What do you guys reckon?"

JB and Rebekah crowd around my hip, jostling for position. I think it's fair to say this is something of an uncomfortable moment for me. JB stands bolt upright. His face has gone white. "Funnel web. You'll be dead within the hour if you don't get to the nearest hospital." He runs to the door as my life flashes before my eyes.

"I don't want to die!"

All three sisters explode with laughter, and I realize, through my crippling fear, that perhaps death is not as close as I thought. Gloria stops laughing long enough to explain why my impending death is so hilarious. "There are no funnel webs in this part of Victoria, Barney. And no one has died of a funnel-web bite since they invented anti-venom in the early eighties. I think you'll be fine."

It's boiling hot in here and I can already feel a sheen of sweat covering my body. "I'm getting kind of cold. I'm going to get dressed." I forget about being Axl Rose and focus instead on getting out of the kitchen without losing my rapidly slipping towel.

"We're going out to dinner, Barney. Make sure you dress up!" Grace calls from behind me.

"Maybe a crop top!" Rebekah yells.

Just as I reach the door of my room, there's a loud wolf whistle and another explosive burst of laughter.

Country people are hilarious.

Then I'm finally safe from the onslaught, door closed behind me.

A few minutes later, when I've got my clothes on, there's a gentle knock at the door. I open it and Gloria is standing there smiling. "Take this." She hands me a tube of cream. "It'll help stop the itching."

"Thank you."

"My pleasure. Sorry about my family. They like to play jokes."

"Yeah, of course. No worries. It was hilarious."

"Nice work by the way."

Is she talking about my body?

"With what?"

170

"The dairy. Grace and Bek were very impressed."

I find that hard to believe, but effect a nonchalant *do it all the time* kind of expression anyway.

"They said you did well...for a city boy."

* * *

The kindest way to describe the pub is "homely." When we walk through the doors, I feel like we've just entered somebody's living room; albeit much bigger and with a disproportionate amount of alcohol. There are some mismatched tables and stools, faded and dubiously stained carpet, and a bunch of old blokes scattered around who look like their names could be Uncle Tom and Cousin Bill. The womenfolk are hardy and strong, and every male under thirty-five is wearing a checked shirt. Unkempt and undisciplined-looking kids play unsupervised around the room, most of them with manicured rats' tails.

We sit down at a table and peruse the menus. A large, apron-wearing woman with curly red hair arrives to take our order. When it comes to my turn, I ask her if the steak is panfried or grilled.

She stares at me like I just blew a fly out of my nose. "You from the city?"

"Barney's staying with us for the weekend," Gloria says. "We've just started working together."

"Well, you've got a fancy one on your hands here, Glory. Next thing he'll want to know whether the chips are hand cut."

That actually was going to be my next question.

"Well, for your information, Martha Stewart, the steak is marinated for six hours, tenderized, and then cooked over a flame grill until there's just the tiniest touch of pink left in the center. We top it with garlic butter or your choice of mustards from the menu. And, yes, the chips are hand cut."

This is a good opportunity to get a local on side with a bit of my trademark humor. I sit back in my chair and rub my chin, pretending to contemplate my decision. "I'll take it," I say. "But only if the chips are cut by a left-hander."

The woman throws her head back and laughs. A warm feeling of satisfaction runs through my body. "Cut by a left-hander," she says, shaking her head and writing down my order. Then she leans in close to my ear. "I'll have you cut by a left-hander."

The warm feeling evaporates. I turn to her face, which starts as menacing, then breaks into a wild grin. "Lighten up, sweetheart."

Seriously, is everyone in the country a comedian?

"So tell us a bit more about yourself, Barney," JB says after the homicidal waitress departs. Where'd you work before you joined Glory at Rogerson?"

This is an excellent opportunity to continue my relationship building with Gloria's family. We talk about my life—which, frankly, I'm surprised they're all that interested in—and I learn about how JB's ancestors have been farming in this district for three generations. Both Gloria's sisters have been to agricultural college, and Rebekah is studying for a master's of agricultural business management online—clearly her strategy to get into hostile corporate takeovers. The whole family is formidable, polite to a fault, and as handsome as the autumn sunrise.

By the time dinner is over, I've well and truly loosened up courtesy of my exquisitely cooked yet appallingly presented steak—daisy-patterned plates and twenty-five-year-old cutlery—and the four beers I've knocked down while eating it. Gloria decides it's a good time to introduce me to some of her old friends, so we hone in on two country-strong lads at the bar.

"Hello, gentlemen," Gloria says to them as we approach.

"Glory," one of the young men says with too much delight for my liking. "Who are these gentlemen you're referring to?" He steps forward and hugs her, and then his mate does the same. I want to annihilate them both on the spot. They look at me like I'm a presumptuous butler who needs his comeuppance.

"Jacko, Stamper," Gloria says.

Who are these people and why don't they have real names?

"This is my friend, Barney."

"Hello, mate." Stamper shakes my hand, breaking twenty-two of the twenty-seven bones therein. Jacko, who is distinguishable from Stamper by his red, rather than blue, checked shirt, then finishes off the remaining five bones.

"So what exactly does 'friend' mean, Glory?" Stamper asks.

That's a bit forward, champion!

"We work together."

"Right. Working late tonight, are you?"

Gloria laughs. "Give me a break, Stamp. Barney's here because we need to work on an urgent campaign pitch. Nothing more."

"Don't get all technical with your fancy city-speak on us, Glory," Jacko says.

I decide this is a good time to add some value to the conversation, and to demonstrate that, although I'm a white-collar professional, I can still relate to the common man. "Actually, the term *pitch* is not that technical at all. While it can have several meanings, in this case it simply refers to presenting an idea for consideration." I think about how to relate to these guys on *their* terms. Sports is the obvious answer. All country people like sports, right? "Like a baseball being thrown to a batter," I say. "An offering, if you like." I raise my hands to either side of my head and shake them like a minstrel, somehow convinced this is an accurate representation of what a baseball would do if it were human. "Hit me if you dare, Mr. Batter!" I say in a voice that the human baseball would use. It sounds like a cross between a chipmunk and an evil spirit.

Jacko and Stamper stare at me like I just announced that Garth Brooks has switched to hip-hop. Gloria's not taking the news that well, either. "Did I tell you Barney's mother is Audrey Conroy?" she says through gritted teeth and a forced smile.

This does its intended trick, snapping the boys out of their shock at Garth's betrayal. "Fair dinkum," Jacko says. "You must be super rich. How big's your house?"

"I live in an apartment."

"How's your mum?" Stamper asks.

"Great. Still working hard."

"Yeah, I watch her most nights. She's awesome. My olds love her, too. Just wait until they hear that I met Audrey Conroy's son." Stamper calls out to the barman. "Hey, Biffo, get us four cans of bourbon, will you? We're having a drink with Audrey Conroy's son."

Biffo produces the requested four cans and we toast to my mother's ongoing success. Gloria takes a few unconvincing sips from her can, and then excuses herself to head back to her family. She makes a face to tell me I can join her if I want to, and I make a face like, nah, I'm cool, I can handle these guys.

"You play pool?" Stamper asks.

"You bet."

"Biffo! Three more cans, mate."

We head to the pool table with enough bourbon and cola to anesthetize a village of pandas. "Winner stays on," Stamper says, and with my bourbon-fueled bravado, I decide to take a gamble.

"No worries, lads. I'm quite happy to play all night."

It pays off. They both make good-natured hooting sounds.

"Look out, we've got a trash talker on our hands!"

"Hope your game's as big as your mouth, city boy!"

This.

Is.

Living.

Playful jests with the most masculine men I've ever met, neither of whom appears to outright hate my guts despite my comparative femininity. Lining up the ball on the pool table. Breaking with the force of my joy and relief at fitting in with Gloria's beloved country folk. Earning their praise because I just sank two balls off the break (I'm actually pretty good at pool—a rare, and largely useless, talent).

"Whoaaa, watch out!"

"What are you, some sort of shark?"

Let me repeat:

This.

Is.

Living.

The next hour is a joyous cavalcade of beautifully executed shots, hilarious insults, and deep octave laughter (theirs, not mine). The bourbon continues to flow through my body like the waters of eternal life, making me strong and confident and bold.

As I line up my next shot, I ask the lads (that's what I'm calling them now) what they do for fun around here.

"Get smashed," Jacko says.

Opportunity knocks!

"Crikey, mate, lucky you boys aren't at the Literal Café!"

They stare at me like I'm speaking a foreign language. I stand up straight after sinking another ball and lean on my cue at the end of the table. "You know, 'cause if you were you'd end up *literally* getting smashed. Like actually, physically smashed. Bones and all. And that's not as much fun as drinking bourbon, let me tell you!"

Jacko is standing right next to me. He starts to sniff like he's on the scent of foul play. "What are you talking about? And why do you smell like a lady?"

I need an out.

"Where are the toilets?"

"Out the back. But the light's been busted for a year, so watch your step."

Jacko wasn't joking. It's pitch-black out here. The toilet block is separate from the rest of the pub but I manage to find it all right, survive the dark, and begin my return journey. As I'm heading back, I hear a familiar and spine-tingling cough. "Gloria?" I call into the darkness.

"Over here, Barney."

I look to the sound of her voice and give my eyes some time to adjust. I can see the faint outline of JB's four-wheel-drive, but no Gloria. I focus in on the spot her voice came from, but the liters of bourbon rushing through my veins are like a waterfall thundering in my ears. That's when I realize how drunk I am, and decide that I need to watch my step. Literally. And metaphorically.

"I'm up here," Gloria calls out, and I see her silhouetted against the night sky, waving to me from the roof of the four-wheel-drive.

"What are you doing?"

"Checking out the stars. Come and have a look. They're beautiful."

I navigate my way across some pretty treacherous terrain and, despite the very real risk of breaking both my legs, I make it to the cleared space of gravel known as the car park. I take my life into my hands by scrambling onto the roof of the four-wheel-drive without a safety rope. My heart does a series of star jumps when I see Gloria's flushed cheeks and sparkling eyes. She might be superhuman, but she's clearly not immune to bourbon, either. Even in the soft light of the moon, she is the most magnificent creature I have ever seen.

"Lie down on your back," she says.

I do, and the world drops away from me. Despite being on the metal, ridged roof of a battered old family truck, I have never been so comfortable in all my life. The sound of the rushing bourbon again rises to a deafening crescendo, but then fades to the background like a passing jet plane. I look to the night sky above and the stars are brighter and more numerous than I ever knew they could be. They awe me with their distance and their possibility. Their disdain and their promise. They remind me that I am so terribly, frightfully small.

"Beautiful, isn't it?" Gloria says.

My bourbon boldness flexes. "Second most beautiful thing out here, Glory."

"Glory?"

"Glorious."

"Don't get too charming, mister. We still have to work together, you know."

There's a lightness to her voice that, combined with the darkness, the blinking stars, the solitude, and the accidental touch of her leg on mine makes me feel like Gloria and I are the only people on earth.

"Speaking of which..." she says, "...I've finished everything Dad needed me to do so we can spend a few hours on the pitch tomorrow morning before we head back after lunch."

"Sounds like a plan. It's fun being on the other side of this process, you know. Normally I'm the public servant waiting to be dazzled by the consultant, so to now be doing the dazzling is more exhilarating than I expected."

"What were you expecting it to be?"

"Terrifying."

"Sometimes it is. Especially when you present an idea to a room and you're greeted by absolute indifference. Tension, objections, anger, even; I'll take those over indifference any day. If you can't provoke a reaction, something has gone terribly wrong."

"Well, if provoking a reaction is the benchmark, then absolutely nothing has gone wrong with you, Glory."

She turns her face to me. The moon is reflected in her eyes, and the corner of her smile is just the tiniest bit lopsided. "Sometimes indifference *is* what I'm going for." She turns back to look at the stars, but her grin remains. I don't speak; nothing I have to say could make this moment any more magnificent.

"So is that why you stayed in the public service so long? Because you were scared of what it might be like on the other side?"

Talk about your mood killer.

But this is what mature adults do, this is how they forge relationships. I usually try to avoid speaking about this, even with Mike, but now that I'm having a midlife crisis, what else have I got to lose? "Actually, I stayed in the public service for so long because I thought I'd only be there for a few months."

Gloria rolls onto her side and raises the top half of her body, using her arm as a headrest so that she is looking down on me. She's wearing a fitted black T-shirt tucked into designer jeans and she flicks her hair back over her shoulder so that it hangs down like a stage backdrop behind her face. The intimacy of her pose makes my heart ache with desire.

"What do you mean?" she asks with apparent fascination.

Apparent fascination is not the routine reaction to conversations with me, so I decide to keep dancing, to keep sharing, to keep drawing from the bottomless well of my insecurities.

"You know that Thirsty Merc song 'In the Summertime'?"

Gloria looks like I just asked her if she remembers her first pet kangaroo (I'm making some assumptions about country folk here). "Of course, I do. I *am* young and hip, you know."

"That song must be at least ten years old."

"Yeah, and I'm *still* young and hip. Now get on with your story."

Man, she's beautiful when she's funny. "So you know how the song starts with a line about not having a job because he never liked them?" This was meant to be a rhetorical question but Gloria cuts me off.

"No, it doesn't," she says.

"What?"

"That's not how the song starts. Before those lyrics, you can hear the lead singer talking. Then he sings the first line."

Thirsty Merc, she's right!

"Are you kidding me? Are they your favorite band or something?"

Gloria shrugs. "No. I just remember stuff."

O to the M to the G.

I think I just met my match. "That's incredible. You're like a superhero and your power is retaining useless information."

"It's not useless. I just used it to prove you wrong."

"Superheroes use their powers for good."

"Like I said, I just proved you wrong." Gloria smiles like Lois Lane but her eyes flash at me like Catwoman. "So you didn't want a job? Why not? Did you think you were going to have a career as a stand-up comedian?" She laughs at the end of this sentence. Because it's a joke, obviously. And then she sees my face. She sits up, tucks her hair behind her ears, and crosses her legs. "Oh, Barney, I'm sorry, I didn't mean to be rude."

Now she pities me, which is not quite what I was going for. I sit up as well. "You don't have to be sorry. It is kind of a joke. I mean, you actually have to keep doing stand-up comedy to have a career as a stand-up comedian."

"So you did do comedy? What happened? Why did you stop?"

"I did a gig at the end-of-year uni ball. It was a disaster. I thought I just needed some time out to regroup so I took a graduate job. A month of regrouping turned into six, six turned into a year, and before I knew it, I was staring down the barrel of long-service leave."

"But why couldn't you do both? Surely, you could work during the day and write comedy at night."

"You'd think so, wouldn't you? But as time went on, I guess I just started to accept that it was the foolish dream of a young man without a mortgage. So I let it go."

Gloria's mouth drops open, aghast. "How incredibly depressing."

"Well, it's not all bad. I *was* good at my job. I know I come across as a completely useless buffoon..." Pause to accommodate Gloria's emphatic denial. Nothing forthcoming. Move on. "...but the department was like my natural environment. I was comfortable there. Capable. A good leader. Until they fired me."

Gloria slaps her hands onto my knees. The pain is exquisite. "They what?" she yells.

Oh no. Critical, bourbon-induced lapse in judgment.

But it's keeping her fascinated.

"Well, technically I resigned. That's what the paperwork says, but everyone knows I got the sack."

"Does Archie know?"

"I doubt it. Unless he's in the trunk right now."

"Why did they fire you?"

I'm about to respond when a voice breaks through the darkness like a sonic boom. "Barney!"

I straighten my shoulders and flick my head left and right like a threatened meerkat. Footsteps approach. "You up there, Mr. Conroy?"

It's Stamper. He's striding toward the car but stops when he realizes I'm not alone. "Glory? Is that you?"

"Yes, Stamp."

"What are you..." he breaks off mid-sentence. "Oh, I see. Sorry, I didn't realize what was going on."

"Nothing's going on," Gloria says. "We were just looking at the stars."

"Is that what you call it in the city?"

"Very funny, Stamp. Seriously, nothing to see here. We were just about to come back inside." To emphasize her point, Gloria swings around behind me, places her feet on my spine, and kicks me down the front windscreen. I tumble, roll off the hood, and land with feline dexterity on my feet. Before overcompensating and falling into the dirt.

"Take it easy, Glory!" Stamper says. "You could have hurt him."

"Sorry, Barney. It was meant to be a gentle shove."

"I'd hate to see your fly kick."

Her laughter twinkles like the stars and, when she places her hand on my back, it takes me to another galaxy. "C'mon," she says. "Let's head back inside. I think I can guess why Stamper is looking for you."

"It's country time," Stamper says.

What?

Stamper leads me back into the pub. I steal a glance at Gloria; she's wearing her lopsided grin again.

"Fire it up, Jacko!" Stamper calls above the noise of the crowd. Then, the most unexpected sound fills the room. Bagpipes. The crowd cheers as though we're at the Edinburgh Tattoo. In Edinburgh. Not in the middle of nowhere. Then there's a long note that sits above our heads. Holding, holding, holding. Every bloke in the pub between eighteen and thirty-five has raised his right arm in the air. They hold them aloft like warriors ready to go into battle. Holding, holding, holding as the bagpipe note sounds.

And then, in perfect unison, their arms drop as one with the beat of a thundering drum. As the drumbeat kicks in, it's joined by a twanging guitar. I recognize the song now. It's Steve Earle's 'Copperhead Road'. The men of the land screw up their faces, tap their feet, and sway their hips, all while taking Herculean swigs of bourbon. Then the group singing begins.

I seek out Gloria. "What's happening?" I ask above the brutal slaughter of the art of song.

"Tradition."

"Thanks. That really clears it up."

Before I get to ask another question, I'm grabbed by the shoulders and dragged into a self-forming circle. It's some sort of natural phenomenon, like the way birds fly together in a pattern, none of them apparently having any idea what's going to happen next. Like me right now.

Things are hotting up in the song and the butchering is reaching fever pitch.

Then the drums take over:

Bam, bam, bam, bam, bam!

Bam, bam, bam, bam, bam!

Bam, bam, bam, bam, bam!

Bam, bam, bam, bam, bam!

This series of sharp, aggressive sounds coaxes out prehistoric man. Every bloke in the circle slams his feet, fists, or head in time with the repeated bamming. Nobody puts down his bourbon, of course, so it's now raining down thick and fast, threatening to undo the excellent job I managed with tonight's hair wax.

The bamming is followed by an extended guitar-twanging interlude and the circle now goes all *Lord of the Dance*, leaping and jigging out of time with the guitar. Then more singing. Then, though I can't hear it, uncontrollable, double-you-over, breath-stealing laughter from Gloria, Rebekah, and Grace, whom I see watching me being tossed up, down, left, and right like a rag doll among the giant men of the country. All my fellow circle-makers are throwing their heads back and singing at the top of their voices now. Even Sebastian, the timid Goliath, has linked arms with the other brutally powerful men and is roaring like a wounded lion.

The verses finally end, and it's now freestyle jumping up and down and chanting "Copperhead Road," sometimes in time with the song, sometimes not. And then, as it began with one long note on the bagpipes, so it ends. The men raise their arms again in salute, and silence falls over the crowd.

There are no words in the English language powerful enough to express my gratitude that this is over.

"Play it again!" somebody yells.

Oh, mercy. Somebody, please, grant me sweet mercy.

The Bell sisters are sent in answer to my prayer. They materialize alongside me, and sweep me away from the Copperhead Circle until we're at the far end of the pub.

"We didn't think you could handle another round up there, Barney," Grace says with tears of laughter streaming from her eyes. "You looked like you were about to burst into tears!"

"I wasn't about to burst into tears. They're just very violent men."

"If only you could have seen your face," Gloria says, wiping away her own tears.

Rebekah hands me her phone. "You can. I got a photo of you just as the drums began. You look like a hunted animal."

"I was a hunted animal." They all laugh. "What was that all about, anyway?"

"It's their favorite song. They play it every Saturday night. I don't know, maybe it just perfectly captures what it's like to be a young man in country Victoria."

"It's about bootlegging in Tennessee."

"Okay, so maybe it's just the drums."

"Look out!" Grace cries, and then I'm in a friendly headlock that's threatening to crush my larynx.

"Come on, mate. You're not getting out of it that easy!" Stamper is dragging me back into the circle, his comradely wrestling blocking the flow of oxygen to my brain. I recommence breathing just in time for the *Lord of the Dance* section. Rough arms wrap around my shoulders. Heavy boots kick me in the shins. Flat voices brutalize my ears.

But this is the country. This is my home. So I let the dancing and the singing and the bourbon wash over me. And then...

... I become one of them.

"Copperhead Road!"

EIGHT

It's fair to say that, the following day, I'm feeling a little dusty. I'm not a big bourbon drinker at the best of times, so it's taken a significant toll on my body, which now aches more or less all over. But I want to put on a good show for the family, so I resist the urge to roll over into the fetal position. It's 7:30 a.m. and I want to prove that I can rise at the crack of dawn with the best of them.

I crawl out of bed, very pleased with this first accomplishment. I poke my head around the bedroom door and sneak a look in every direction. No sign of McLeod or his daughters. Maybe I've woken up before them—wouldn't that be a turn-up for the books if they all got out of bed to find me showered, fresh as a daisy, and ready to make their breakfast?

I tiptoe into the kitchen so I can get to the bathroom without waking anybody up. Then I hear tires on gravel, the cut of an engine, and the creak of a door. Rebekah bursts into the room. "Here he is, Sleeping Beauty! How are you feeling this morning, sunshine?"

Before I'm able to respond, old man McLeod arrives. "Ahh!" he booms. "Rip Van Winkle awakes!"

Give me a break, don't these people ever sleep in?

Grace follows them, says good morning, and ruffles my hair like I'm the family dog. They're all in their milking gear. Then Gloria appears from another room, dressed in a different pair of jeans from last night, brown boots, and a red shirt, which, to my great surprise, is checked. She's becoming more and more country the longer we're here. She's also sporting the kind of fresh face that only comes with a solid, non-alcohol-affected night of sleep. Why does she look so radiant? I saw her drinking bourbon as well!

"Morning, Barney. How are you feeling?"

"Fine," I say, shrugging my shoulders like it's a bit of an insult to even be asked. "How are *you* feeling?"

"I feel great. But I'm not the one who got myself into a round with Jacko and Stamper."

A memory returns. It's Jacko talking to me about tweenies. They're a drink you have in between a round when somebody is drinking too slowly. Somebody being me.

"Yeah, well, you know. I can hold my own."

There's a moment of silence, then Gloria's sisters burst out laughing.

"Seriously, am I that funny?" My head has started to ache so I can't keep the petulance out of my voice.

"Oh, Barney. Don't get upset. We think you're adorable," Grace says.

This isn't the world's worst result, I guess.

"I'm hungry," Gloria says. "I've done about an hour's work on our pitch this morning..."

Is she serious?

"... so let's pick it up again after breakfast."

We do just that and, after I've showered and eaten, I'm feeling a lot more capable of making a contribution to the success of this project. Gloria and I sit side by side at a lounge room table covered with some sort of lace tablecloth that looks like a giant doily. Her laptop is fired up and we work on the presentation for much of the morning. It's basically my dream come true. Maybe minus the doily.

When we've finished a complete draft, Gloria leans back in her chair, stretches, and yawns. It's exhilarating to watch. "Nice job, Barney." She smiles at me. "Thanks for coming up. I really appreciate it. I know it was hard work last night."

"Don't be silly. I had a great time."

"It did seem like you were having fun." She gives me a part fond, part mocking smile and I experience the very familiar sensation of suspecting I did something the night before that warrants me being ashamed, humiliated, regretful, or all of the above.

"What did I do?"

Gloria laughs. "Nothing. Nothing you need to worry about."

"Nothing? Or nothing I need to worry about? They're not the same thing."

"Nothing you need to worry about."

"Oh, no. Please tell me. What did I do?"

Gloria cocks her head and looks at me like I'm a newborn puppy. This is going to be bad. "You asked me to marry you."

I have a slight convulsion. "When did I do that?"

"Right after you told me you love me."

My spleen explodes. I drop my head into my hands. "Was this before or after 'Copperhead Road'?"

"After."

"I can't remember much following the forty-fourth rendition."

Gloria must sense the spontaneous combustion of my internal organs because she reaches out and pats me on the arm. Even in the mortification that is bringing on my premature death, I revel in her touch. "Don't worry, Barney. I know you don't love me."

I consider protesting but my trachea has dissolved.

"You just had a little too much to drink. Those boys are seasoned performers. Getting in a round with them was always going to end in disaster."

"Jacko and Stamper?"

"Yeah, Jacko and Stamper. They're nice guys, but like most nice guys they turn into obnoxious bores when they've had too much to drink."

"*Most* nice guys?"

"Oh, I wasn't talking about you, Barney. You're a perfectly obnoxious bore when you're completely sober." She delivers this line deadpan, so I have no idea whether she's being serious. Until she shakes her head in mock despair. "Mate, for a wannabe comedian, you really need to work on your sense of humor."

"Yeah, nah. I knew you were joking."

"There is one thing you didn't tell me, Barney."

"My most crippling regrets?"

"No, but I can pretty well guess what they are."

What does that mean?

"You didn't tell me why you were fired from the public service."

"That's because I was press-ganged into the sing-along."

"So what happened?"

"Do I really have to tell you?"

"No. Not if you never want to speak to me again and would prefer to catch the bus home."

"That's a tough deal. I hate buses."

Gloria folds her arms in a challenge and stares at me. I notice that her ponytail is just slightly off center, a little too far to the right. And yet it does nothing to detract from the absolute perfection that is her.

"If I tell you, will you promise not to ask me any more questions?"

"No."

I take a deep breath. "One of my junior staff, Sylvia, was in a meeting with a senior exec Warwick Harmen. He was a really nasty piece of work and known for his bullying behavior. I should have been in the meeting, but somehow it got past me and she ended up with him alone. Long story short, she was passing on a decision I had made that he didn't like. He abused her, promised retribution against me, and ordered her out of the room. She came back to her desk in tears."

"Wow."

"Yeah, I still feel bad about it. She's only twenty-two."

"So did they fire you for not kowtowing to what he wanted?"

"No, no, nothing like that. You can't get fired for being oppositional in the public service."

"So why'd they fire you?"

"Because of what I did next."

Gloria tenses the muscles in her neck and sucks in a noisy breath. "That sounds ominous."

I sit back and stare at a spot on the wall just over Gloria's shoulder. I wouldn't be able to concentrate on the retelling if I was looking into her eyes. "Let me give you a bit of context first. Harmen's one of those guys who feels like he has to oppress everyone around him. He's aggressive, rude, intimidating. A real piece of work. And what got me the most is that he's part of the executive leadership team. These are the guys who came up with the departmental values of honesty, respect, and accountability. The hypocrisy was breathtaking."

"Why'd they tolerate it?"

"Because he might have been a jerk, but he was smart about it. He never behaved like that when anyone more senior than him was in the room. He was your classic two-faced creep."

Gloria grunts. "I've worked with one of those. So why did he hate you so much?"

"I embarrassed him in a meeting once. I didn't mean to, I just corrected a statement he was making about one of our campaigns. He didn't take it so well."

"He didn't appreciate the lion cub challenging the lion?"

"I wouldn't quite put it that way. You might have noticed that I'm not exactly an alpha male."

"Yeah, probably not even a Bravo or a Charlie. You're more like a Delta. Or a Juliet."

I love it when she insults me. It means she cares. "Well, alphas don't like being shown up by Juliets, and they have long memories, too. He was looking for a chance to get back at me. In typical bully fashion, he targeted one of my staff. After Sylvia came back from the meeting in tears, I went into a rage."

"I can't imagine you in a rage."

"It doesn't happen very often, but I couldn't let him get away with it. That's what people had been doing for years. So I went straight up to his desk to call him out. It didn't even take the wind out of my sails when his secretary thought I was from IT."

Gloria laughs. "So who threw the first punch?"

"No punches, but he did trade the first insult, claiming I sent a girl to do a man's job."

Gloria bares her teeth. "I would have punched him."

"I opted for calling him a filthy piece of scum in front of his entire team."

Gloria throws hand to her mouth. "What did he say to that?"

"He told me I had one chance to publicly apologize, so I raised my voice even louder and explained that he was the filthiest kind of bottom-dwelling scum, and that scum that grows on scum was better than him."

Gloria laughs. "Oh, Barney, I'm sorry for laughing, but that is brilliant."

"Well, I don't know about that, but I'd passed the point of no return, so I went on a diatribe about him being a disgrace to the department and a blight on the public service."

"Wow. You really were committed to destroying your career."

I look away from the wall and into Gloria's eyes. There's astonishment, laughter, and just a hint of respect in them now. "The moment I finished, my heart was beating so hard I thought it was going to explode. You survive in the public service by keeping your head down. You don't rock the boat. You don't put your neck on the line. But something about Sylvia's tears pushed me over the edge. It was like I had to fight the injustice of it all." I scoff and shake my head. "That sounds ridiculous now, but adrenaline messes with your mind in the heat of the moment."

"Well, I say good for you, Barney. We could use a few more Juliets to stand up to the two-faced alpha male creeps we've all had to work with." Gloria's voice cracks and she swallows hard.

"Who are you talking about?" I ask.

Now Gloria looks over my shoulder, weighing up her decision. "Just a former boss who didn't respect me. He was part of the reason I ended up at Rogerson."

"What happened?" I ask on impulse, before raising my hands in apology. "I'm sorry, that was rude. It's none of my business."

Gloria looks down at the floor. "Let's just say it didn't work out, and because of that I quit and moved home. Then Mum got sick and my whole life seemed to be falling apart. After she died, I thought about giving up my career and coming back to the farm for good. It was Archie's offer that turned it all around. When he asked me to join his start-up, I felt like I was being given another chance." Gloria breathes out and relaxes her shoulders. I wonder if this is what she didn't want me to find out from her sisters. "Enough about me," she says. "I completely hijacked your story. I'm sorry. What happened after you called Harmen scum?"

I don't want to tell my story. I want to hear more of hers. I want to hear every story about every moment of her life. But I can see that she's done talking about her past. The wall she puts up is like a physical presence. I once mistook it for professional detachment; now I know it's for protection.

"My boss told me I had to resign before Harmen had me fired for unacceptable conduct. It was the only way I would get my leave paid out and maintain some shred of a professional reputation...at least to anyone who didn't know the story. Word moves fast in the public service, and this was a scandal worth spreading. That's why I wanted a private sector job."

"And now here we are," Gloria says, sweeping her arm across the room and pointing out the window to a cow paddock. "Working at the very epicenter of the communications industry." She grins, and I laugh.

Because, right now, I can't imagine any place I'd rather be.

* * *

We get back from the farm late on Sunday afternoon. I haven't got anything to eat, so I give Mum a call to see if she wants to come over, with dinner. She arrives with Chinese take-away from a restaurant next to my apartment building. "I guess I could have got that myself," I say.

"That would have taken the fun out of it." Mum places the food down and hugs me. She's wearing a sleeveless floral print dress and her dark hair is piled high on her head, held in place with a black diamante-studded clip. Nothing too fancy, but enough to still look stylish for an unexpected photo opportunity. "How was your romantic getaway?" she asks.

"More romantic than I expected."

Mum makes an absurd humming sound. "Do tell," she says, taking off her sunglasses, which she probably could have done after she entered the lobby, but she is famous, after all.

Mum sits down at the table and I start scooping rice and stir-fry into bowls. "Is this braised beef?"

"Do you need to ask?" Fair call. I've never eaten anything else from a Chinese restaurant since I accidentally swallowed duck neck at age eleven.

I serve up the food and sit opposite Mum.

"Do you have any wine?" she asks.

"Sorry, no. That was Lucien's specialty."

"How is Lucien?"

"He's doing well. He texts me nearly every day to make sure I'm coping all right without him."

"I always liked that boy. Now tell me about the weekend. Should I be shopping for an engagement party dress?"

"Perhaps I gave you the wrong impression. When I say it was more romantic than expected, what I mean is that Gloria didn't try to have me deported."

Mum laughs.

"We got the pitch done and I had fun with her friends. Her family is pretty formidable, though. I wouldn't fight either of her sisters."

"They're from the country. You don't fight anyone from the country. What about her parents?"

"It's just her dad. Her mum died last year."

"How awful," Mum says. She takes a mouthful of dinner and dabs at her eye. She's always been so sensitive to other people's pain. I think it's this innate empathy that makes her such an outstanding actress.

"Her dad is putting on a brave face but I could sense the sorrow beneath his salt-of-the-earth smile."

"No wonder his daughters are so impressive. Every little girl needs a strong male figure when she's growing up."

"And every little boy." I whisper the words, committed to the thought but not to saying it out loud.

Mum places her hand on mine. "And every little boy," she whispers back.

I scoop food into my mouth and keep my eyes down. We never talk about this, but only because I never want to. Now, though, the injustice of Gloria's family being split by tragedy makes me even angrier about the selfishness that tore my own family apart.

"I'm sorry, Barney," Mum says. "I'm sorry I couldn't give you what you needed."

Heat rises from the pit of my stomach, burning like acid in my chest. "It's not your fault. He's the one who walked out. He's the one who should be saying sorry."

"He never did, you know."

I haven't seen my father for more than twenty years and I have no desire to ever see him again. My greatest fear, though, is that I can't escape him.

That he's a part of me. That my own life will forever be colored by his weakness.

I fold my hands together and rest my elbows on the table. "Am I anything like him, Mum?"

She doesn't hesitate. "Nothing. You are nothing like that man, Barney."

Talking about this deep-seated fear crumbles my defenses and self-control. My words come out in a rush, like an undammed stream. "I can't hold down a relationship, I gave up on my comedy, I'm terrified of everything, all the time..."

Mum cuts me off. "I said *nothing*, Barney. You are nothing like him."

My voice cracks. "Then why am I like *this*?"

Mum's eyes fill with tears. She wipes at them, swallows, and speaks in a voice I can barely hear, and don't recognize. "Because of me, Barney. Because I didn't protect you from them."

I know what she's talking about. Them; the people who would never leave us alone. The people who thought they knew us because they'd seen my mother on television or on stage or read about her in a magazine. The people who thought they had a right to a piece of us. In the street, at school, at the supermarket. Always there, always them.

"I'm sorry, my boy. You were so lost when your father left..."

I still remember the scent of his aftershave.

"...and you shouldn't have had to share me with the world when you needed me all to yourself."

I was on the front cover of a gossip magazine. A family photo, torn in two.

"But it was all I knew how to do, Barney."

I don't blame her. She doesn't need my forgiveness. "I understand, Mum. You don't have to defend yourself to me."

She draws her shoulders back and raises her chin as though she's projecting her voice to a crowd. "Do you know why I love the theater? Because in the theater, you can be anything to everybody; confidant, lover, enemy even. And you don't have to know a single one of them. All that intimacy, and not one ounce of commitment. It's the ultimate emotional high, Barney." She looks away from me. Drops her chin. "Until it ends."

We sit together in silence. Mum shuffles her food around in the bowl. I stare at mine.

"It's like a drug," Mum says.

I look up and her eyes are blazing again.

"The more you have, the more you need. That's why I couldn't protect you from them, my baby. I *needed* them. I was addicted." A tear rolls down her cheek. "I'm sorry."

I can't watch her cry. Not because of me. "It's okay, Mum. We're going to be okay." I clear the table and take our bowls to the kitchen sink.

"Of course, you're going to be okay, Barney. You're braver than I'll ever be."

This is the kind of factually incorrect, though welcome, maternal encouragement that has helped me make it to my thirties. "Thank you. But that's ridiculous."

Mum starts projecting again. "When I'm on stage, I'm hiding behind a character. Even more so on the screen. I don't have to reveal anything of myself. I don't have to be vulnerable as me. It's a safe place."

I turn off the tap, the bowls not yet rinsed. "I'd never thought of it like that."

"But you, when you're doing stand-up comedy, you have *nowhere* to hide."

My most recent gig flashes before my eyes, the terror of the whole experience returning to me in an instant. "Don't I know it."

"That's true courage, Barney. Standing up there with nobody else to blame...no director or writer or cameraman..." She casts her hands around the room as though these loathsome creatures are in every corner of my apartment. "...that would be terrifying. And yet, you do it anyway. It's the true definition of courage."

She's right. It's terrifying and I do it anyway, because with the terror comes the incomparable rush of hearing them laugh. But...

"I gave up, Mum."

She stands. "No, you didn't. You just took a break. And now the drifting is over. You're pursuing your passion again, which means you're living a worthy life, Barney."

The acidic heat that was in my stomach is long gone, replaced now by the warm glow of comfort.

Mum smiles at me. "Well, this is altogether too dramatic for a Sunday evening. I want to hear more about Gloria." She picks up her sunglasses. "Let's go out for a drink."

NINE

I keep my head down, eyes on the floor. I figure there's nothing so distinctive about the top of my skull that it will give me away to a former colleague. Gloria, Achal, and I are sitting in reception, waiting to be taken upstairs.

I steal a quick glance up at my new colleagues. Gloria's nervous. She looks the consummate professional in her charcoal suit, but I can tell by the tiny quiver of her hands that she's on edge. I'm wearing the traditional private sector, navy, single-breasted number to project integrity and gravitas, and because it's the only type of suit I own. Achal has made a special effort by wearing what could possibly pass as smart casual pants and a very respectable bright purple business shirt. As long as nobody looks at his skateboarding shoes, we may be able to give the impression of a professional outfit. They're seated opposite me and we're all marked as outsiders by our plastic visitors' passes.

I worked hard to get out of this meeting. Despite my moment of madness with Warwick Harmen, I'm actually a very nonconfrontational, peace lover. Or weak dog, as I was repeatedly called during my short and uninspiring junior football career.

I have tried to reconcile what it was that tipped me over the edge that day. I have tried to understand how my cultivated prudence could evaporate in the face of my rage at Sylvia's treatment. Many times, I have lain in bed pondering these questions. Sometimes, just before I fall asleep, at the very moment I cross into unconsciousness, I think the answer comes to me from somewhere deep inside the dank shadows of my subconscious mind. It tells me that my stage-managed persona of a happy-go-lucky, respectful, and docile man is a front for the man who lives inside. It tells me that I'm basically a fraud, and if I actually followed my passions I'd be an altogether different Barney Conroy. Possibly a much, much improved version of the one I am now.

Thankfully, though petrified, I am wide-awake at the moment and have no unrealized desire, conscious or not, to be anything more than my current, mediocre self. Right now, I just want to get to the eighth floor without being spotted by Warwick Harmen or any of his allies.

In response to my cowardice, which I have framed as business acumen, Gloria has explained that I cannot get out of this meeting because it is the whole reason Archie hired me. If I bail on the account, Archie will either get suspicious and do some further investigation into what happened at the department, or simply fire me on the spot, hopefully without a physical confrontation. Chad has been moved to a new account he landed him-self—thankfully, because I was starting to get *really* sick of him knowing more about everything than me—so I have nowhere to hide. Mandela had to go home.

"Gloria Bell?"

I snap my head up to see Gloria standing at the sound of a man's voice. A man I've never seen be-fore.

"Yes, I'm Gloria."

"Samuel Ebenstar. Pleased to meet you."

Who is this Samuel Ebenstar?

Gloria shakes Ebenstar's hand and introduces Achal, and then me.

"Ahh, yes, Barney. I've heard all about you," Ebenstar says this as he's shaking my hand. He's my age, my height, more muscular, and slightly better-looking. I hate his guts.

What is "heard all about you" supposed to mean, anyway?

"We haven't met, have we?" I say as our hands drop away.

"No, I only started here a few weeks ago. I'm in your role on a short-term contract until they find a permanent replacement."

"They didn't waste any time."

Ebenstar laughs, and because he's smiling at me, I have no idea whether he is a friend or foe. "All right, let's head up, shall we? I can't wait to hear this pitch." He turns and begins to walk away. I can't move, suddenly paralyzed like a weak dog at the thought of crossing the lobby to get to the elevators, and then riding said elevators while trying to do an impersonation of someone who is most definitely *not* Barney Conroy.

I consider running away. Not metaphorically, but literally, physically *running away.* I could get out the front doors as everyone else turns left to the lifts. As I'm planning my escape, I feel a nudge in the small of my back. I turn to see Gloria alongside me. The only reason I'm moving is she's pushing me with the palm of her hand.

"Come on," she whispers. "You'll be fine. Remember, you did nothing wrong."

Even though I'm experiencing a mild case of sciatica at the country-strong pressure of her hand on my spine, her touch sends all the nerves that aren't associated with my sciatic pathways into overload. I keep my eyes down and we make it to the eighth floor and into an empty meeting room without any trouble.

"I'll be right back," Ebenstar says after we settle into our ergonomically approved chairs.

The next person we see is Sylvia. She enters the room like a little kid sneaking out at bedtime. She rushes straight to me, ignoring Achal and Gloria, and wraps me in a hug. "I'm so glad you found a job. I nearly cried with relief when I saw your LinkedIn update. We all miss you heaps, Barney. Make sure you get this pitch so we can work together again." Sylvia says all this into my shoulder and then, just as quickly as she appeared, she disappears.

"Was that her?" Gloria asks.

"Yes."

"Very fond of you."

"She's only human."

Gloria laughs and it helps galvanize my nerves. We wait in silence for a minute before somebody else enters the room. It's my former manager, Margaret. She is more refined than Sylvia in her greeting. "Lovely to see you, Barney. Looking forward to finding out what you've got for us today." And then some more of my former colleagues come in, greeting me with smiles and handshakes, pretending I didn't get fired.

Ebenstar is the last in and closes the door behind him. "All right, thanks for coming in, guys. I can see you've done all the introductions. Achal, do you need any help connecting to the projector?"

"Already hooked up."

"Great. Well, we're in your hands, Rogerson. Over to you."

And just like that, I have conquered my fear. Not only is this not as bad as I thought, but as Gloria begins to launch into the pitch, I actually start enjoying myself. She is magnificent, commanding their attention, engaging them with the idea, humoring their risk aversion.

Achal performs a cameo to discuss the technology component of Track Your Attack (my idea) and then I am on to present one slide on the campaign key messages. I line myself up underneath the projection screen and take hold of the remote clicker. "Good afternoon," I say, channeling Clooney.

The door to the meeting room swings open, severing my connection with George. Warwick Harmen walks into the room. Everybody stares at him, their confusion clear. Everybody except Ebenstar, who is smiling like he just got my permanent job.

"Oh, don't mind me," Harmen says with the politeness of a psychotic, Tchaikovsky-listening despot. "I'm just here to observe the pitch."

Why is he here to observe the pitch?

This has never been done before. And if there's one thing I learned from ten years in the service, if it's never been done before, then it should never be done at all!

"Warwick is representing the Executive Leadership Team's interests," Ebenstar says. "With such a major project, we want to ensure executive approval before making any commitments."

I look at Margaret for support, an instinctive but pointless reaction, really, because what is she going to do? She can hardly chuck him out. He's executive leadership, he can do whatever he wants. She looks into my eyes, narrows her own, and gives a slight nod.

Harmen sits down beside Ebenstar and I note that he would have to get past six people before he had the opportunity to punch me in the face. But he doesn't look at all like he wants to punch me. He looks like he wants to be my best friend, which is even more alarming.

Ebenstar hands Harmen a hard copy of our pitch. He ignores it completely and continues to stare at me in the manner of the aforementioned, Tchaikovsky-listening despot.

"Please, Barney. Carry on," Ebenstar says.

Gloria smiles at me a little bit like a mother willing her child to take its first steps. Achal is motionless, except for the small movement of his hand resting on his knee. He gives me the thumbs-up.

"All right. So, key messages. Let's start with the most important, and the simplest." I hit the button on the clicker to bring up my slide. Our first memorable campaign take-away transitions onto the screen. "Your health—You're in control." I pause to let it sink in, to give them a moment to digest it. "As Gloria highlighted earlier, a critical tenet of this campaign is giving people control of their own health. It's not a government department telling them what to do. It's not a health expert guilting them into action. It's a campaign of empowerment. When you sign up to be part of Track Your Attack, you're acknowledging that it's your health, and you're in control."

I deliver this speech like I work at Apple, which vindicates the 18.5 million times I rehearsed it in the lead-up to this meeting. Gloria is smiling again. I've just taken my first steps. The rest of the crowd is nodding and chin rubbing. I'm ready to run.

Which I don't do literally, but I do launch into key messages two and three. They are greeted with the same noncommittal enthusiasm that is the staple of the neutral public service stalwart. I pretty much invented the move, so I know that it's about as positive a reception as we're going to get before they tally their scores. By the time I finish key message three, I'm so enthused by their ambivalence that I wish I had more to say.

But now it's back to Gloria to take the stage, wrap up the pitch, and call for questions. Achal gives me a pat on the leg as I sit down next to him, which is encouraging, and a little disturbing at the same time. I feel great, though. Maybe my paranoia was unjustified. Maybe I won't be the reason Rogerson loses this pitch. Maybe Warwick Harmen is a better man than I gave him credit for.

It's Harmen who responds when Gloria opens up the floor to questions. "How do we know we can trust you to act professionally, and with respect?" he asks, sitting back in his chair with his hands behind his head.

Gloria is thrown off balance. I long for Achal's reassuring squeeze of my thigh.

"I'm sorry, what do you mean?" Gloria asks.

"Professionalism is very important to us here at the Department of Healthy Living, and respect is one of the core pillars in our Code of Conduct."

Gloria regains her composure, but her hands develop the almost imperceptible quiver again. We both know where this is going. "Respect is also a core pillar of the way we operate at Rogerson. But don't just take our word for it; we'd be happy to provide references for the way we work."

"Yes, I'm sure you would," Harmen says. "But what about personal references? How do we know that we can trust your team to act professionally?"

Gloria hesitates. Then her words are measured. "Well, that goes without saying. Everyone on our staff maintains the highest professional standards."

"What about him?" Harmen points at me.

Gloria smiles but doesn't even look my way. "Perhaps we could finish answering questions about the pitch and then move on to the team makeup if you're satisfied with the idea."

"The team delivering the idea is just as important to us, Gloria, as the idea itself. If we can't work with your team, it doesn't matter how brilliant the concept is." Harmen stands up. "Let's speak frankly. We'll assess your idea on its merits against the other two pitched this morning. But we will only do that if you can guarantee that Conroy won't have anything to do with the account."

This is outrageous. I don't even work there anymore and Harmen is still trying to control me. We're desperate for this account, and I'm desperate to be on the team, but he's made sure Gloria can't deliver both.

I wait for Gloria to decide my fate. She looks at me, and then back at Harmen. I think she's going to support me even if it costs us the job. I can feel it. I just know she wouldn't compromise her integrity to secure a client.

"Barney is the architect of this idea."

Right on.

"It was his vision that helped us create the pitch."

Tell him, sister.

"And his passion for the project and the department would be invaluable."

Would be? What? Why the qualifier?

"But it's your prerogative to have input into your team's make-up. If you don't want Barney on the account, he won't be."

Remember that bit in the second *Indiana Jones* movie when that guy gets his still-beating heart ripped out of his chest?

"Thank you, Gloria," Harmen says as he makes for the door.

"Our pleasure." Gloria sits down and directs her next question to Ebenstar. "Perhaps we could go through some details about the timing of your decision?"

Harmen opens the door. Everybody else is focused on Ebenstar, waiting for his response. I'm the only one looking at Harmen as he backs away. Before disappearing, he smiles at me and mouths three silent, yet deafening, words.

"You're scum, Conroy."

* * *

"I'm finished."

Gloria takes a bite from her hamburger and speaks through a mouthful of food. "What are you talking about?"

"My career. It's finished. Archie recruited me to work on the department account. The department won't let me work on the account. Ergo, I'm finished."

Achal sighs. "You are a real pain in my neck sometimes, Barney. We just delivered our best pitch ever. We've got a real chance of winning this account and all you can think about is yourself."

"It's all right for you, Achal. You still have a job!"

"So do you, Barney," Gloria says.

"Not for long."

Now Gloria sighs. "Achal's right, Barney. You're really killing the celebratory mood of this gourmet hamburger. I'm going to ask you to stop talking now until Achal and I have finished eating. We like our celebrations unmarked by self-indulgent whining."

Is she serious? What is there to celebrate other than my impending doom?

I try not to sulk, but it's impossible so I give up trying and sulk very enthusiastically. This has no effect on Gloria and Achal, who continue relishing the celebratory lunch.

Fourteen days later, when Gloria finally finishes her last chip, she sits back, smiles, and pats her stomach. "Now that is what I call a hamburger. How were the chickpeas, Achal?"

"Exquisite."

Now I know they're messing with me. My steak sandwich was pretty good, but nobody, anywhere, ever in the history of the world ate "exquisite" chickpeas.

"Barney, here's what we're going to do if we get the job." Gloria leans forward and rests her elbows on the table. "You're staying on the account."

"But..."

"Quiet!"

I obey.

"You have to stay on it to keep your job. And, despite your river of insecurities..."

Achal: "More like an ocean."

"...you've actually proved, repeatedly, that you're going to be critical to our success. You just demonstrated that again during the presentation. You know exactly how to connect with them, Barney." Gloria jabs at the air with her unused fork. I think it's supposed to reinforce her point, but it's making my eyeballs nervous. She jabs again. "And that's the kind of expertise I'll be relying on, especially if things get tricky toward implementation, as they always do."

My sulking turns to exultation. I repeat Gloria's words in my head: *...that's the kind of expertise I'll be relying on.* She basically said she wants to marry me.

"But what about Harmen?"

"Forget him. He doesn't need to know you're advising us behind the scenes. As long as you don't come to any client meetings or deal with the staff directly, we'll be fine."

"And Archie?"

"He wouldn't have a clue. He's not exactly what you call a hands-on boss when it comes to real work. We're in the office most of the time, anyway, and when we go to meetings, just pretend you're coming with us. Spend a couple of hours in a café or something."

"And if he asks?"

Gloria sucks in a deep breath and bares her teeth. "I'll tell him you're on the account."

"So you'd lie for me?" Now I know marriage is on the table.

"No, Barney, I won't be lying. You *will* be on the account with us. End of story."

I don't care what she says, Gloria just admitted she'd compromise her professional standards for me.

I feel like a god.

* * *

Sometimes in life, things just go your way. They line up, they work for you. They come together. I have read about this phenomenon but never experienced it personally. Until today. Back at the office, among the familiar whirr of the air-conditioning and the tangled mess of Snake Valley, I am the conquering hero.

Chad, Archie, and Diana stand to greet us as we enter the office.

Chad folds his arms, puffs his chest out, and tilts his head back like he's about to challenge us to a *Step Up*–style dance-off. "How'd it go?" he asks Gloria.

"Pretty well. They seemed to like the pitch but didn't give us any indication of how it stacked up against the other agencies' ideas."

"Good to hear. Nice work, Gloria."

"Did you use your local knowledge, Barney?" Archie asks. "Did you twist and turn and duck and weave until you had them begging for mercy?"

He knows it wasn't a prizefight, right?

"He was brilliant, man," Achal says.

Archie looks at Achal like he's not sure who he is or why he's standing there. It takes the enthusiasm out of Archie's charge. "Right, well, okay. Let me know when you hear a decision."

Gloria's desk phone rings. I check the prefix on the caller ID display. She sees it, too. It's the department.

It's all lining up.

We share a moment of delicious excitement in a glance. Gloria reaches down to the phone.

"Quiet, everybody!" I say. "It's the department."

No one is talking, so no one reacts.

"Rogerson Communications. Gloria speaking."

I hold my breath. I watch her bite her lip. "Uh huh," she says, her expression unreadable. "Yes...Thank you for the opportunity." Her lips part just enough to allow shallow breaths. Her eyes are distracted. "Absolutely." Her lips start to turn up in a smile. My heart thunders in my hollow chest. "Yes, definitely." Now her eyes turn to me and they are alive with joy and promise. "Sure...Okay...Great, I look forward to it...Yes, likewise...Okay, thanks again. Good-bye." Gloria hangs up the phone. "We got it," she whispers.

I feel tears sting at the back of my eyes. I want to wrap my arms around her and celebrate in a loving embrace. Which is apparently what Archie wants as well because the next thing I know I've got two hairy arms encircling my rib cage and I'm being lifted up in the air by my diaphragm.

"I knew it!" Archie cries from below me. "I knew taking a gamble on a public service nobody would pay off! You've just saved the agency, team! Without that contract, we would never have made it to the New Year!"

He lets me go and I hit the floor hard enough to twist my ankle, which sends me sprawling onto my desk. Archie is making a sound that lands somewhere between a war cry and wailing for the dead.

He fades to nothing, though, as Gloria reaches out for my arm and helps me back to my feet.

Her touch makes me hope in eternity.

"Congratulations, Mr. Public Service Nobody." She shakes my hand. Hers is warm and soft. "You did a great job." I wonder if this is the part where I should kiss her. That's what would happen if this was *Love Actually*, isn't it? Or would it be workplace harassment? I err on the side of the law and thank her for her praise.

"Diana, open the champagne!" Archie yells, rubbing his hands together and grinning like a wild baboon. "The Finisher!" he says to me. "That's what we'll call you from now on, The Finisher!"

"Well, it wasn't just me, Archie. Gloria and Achal were the ones who got us over the line."

"Now's not the time for modesty," Gloria says, before launching into a spirited retelling of how the pitch unfolded. Tears form in Archie's eyes. He hugs me again like I might actually be his son.

Diana hands out glasses and Chad pours our drinks. Archie proposes a toast. "To Rogerson and her continuing success." He's beaming like he just delivered his Oscar acceptance speech.

"To Rogerson," we all chant. And I take a rather too enthusiastic swig that causes me to snort at precisely the moment the champagne is about to

slide down my throat. It goes to my nose instead
and I get a buzz like somebody just exploded three
sherbet packets in each of my nostrils.

It feels magnificent.

TEN

Archie promised that if I make this campaign a success, he'll give me a permanent job. That was three weeks ago. Since then, I've worked harder than I ever have in my life. It's not unusual for me to still be at my desk at 6:45 p.m. I'm enjoying the job, sure, but what I'm enjoying infinitely more is spending a serious amount of time with Gloria. Once, our hands accidentally touched as I passed her my stapler. If felt like my life was complete.

My phone rings. It's the bagpipe intro to "Copperhead Road." Gloria is sitting next to me, her eyes focused on her computer screen. She doesn't look at me as she speaks. "You can put that on silent, you can change your ringtone, or you can watch your phone smashed to a million pieces before your very eyes, Barney."

I select option A and stand up to take the call in private. It's an unknown number, which always makes me nervous. Why are unknown people calling me?

"Hello, Barney speaking." I hold my breath.

"Barney, it's Jake MacIntyre from MacDaddy Communications."

What? MacDaddy is the coolest agency in town. Everyone either wants to work with them or for them. Their founder, Jake, is a cult hero. He has rolled out some of the most innovative and awarded campaigns of the past three years. They're basically the David Guetta of communications agencies.

"We haven't met," Jake says, "but I've heard about some of the great work your team has been doing with the Department of Healthy Living."

"Really?" I can't help sounding incredulous. Partly because he's heard about the great work, and partly because he thinks I have a team.

MacIntyre laughs. "Don't sound so surprised. Listen, I want to talk to you about a job."

OMG. Oh My Gandalf.

"Why don't you come down to my office and we'll grab some lunch."

Oh My Gandalf.

"Barney, are you still there?"

"Gandalf."

"What?"

I make one of my trademark gurgling sounds before recovering my voice. "Where's your office?"

Jake gives me the address and we agree to meet in an hour.

"What was that all about?" Gloria asks when I get back to my desk. She obviously didn't take the Privacy Basics course.

"What?"

She narrows her eyes at me. "Your secret phone call. The one you just rushed off to take."

"A man's allowed to have secrets, isn't he? It adds to the mystique."

Gloria scoffs. "No offense, Barney, but you've got about as much mystique as a dry biscuit."

"You know that just saying 'no offense' before an insult doesn't make it any less offensive, right?"

"To you or dry biscuits?"

"Now you're just being hurtful."

* * *

MacDaddy Communications is in Richmond, which is just outside the city. It only takes me fifteen minutes to get there on a tram.

I find the building, take a deep breath, and open the door. I'm getting better at this. I search for a receptionist with whom I can build rapport—old habits die hard—but am confronted by a lack of reception and an assortment of desks, beanbags, and Apple computers that shatters my self-confidence. The offices are, of course, more your gutted warehouse than the traditional corporate digs, and I feel like Owen Wilson in *The Internship*. I need Vince...

Nobody seems to notice I've arrived so I look around for the MacDaddy. I can't find anyone who looks like they might own the business, but my curiosity does attract the attention of a dude— seriously there is no other way to describe him— who looks up from his computer, smiles, and bounds my way. He's got the facial hair of a third-year uni student—with possible guarana overload issues—and the hair of a nineties Seattle grunge band drummer, updated for the new millennium with some product and a hint of highlights. He's a big man, over six five, easy, and he'd be about my age, maybe a little older but it's hard to tell behind all the hair.

"Hello, mate. Welcome to MacDaddy. What can I do for you?"

"I've got a meeting with Jake MacIntyre."

"Lovely," he says, a little more enthusiastically than is necessary IMHO. "I'm Anton."

Of course he is.

"Barney Conroy."

"All right, Barney, let me take you to meet Jake."

On the way through the office, various young women look up at me and smile. Young men nod and one guy even throws me a wink. MacDaddy appears to be the *Cheers* of communications firms. Anton leads me to a room called the Ideas Station (not kidding), where there is an assortment of mismatched couches—pink, blue, and green—and naked lightbulbs hanging from the ceiling in a trendy *get too close and you'll be electrocuted* kind of way.

Walking through the valley of the shadow of death is a man, about my age, in a devastatingly navy suit—pure white shirt, no tie. He's on the phone and turns to Anton and me as we walk in. When I see his eyes for the first time, I'm pretty sure I fall in love. In contrast to the rich depth of his navy jacket, his eyes are a piercing, pale blue. He smiles with teeth so white I almost fall to my knees in worship. He holds up a single finger to indicate he'll just be a minute. Either that, or he has mistaken me for the coffee guy and wants a macchiato. Anton pats me on the back. "I'll leave you to it," he says, before walking out of the Ideas Station and closing the door behind him.

Now it's just me and the MacDaddy. The bromance is on. I can't hear what he's saying but I'm pretty sure it's charismatic and convincing. I watch the way he walks as he talks. It's the casual, yet assured, stroll of a man who is in charge of his own destiny. He ends the call and walks toward me, hand extended.

"Barney, it's great to meet you in person." As you'd expect, his handshake is cool and with the expert level of pressure.

One MC Hammer, two MC Hammer.

"Sorry about that," he says. "I was just settling the nerves of a jumpy client. You know what that's like."

No, actually, I have no idea what it's like to deal with jumpy clients, or any clients for that matter.

But in the spirit of rapport-building—which is already through the roof by the way—I meet Jake's conspiratorial wink with a knowing smile. "We all know what it's like in this game."

Jake laughs.

Mission accomplished!

"Indeed, we do, Barney. Indeed, we do." He motions to the green couch. "Have a seat. I hope you don't mind, but I took the liberty of ordering lunch in."

"Not at all," I say, as though I pretty much order lunch in every day. Whatever that means.

Jake sits down opposite me. "So how are you enjoying working at Rogerson?"

"It's pretty good. Good people, good culture, good clients."

"Archie still as mad as ever?"

"You know Archie?"

"Everybody knows Archie!" Jake says this in a way that leaves me unsure of its hidden subtext. I can't tell whether everybody knowing Archie is good because he's the most popular kid in class, or bad because he's the only kid that ever had to do athletics training in his speedos because he got his timetable mixed up and brought his swimming gear to phys ed instead of his track gear. (Not me).

"How did you know I worked at Rogerson?"

"I know people."

A thought occurs to me. "How did you get my phone number?"

Jake smiles and spreads his beautiful hands in a gesture so charming it feels like he's asking me to dance. "I know people."

"None of them criminals or crackpots, I hope!" I'm only one-quarter joking, but Jake thinks this is hilarious.

"You're funny, Barney. You'd fit in well here."

My heart begins to flutter at the compliment and the job inference.

"Let me tell you some more about MacDaddy. I started the company six years ago. It was just me and my future ex-wife back then."

Ex-wife? He's my age and he has an ex-wife? He's even more accomplished than I thought!

"The business has lasted three times as long as my marriage, and in that time we've built up an enviable stable of clients and a reputation as an innovative, results-focused agency."

"I'm all about results."

"We're a major player now, and we're looking for the right talent to take us to the next level. When I heard about your work with the department, I was impressed. I thought, now there's a man we could use at MacDaddy."

I wonder how much he knows about the agony and ecstasy of my relationship with the department. Given that it's enough for him to get me down here and basically throw a job at me, I'm guessing he hasn't got the full story. And I'd quite like it to stay that way.

"Well, I think my public service experience put me in a good position to understand their needs."

"I like it, Barney. If we can't understand the client's needs, then what hope have we got, eh?"

Our philosophical musings are interrupted by a knock on the door. A woman enters carrying two trays of food. "Lunch is here," she says.

"Thanks, Zara. Come and join us. I'll introduce you to Barney."

Zara turns to me and smiles. "Well, I can do that myself."

Hold the phone!

"I'm Zara. Barney, right?"

"Right on."

Stop speaking, Barney.

Zara is dressed in a smart gray skirt and white shirt, which I think is too businesslike for a workplace that has a room called the Ideas Station. She's attractive, if you like women with long hair tied back in a ponytail the color of a tropical sunset who wear trendy black-rimmed glasses to emphasize their smartness *and* contemporary fashion sense. Which I've just discovered I do. Zara sits down opposite me, next to Jake. She's so close to him that their upper arms are touching and, when he turns to her to talk, their faces are close enough to require breath mints. No wonder his marriage didn't last.

"Zara's our Senior Account Director. She takes care of our biggest clients. The role we're thinking of for you would work very closely with her."

Zara has leaned forward to pick up some sort of Japanese-looking food, which she places onto a small plate. It distracts and threatens me with its complex presentation. I mentally shake my head to cast off the fear of the small, vibrantly colored portions.

"You all right, Barney?" Jake says.

Is he on to me? Does he know I have the palate of a twelve-year-old?

"Yes, of course, why?"

"You look concerned."

I laugh like a tormented alpaca, which seems to throw Jake off the scent. "Have something to eat," he says.

His offer of "something" is actually spot-on, because who knows what this collection of alleged foodstuffs is? I presume it's Japanese because there's a fair bit of sushi-looking gear, and a few concoctions wrapped up in what I believe is rice paper.

"Can't decide, hey?" Jake says. "Everything looks so good."

"Do you know the Luncheon Locomotive?" Zara asks, as though we both listen to the same underground indie rock band.

I try to give the impression I'm trawling through a catalog of sushi restaurants in my brain. "I...don't...think...so."

Zara's eyes blaze with evangelistic fervor. "It's amazing. There are dozens of exquisite dishes that go around the restaurant on a mini train. You watch as each carriage brings past a dish and you just reach out and take the one you want."

What poor Zara doesn't realize is that she has just described my own personal version of hell (well, another one of them anyway). Unfortunately, my instinctive repulsion to my own eternal damnation overcomes my fakeness and I forget to act tolerant and cultured. "So you mean the food goes past all those people who stare at it and breathe around it and sneeze on it before it gets to you?"

Jake and Zara stop eating and look up at me, both their mouths open wide. They're on the cusp of writing me off. I can see it in their eyes. I've seen it so many times before. I need a save. A mega save. A once in a generation save. Which. I. Deliver!

"Said no one, ever, anywhere in the world when the food is this good!" To reinforce the point, I pick up two of the roll things and put them into my mouth. They're deceptive little wretches and take up more space than I anticipated. While they're not entirely repulsive, one part of my brain still sends *spit that garbage out* signals to my tongue. Thankfully, it's overruled by the more financially astute part of my brain that sends *eat that garbage and be happy about it if that's what it takes to get a permanent job* signals.

While I try not to gag, Jake continues to talk about MacDaddy. "We ascribe to the fail fast, fail often theory."

I can deliver failure.

"It's the only way to truly break through to the great ideas. Otherwise, you get stale and you start rolling out the same campaigns in different colors. We've set this office up to foster creativity. We hire people who are prepared to challenge themselves and our clients. That's how we ended up with four of the top five industry awards last year. And we have no intention of slowing down. We want big ideas, Barney, and we want you on board."

This is absolutely worth eating garbage for, and, most importantly, he hasn't used the phrase "short-term contract." He's talking about improving my financial security and status all at once. I'll be sorry to leave Rogerson, but things are heating up so much between me and Gloria that it would probably have become awkward for us pretty soon, anyway.

They don't ask me much about myself, but seem very happy just to talk about MacDaddy and the proposed role. I find this a little unusual, but not unwelcome. If they're thinking of hiring me because of word of mouth (how good is the private sector!), then anything I add will only dilute my chances.

Lunch ends and Zara bids me farewell. "Lovely to meet you, Barney. Hopefully, I'll see you soon."

Emboldened, I throw Zara a familiar phrase to let her know I'm effectively one of them. "Not if I see you first." She hesitates as though she's going to respond, but then decides to walk away. A very common female response to my charm.

"Thanks for coming down, Barney," Jake says. "We've got a few things to tidy up on the job, but once that's done, I want to offer you the first right of refusal. I'll be in touch again soon."

I do a quick mental assessment of whether he's given me any signals to indicate he's up for a bromantic hug, and decide he hasn't. We settle for the safety of a handshake, but I calculate that we're only a shared pot of peppermint tea away from taking it to the next level.

* * *

When I try to sneak back into Rogerson without being noticed, everybody is standing at Archie's desk buzzing.

"Where have you been?" Archie asks.

"Nowhere."

"Why do you look so guilty?" Achal says.

"I don't."

"How do you know you don't look guilty if you can't see yourself?"

He's got me there.

Gloria rescues me. Her smile has taken over her whole face. If I had to describe her as a type of beverage right now, I'd go with effervescent. "Barney, you won't believe it, but while you were out, we got a call from the Department of Youth. They want us to pitch on next year's Youth Alive campaign."

Youth Alive is a massive weeklong celebration of Victoria's young people that would be a miraculous coup for a small agency like Rogerson. "Are we big enough for Youth Alive?"

Silence falls on the room like a concrete slab. Chad steps out from the group. "Some of us in this agency have been working toward this moment for a long time, Barney. Some of us know that with the skills and capabilities of our team, we can deliver Youth Alive better than anybody. Some of us believe in Rogerson Communications."

"Amen to that, Chad!" Archie roars. "You might have done a good job getting us on board with Healthy Living, Barney, but if you want any chance at a permanent job around here, you need to deliver more than once in a blue moon."

Once in a blue moon? I was here five minutes before securing your biggest ever client, you sanctimonious tyrant!

The group breaks up and everyone heads back to their desk. I watch Archie stare at his computer screen like it's an alien life-form, and it gives me a thrill of satisfaction to know I'll soon be telling him to keep his permanent job because I've got a better offer from Jake MacIntyre. That's right, Jake MacIntyre. You may have heard of him, Archibald, he runs a real communications firm with a real office, and real clients.

Archie stands up, picks up his bag, and strides toward the door. He doesn't make eye contact with anyone, but raises his right hand high in the air, index finger outstretched and wagging like he's cheering a ball through the goals. "All right people!" he booms. "See you all tomorrow. Roger that!"

I make eye contact with Chad, who stares at me for a moment before looking away. Achal is eating from a box of Cheetos, and, with his headphones on, it's unclear whether he knows the rest of us are in the room. Diana has used Archie's departure as an opportunity to get stuck back into her weekend crossword.

And Gloria, well, Gloria is as magnificent as ever. Focused on her computer screen and biting her bottom lip, she is the very essence of professional beauty. Her simple ability to stay focused, a trait that has always eluded me, is inspiring. I could watch her until the sky falls into the ocean, and the days melt away like wax on the candles of time.

"You're creeping me out, Barney."

Did I say that candles thing out loud?

"But I didn't say anything."

"You're staring at me like you're disturbed. Give it a rest and get onto the Youth Alive website will you. We need to prepare as much background information as possible before the brief comes in this afternoon. We've got an extended period before we pitch because it's such a huge campaign, but I don't want to leave anything to chance. Find out everything you can about what they've done for the past three years. You'll need to know it for our creative proposal."

"Of course, Gloria. Your wish is my command."

"Chad," Gloria calls over the snake pit.

He pops up like an obedient meerkat.

Suck.

"I'm going to flick you the brief when it arrives. Can you start turning your mind to strategy?"

"On it. I've just downloaded the department's vision and mission statement."

Suck.

"Great. I think we might need some expert insight around young people so I'm going to see which of our partners might be able to provide the right audience profiling."

"Good idea," Chad says.

Suck.

"Achal," Gloria says. No response. "Achal!"

He looks up.

"Can you start thinking about the technology most used by sixteen- to twenty-year-olds? We want to make sure our technical offering lines up with their device and consumption preferences." Achal nods, which is as good as a declaration of love from that hostile bogey.

Gloria turns her attention back to her computer and I do the same, trying to feign enthusiasm about a project I'm not going to be around to deliver. I don't really feel bad about it because a man's got to do what a man's got to do in this world. And if that means walking away from a disrespectful, unappreciative employer and into the hands of one who smells like a hairdressing salon, well so be it.

"It wasn't fair, what Archie did to you earlier." Gloria speaks so that only I can hear, and she doesn't turn to look at me. "I'm sorry. You didn't deserve that."

Maybe I should give my departure some more thought. Although she might not be ready to tell me in quite these words, Gloria has basically just admitted that she loves me. It gives me the kind of courage I usually get from two beers and a refreshing switch to a lemon spritzer. "Let's have dinner tonight," I say in the same conspiratorial tones. "To continue the campaign planning."

She gives me her shrewd eyes. "Shall we invite Chad and Achal?"

"Only if you want them to die."

Gloria chuckles. "All right. We'd just be here working anyway, so we might as well do it over a meal. My choice of venue, though."

* * *

Gloria chooses a restaurant so platonic, married couples leave in separate cabs. It's a little Italian joint around the corner from our office with just enough people to not make it romantic, and just few enough to not make it one of those ghastly chains.

"Where can I put this beautiful couple?" some young, handsome, Italian-looking shonk asks us, staring into Gloria's eyes as though he can see her soul.

She blank-faces him. "Anywhere but the window."

"But, no, such a beautiful woman must be put on display. She should not be hidden from the world."

Oh man, this bloke doesn't know who he's dealing with. I actually feel a moment of sympathy for him, as I visualize his inevitable kneecapping.

"Over there will be fine," Gloria says, pointing to a table against the wall, under some heavy-duty fluorescent lights. Mr. Italy shows us over, rambles off the specials, staring at Gloria's body the entire time, and then leaves us in peace.

"What a chauvinist," I say, all Germaine Greer–like.

Gloria looks confused. "Sorry, what?"

"That waiter, the one who said you should be on display. He spent the whole time treating you like a showpiece!"

"You know what that is, Barney?"

I shake my head.

"Life. Everyday life. Ninety-five percent of you treat me like that."

Am I in the good five percent?

"If I got outraged every single time it happened, I'd be permanently outraged."

Am I in the good five percent?

"And that would mean I'd never get anything done."

"Am I in the good five percent?"

Gloria chuckles, then looks at me with her head tilted to one side. "Yes, Barney Elvis Conroy. Yes, I believe you just might be."

Somebody, somewhere in the world lets off a firework. I dedicate it to me.

Mr. Italy reappears with his objectifying eyes, decisively ruining the moment. I silently declare war on him. He leans on our table like we're privileged to have him there, takes our order, and then throws me a wink as he walks away. Warmonger.

Gloria's eyes open wide as she starts to talk about the upcoming campaign. She's already mapping out the roles we'll all play. I decide not to dampen her enthusiasm with the truth, convincing myself, unconvincingly, that whatever role she has designated for me, somebody else can easily pick it up. I don't want anything to interrupt her, or to take the shine out of her eyes. Even the arrival of our suspiciously quickly prepared meals (anybody else thinking microwave?) doesn't slow her down.

"I know we shouldn't jump straight to creative ideas, but I think there are so many great possibilities. Have you given it any thought?"

I have, and I haven't got a single idea. The problem is that I don't really know how to generate ideas, I only know when they arrive in my head, which is less often than I'd like. "I probably need a bit more time to think about it."

"Yeah, of course, I'm sorry. I'm just really excited, and I know you need time to brainstorm. Maybe we could just spend a moment in silence thinking about it now."

This is one of the weirder requests I've had over dinner, but I acquiesce with a nod of my head and try desperately to come up with a moment of creative genius for a campaign brief I've only half read. What with me basically working for MacDaddy now and all, I didn't think there was much point getting too immersed in the project.

"Anything?" Gloria asks, thirty seconds later.

Not exactly a doyenne of patience.

"No."

"Me, neither."

Her energy drops, and she falls quiet. It's nice, really nice just to be sitting here eating together, like an old couple who have no need for words to express that they are just where they want to be.

But we're not an old couple, and I'm basically an idiot, so I start trying to make conversation. All I can think about is MacDaddy, though, so I risk showing my hand, figuring it won't hurt to find out what Gloria knows about the company I'm going to work for.

"What do you know about Jake MacIntyre and MacDaddy Communications?" I'm playing this very cool and I take a sophisticated bite of my pizza.

Gloria is twirling some linguini onto a fork and has her head down, concentrating on the task. She looks up at me with her eyes only. She still has half a mouthful of dinner, but speaks through it, none-theless. "Is that a joke?" There's a hard edge to her voice that makes me nervous.

"No."

"That's a serious question?"

"Yes."

Although the smoldering anger in your eyes is making me wish I'd never asked it.

"Why do you want to know?"

I think it's time to get out of this conversation before it ruins the evening.

Initiate exit strategy.

"Just interested because I heard they'd won a swag of industry awards last year." Gloria twirls some more linguini onto her fork and looks at me less like she wants to garrotte me with her pasta. She's studying me now as though she's assessing my character, which I really don't want her to do. Then she speaks.

"I used to work at MacDaddy."

My throat evaporates and the pizza that was in it drops into my windpipe. "Man down!" I try to cry, but I can't speak. Or breathe. So I just flail my arms and make a gurgling sound.

Gloria drops her fork and leaps out of her seat. It makes a clattering sound on her bowl, perhaps the last sound I will ever hear, and then I feel overwhelming blunt force trauma between my shoulder blades. And then again. And again. Until the offending piece of margherita flies out of my mouth and into Gloria's pasta.

"You all right, man?" It's my archenemy, the warmonger. The one who's been trying to finish me off with an open palm on my spine.

"Fine," I try to say, but it comes out as "urrchh."

Mr. Italy looks at Gloria.

"You okay, Barney?" she asks.

I nod and, to demonstrate my faculties are still intact, I take a giant swig of water. This seems to satisfy Italy, and the rest of the patrons who had all stopped to stare at my untimely death. I wave a hand to my fellow diners to indicate I'm going to make it. "Nothing to see here!" I say, trying to effect a jovial *I have near-death experiences all the time* kind of air.

And then, trying to maintain the lightness of the mood, I turn back to Gloria and smile at her with tears still in my eyes. "I didn't know you worked at MacDaddy," I say, as though it means nothing to me, when this piece of information actually has the potential to change everything. If Gloria worked for Jake, he must know she's at Rogerson. And if he knows she's at Rogerson, why is he trying to headhunt me, yet making no mention of her at all? Something's not right, but I have no idea what.

"Why would you?" Gloria's not jovial.

"I just thought that we'd been getting along pretty well so, you know, it might have been something that you'd tell me."

"Why?"

I think about this for a moment. It's a fair question. There's no reason for her to have given me a list of her former employers. Before tonight I had barely given it any thought myself. We haven't known each other that long and, despite my romanticized notions of our burgeoning relationship, we're still just work colleagues.

"Because I thought we were friends."

Gloria drops her guard and smiles. There's a
piece of green leaf covering one of her top front
teeth. She looks like a pirate. I consider reaching
over and dabbing it with a napkin, when I remember that I'm not Captain Jack Sparrow.

"We are friends, Barney."

I'd like to celebrate this elevated status of our
relationship but my mind is crowded with doubts
and questions that are dogging me into an anxious
stupor. Why didn't Jake tell me about Gloria working for him? Did he target me *because* of Gloria?
But why? What would be the value in that?

"Can I offer you another drink?"

I never thought I'd be happy to see my old war-
time foe, but Mr. Italy arrives just in time to save
me from self-destructive reflection. "Another beer,
please."

"Me, too," Gloria says.

Italy's interruption has left us in no-man's-land.
Gloria is staring at her hands, and I'm not game to
say anything that would compromise my opinion
of MacDaddy—my career salvation—or our new
"friend" status.

Our drinks arrive and Gloria and I chink bottles.
Focus descends on her again like a Jedi mind trick.
I really wish I could do that. She looks at me with

Yoda eyes. "To working together. And to friendship," she says.

After dinner, when the taxi pulls up outside Gloria's apartment, there's a moment of magic. She puts her hand on my upper arm. "Thanks for dinner, Barney. I had a really nice night." She shuffles her way out of the cab and leans back through the door. "I'll see you bright and early tomorrow." She throws a twenty-dollar bill onto the seat, slams the door, and disappears around the back of the taxi.

The driver catches my eye in the rearview mirror. "Where to, mate?"

"There's nowhere else I want to be," I say, slouching back into the seat as though I've just kissed Juliet.

"Well, then, get out of the car."

"Yeah, right, sorry mate. Port Melbourne, please."

* * *

I leap out of bed at the sound of my phone. I know it's sitting on my bedside table—I can see it flashing—but my legs refuse to obey my brain's commands and I walk straight into the wall. It is two a.m., after all, not traditionally my peak time of day. Just before collapsing onto my bed with a suspected broken nose, I grab the phone.

It's Gloria.

"I've got it, Barney. I've got it!" she says in lieu of a greeting. Her voice is so loud, it bounces off my bedroom walls like a sonic boom.

Despite the physical pain surging all through my body as it revolts against this unscheduled wake-up call, I can't help but be excited. About what, I have no idea, but Gloria's so enthused, I can't help myself. "What have you got?"

"The campaign execution, Barney! I've been working on it since you dropped me off. I couldn't sleep."

"Me, neither."

"Are you ready?

"I think so."

Gloria launches into her idea, for about ten seconds, anyway, before she breaks off. "Are you writing this down? Why aren't you writing this down?"

I'm not yet convinced I'm actually conscious, let alone capable of writing down words that are rocketing toward me like a Keanu Reeves bus ride. "I'll record it on my phone."

Bang, I'm back!

"Is that legal?"

"Gloria, it's two a.m., can we stay on topic?"

"Sorry, okay, so as I was saying..."

After ten minutes, she stops for breath. That's when I wake up. I just lay down to get a little more comfortable and, because I wasn't a required participant in the conversation, my body betrayed me. I have absolutely no idea what her idea is. I play the percentages. "Gloria, that is brilliant. I love it."

"Really? You really think it will work? I know you're the creative in this partnership, but I just had a moment of inspiration and couldn't help myself."

"Trust me, it's fabulous. I can't wait to be part of the team that makes it happen."

"Thanks, Barney. That really means a lot to me." She lets out a long, luxurious sigh. It's such an intimate moment in the dark and the quiet that I almost feel like Gloria is lying next to me, her hair tousled across her face. The heat of her body warm on my skin. "Well, we better get some sleep," she says. "It's pretty late."

"Yeah, of course. I'm starting to feel a little weary."

"Good night, Barney."

"Good night, Gloria."

I reach out to touch her beside me, but my hand falls onto the cold, untouched sheet. Maybe one day.

For now, I've just tied myself to an idea about which I know absolutely nothing. I'm going to have to stand by it tomorrow, though, no matter what's recorded on my phone.

Good idea or not, I won't let Gloria down.

ELEVEN

Gloria's idea, just quietly, is very good indeed. So good that it makes me seriously question my decision to leave Rogerson. This is way better than Track Your Attack. I've actually got an opportunity to be a recognized front and center player with the Department of Youth. I've got an opportunity to add a very serious line item to my LinkedIn profile. And, of course, I would get to see Gloria every single day.

It's been more than two weeks since I met with Jake MacIntyre and I've heard nothing. In the fast-paced world of communications, two weeks is about seventeen dog years. It means the bromance is over. I haven't called him, of course; that would make me look needy and desperate.

But I have spent many long hours pondering what it was I could have done wrong. Did I come on too strong? Was I trying to be too funny? Should I have eaten more from the hygienically compromised Japanese food train? I may never know, but the blow of rejection has been softened by the sweet sound of Gloria's project management-speak, and the promise of a key-player role in our upcoming pitch. I've also convinced myself that something very fishy was going on down there, anyway. I haven't asked Gloria about it again, but clearly, MacDaddy was some kind of criminal enterprise. Or advertising agency.

It's five o'clock on Friday afternoon and my mind has packed it in for the week. Gloria is the only reason I'm still here. I don't want to be on a tram home when she has the epiphany that she's loved me all along. A quick sidelong glance at the way she is interrogating a spreadsheet from hell suggests this is not the night for epiphanies. So I decide to log off and head home for the perfect Friday night in: two-minute noodles, a couple of low-carb beers, and a classic movie. I haven't decided which DVD I'll select from my collection, but I'm in a Demi Moore kind of mood, so it'll be *Ghost* or *GI Jane*, I suspect.

An e-mail hits my in-box. It's from Chad, who sits eight feet away: *Fancy a Friday night drink??*

This is an astonishing development in our hitherto 1960s US/USSR-style relationship; Chad has mostly ignored me since I won the Track Your Attack pitch-off, and Gloria has managed to give us discrete components of work on the Department of Youth pitch. The main thrust of Chad's communication to me has been hostile glances over the snake pit, though he may also be working on a nuclear bomb. Gloria and Achal have been copied in as well, and I see Achal pop his head up and look at Chad with the same suspicion as me.

If there's a chance Gloria's going, though, I'm all about reconciliation: *Sure! What time?*

Achal stands up: "We go right now or I'm out."

Gloria untangles herself from the spreadsheet's tentacles. "Out of what?"

"Check your e-mail," I say.

She does. She smiles. She stands. "Give me two minutes to pack up, Achal."

He rolls his eyes but nods; she really has a power over him. I spend the next 120 seconds working myself up into an epiphany-ready lather.

At school, I was never one of the cool kids. But I was never a persecuted smart kid, either. I managed to tread the fine line of inoffensive, non-attention-grabbing behavior that allowed me to walk past the footy players without being given a crippling dead leg, and yet still sit amiably at a tram stop with the guys studying university-level math. I used to slay them with my mathematical humor: "Calculus? Makes me feel cal*cluess!*"

But now, as I stride down Melbourne's thriving city streets with the impossibly radiant Gloria on one side of me and the infuriatingly handsome Chad on the other, I feel like one of the beautiful people.

Achal is walking three paces ahead of us and, despite being the only nondrinker in the group, has chosen our destination. Because he "likes the decor." Whatever. As long as Gloria's there, we could be sitting on a bed of thumbtacks and I'd be happy.

We arrive at the door of the bar and I'm almost expecting some sort of VIP welcome because we're so beautiful. We get a hostile glance from the bouncer instead. Gentleman that I am, I let the others go in first. Just as Chad is swallowed up by the promise of Friday night revelry, my pocket begins to vibrate. I take my phone out as I'm about to step through the doorway of the bar. Then I stop.

Then I turn around and walk from the entrance.

Then I take a deep breath.

It's him.

It's the MacDaddy. *My* MacDaddy.

I knew he'd call! I knew there was never any doubt. And as for that nonsense about something not being right, well that was just post-rationalization because I thought I wasn't going to get the job. But now I am going to get the job. Surely, he's ringing to offer me the job. Whatever the job is!

I play it cool. "Hello, Barney speaking."

"Barney, it's Jake MacIntyre."

Me (surprised but delighted): "Oh, hi Jake. How are you?"

"Mate, I'm fabulous. Listen, I know this is short notice but what are you doing right now?"

I look back at the bar and wonder if Gloria has noticed yet that I haven't gone in. "Um, nothing, not right now. I was going to head out for a drink with some friends a bit later, but right now I've got some time on my hands."

"Excellent! Get yourself down here. It's Friday night drinks and I want you to meet the rest of the team. It's also my way of apologizing for the lack of contact over the past two weeks."

"Two weeks? No way, has it been that long? Don't worry about that. I'll be there in twenty minutes."

"Perfect. I'll have a cold beer ready for you."

Oh man, oh man, oh man, oh man. Stay calm. Stay calm. You're on the cusp of permanent employment. But you have to stay calm!

I make it to MacDaddy in record time and I'm not sweating even the slightest bit. Not even on my upper lip or brow, a masterful feat that I am taking as an irrefutably positive omen. This is totally meant to be. On the way over, I sent Gloria a text message to let her know I just had to run a quick errand and would be back soon. She replied with "ok." A little ambiguous, perhaps, but I'm confident I haven't killed off the epiphany just yet.

I stand for a moment at the threshold of a new life. Then I walk into paradise. I know I've said that before, but that was seven weeks ago when I was fresh out of the public sector, green and naive. This time, it's the real thing. There are highly educated, highly styled, wickedly fashionable young men and women sprawled across the office, all drinking designer beers or golden, bubbling champagne, French no doubt. Most of them are congregated in the Ideas Station, where, just between you and me, I reckon the ideas must be flowing thick and fast.

Jake is on the pink couch receiving a neck and shoulder massage from a young woman in a T-shirt emblazoned with the slogan "Relax!"

Don't mind if I do!

Jake vanquishes me with his smile. "Barney!" he calls, raising an arm as high as he can while having the knots in his shoulder luxuriously annihilated. He beckons me over and makes some room next to himself on the couch. "Great to see you, mate."

"You, too, Jake."

"You remember Zara?"

I turn to my left and there's Zara sitting next to me. She has her eyes closed and is groaning at the treatment of one of the "Relax!" ladies. "Hi, Barney," she breathes, without opening her eyes. She raises her hand in an unconvincing attempt at a wave but then lets it capitulate onto her leg, which I notice is touching mine. It sends an uncontrollable current of pleasure through my body. I'm not doing anything wrong, of course. Space on this couch is at such a premium, a half-crooked real estate agent could flog it off for three hundred grand. With a view. But the inadvertent pleasure at her touch does give me a pang of guilt. What would Gloria think about me being wedged between her ex-employer and a beautiful woman receiving a neck and shoulder massage?

But I don't have time to ponder the question, or feel anything other than exquisite pleasure myself, actually, because I am transported to the afterlife by the deceptively strong and disconcertingly knowing fingers of my "Relax!" angel. My cares, my anxieties, my insecurities, they all melt away at her touch. I'm aware that Jake is saying something, but it comes to me like the sound of a muted stereo a thousand meters below the sea. I float, I dream, I believe.

A year and a half later, my relaxation is complete and I slump on the couch like a well-worn beanbag.

Jake is laughing. "I thought we'd lost you for a minute there, Barney."

"That was amazing." A beer has appeared in my hand. Not sure when that happened, but I take a swig in the spirit of appreciating my hosts' hospitality.

"So tell me, Barney," Jake says. "Have you given much thought to working with us?"

"Every waking minute and in most of my dreams" would probably come across as too eager for a professional response, so I run with something more measured. "We've been pretty busy at Rogerson, but I have given it a bit of thought."

"Not playing hard to get on us, are you?"

Backfire!

Salvage!

Laugh forcibly!

"Ha, no, no way, of course not, Jake. No way! I would start work here tomorrow if you asked me to, even though it's a weekend!"

"Well, I don't think we'll quite need you to do that, but let's find somewhere we can talk a little more privately. I'll introduce you to the rest of the team on the way through to my office." He does, and I never knew my heart was capable of so much love. So many loveable people. So many people I want to be seen with.

Jake takes a seat behind his desk, which manages to be both minimalist and imposing, and I take the chair opposite. "How's your beer?" he asks.

"Nice and cold. Just the way I like it."

Jake smiles, but I see a change in his eyes. I think he's about to say something serious. I think he's about to make a proposal.

"How's life at Rogerson, really?"

"It's okay."

"You permanent down there?"

"Not yet, but I think Archie's pretty close to offering me a role. I probably just need to get another campaign under my belt first."

"Right." Jake tilts his head back and looks at me down his sculpted nose. "You wouldn't need to do that here, you know. I like to think I can spot talent, and your work with Track Your Attack speaks volumes."

"Thank you."

"So what's the next one Archie wants you to get under your belt?"

"What do you mean?"

"The next campaign. What are you working on?"

I hesitate. I'm pretty sure this is *not* something I should be telling our competition. But I need to keep Jake on my side, so I compromise. "It's another government gig."

"Who with?"

Now I have to dig in. "I probably can't tell you that, Jake. You know, commercial-in-confidence and all that." I shrug and roll my eyes to indicate that it's all the lawyers' fault.

He raises his eyebrows in a challenge. "Don't you trust me, Barney?"

I laugh very loudly and fakely. "Of course I do, Jake!"

I want you to be my BFF!

"It's just that it's not really my campaign to tell, you know. Not my creative concept. If it was, I'd give it to you straightaway."

"Is it Gloria's idea?"

Here's my out. "Yeah, it is, so I'd need to check with her before saying anything."

Jake stares at his desk. I take a swig of my beer and my gulping throat sounds like a church bell at a funeral. Jake looks up at me. His eyes are dark and unreadable. "Did you know she used to work for me?"

"I did."

"Did she tell you why she left?"

"Not really."

"You fancy her?"

This is getting weird. Say something noncommittal.

"Um, well, she's been very nice to me since I arrived."

Jake laughs. It's a bitter sound. "Well you're doing better than me, Conroy. He picks up his beer and takes a long swig. His Adam's apple pumps as he drains the bottle. He sighs and wipes his snarling lips.

I'm not entirely sure why—maybe women's intuition—but I need to get out of here. "I better go. My friends are expecting me."

Jake looks at me like I'm a cockroach that just crawled out from under a drainpipe. "Righto, mate. We'll be in touch."

I scurry through the office. As I meet the eyes of the beautiful people along the way, they ignore me, and I realize that they are so young. So very young. Zara is prowling the room with a champagne glass in hand. She looks at me, but doesn't smile, before turning her back. When I get to the exit, I look back on MacDaddy. Jake is standing at the door of his office like an oppressive king surveying his subjects.

I close the door behind me.

* * *

I feel shaken *and* stirred as I head back to the bar to meet my Rogerson colleagues. I'm not sure what just happened. Not sure whether I just made a massive mistake by talking to Jake about our pitch. Not sure why Jake's sudden change in character made me apprehensive, afraid even. Not sure why he looked so full of vitriol when talking about Gloria. So I decide to confront this brewing personal crisis with my most effective and long-standing defensive tactic.

Pretend it never happened.

This is pretty easy while I'm standing in the queue waiting to get into the bar, but may prove more of a challenge when I have to confront my workmates. I look around at my fellow would-be patrons and notice, with alarm, that they are all male. A couple of minutes of astute observation confirms my worst fears. The bouncer is applying the gender selective entry technique and is only letting women in the front door. This is a not uncommon practice that I have come up against many, many times in my bar/pub/club-hopping career. I have resolutely and publicly asserted, on many occasions, usually when drunk, that this process is discriminatory and, therefore, un-Australian. My primary purpose, of course, is always to get another drink before I remember the emptiness of the life that awaits me the next morning. To date, the tally in this sixteen-year battle stands at Bouncers 336, Barney 0. Or thereabouts. Tonight, though, is my night to get on the board. And I'm going to use my secret weapon to do it.

Unfortunately, my secret weapon doesn't answer her phone. So I send her a text message and wait one and a half minutes before sending her another one. No reply. Does she know about me and Jake? Of course not, that's ridiculous. But I have to know for sure if she knows about me and Jake!

I take my life in my hands and push my way to the front of the queue, buoyed along by a series of witticisms including:

"Oi, you right, mate?"

"I'm not standing here for my health."

And: "Wait your turn, maggot."

The bouncer doesn't appear to remember me. "You can't get in with those shoes," he says, looking down at my casual-Friday sneakers. This is a standard security ruse that I parry with an expert thrust.

"They're exactly the same shoes I was wearing half an hour ago when you were happy to let me in."

"That was then, this is now."

Is he quoting the S. E. Hinton book and movie adaptation of the same name?

"Are you quoting the S. E. Hinton book and movie adaptation of the same name?"

The bouncer looks at me with a sudden surge of interest. "You like S.E. Hinton?"

I read half of *The Outsiders* and only know about *That Was Then, This Is Now* because Mike made me watch the movie when we were at school and he was going through a *tough on the street* phase. But I sense an opportunity here. "I love S. E. Hinton, man. He's my favorite author."

"She's a woman."

Seriously?

"I know. And now I know that you're also a true fan."

The bouncer launches into an extended and painful series of book reviews during which he uses phrases including "life-changing," "gritty," and "literary genius." The appraisal goes on for so long that I almost forget my mission. Behind me, there's a groundswell of discontent forming along the queue as the thirsty revelers watch patrons leaving, but no one going into the bar in their place. The sacred one-in, one-out rule has been abandoned like a worthless idol.

"Come on, mate, we haven't got all night!" someone down the line yells.

The bouncer looks up and is snapped out of his literary trance by the sight of a dozen or more Friday night beauties waiting in the queue. He lets all of them in.

And me.

It takes me ten minutes to find Chad and Achal, and these are ten of the more harrowing minutes of my life. Despite the bouncer's temporary insanity, the joint is absolutely jam-packed with loud, obnoxious blokes, and contemptuous, haughty women. This is not judgmental on my part, but observational, a key skill of both a communications professional and a successful comedian. Neither of which describes me, of course, but I'll need those skills if I'm ever going to actually *live* the dream instead of just dreaming it.

"Where's Gloria?" I ask Achal.

Chad: "Where have you been?"

Achal: "She's gone home."

Me: "What? Why?"

Achal: "She stayed for an hour and a half. What more did you want from her?"

An hour and a half?

I look at my watch. He's right. I had no idea I'd been away so long.

"So where have you been?" Chad asks.

"Errands."

He screws up his face. I'm sure he's going to challenge my lie.

"Why don't you get a beer? We'll be here for a little while longer."

Why is he being so nice?

Not important right now. What I need is alcohol. I get a beer, and then another. And then I start feeling good as the anxiety brought on by my meeting with Jake melts away in direct proportion to my inebriation, like the water overflowing from Archimedes' bath. And then I get another and I'm actually getting on quite well with Chad and Achal. And then I get another and the volume and the haughtiness embrace me until I become one of them. And then I'm pretty much slaughtered, standing in an alcohol haze looking around at what might be the world's most ridiculous decor. This bar is so trendy there's red velour everywhere and, I kid you not, stuffed, life-size wild animals. Truly.

I've got this ridiculous great giraffe staring down at me with the most beautiful long eyelashes. If it weren't so terrifying, I might crane my neck and give it a kiss.

As I mentioned earlier, Achal chose the place. He's a shifty one because he doesn't drink booze, yet somehow managed to select the most obscenely priced venue in Melbourne. So while he's been enjoying a single, six-dollar lemonade, Chad and I have been losing cash like it's the Black Friday stock market crash.

As cataloged, I'm five beers down (including the one I drank at MacDaddy). It's my round. Despite feeling pretty good, I can't drink another beer, so I decide to switch us to spirits. There's a fair bit of jostling going on at the bar, and the barman, a part-time model with intimidating triceps and perfect hair, waits until every other person in the venue has been served before turning his disgusted eyes on me.

"What do you want?" he shouts over the noise of the music and the crowd.

He's not exactly Jamie Oliver's *Fifteen* material, but I decide not to raise it with him, given that I am now desperate to get to the toilets following my excessive beer consumption. I still manage to play it cool, though.

"Two rum and Cokes." I don't say please, because I'm pretty sure matching his obnoxiousness is the only way to win his respect.

He looks at me for a moment like he wants to spit in my face but then ups the ante in our silent battle for masculine ascendancy. "What sort of rum?" His triceps flex beneath his sleeveless vest.

"What have you got?"

Booya, barman!

I try to flex my abs, but it almost makes me wet my pants on account of my over-capacity bladder, so I settle for a curl of my lips instead.

He throws a drinks menu in my face and goes off to serve someone else. I find the spirits page and get about halfway down the list of nine thousand different rums before the throbbing pain beneath my belly moves to critical. I abort the mission and scurry, bent over like a primate, toward the gents.

It's much quieter in the toilets with only the muffled sounds of the crowd penetrating the walls. Only when the door is opened does the sound of joy and revelry flood in like a murderous wind. It's also much brighter, which, as you'll know if you've ever entered the men's toilets at any venue, ever, anywhere in the world, is not a good thing. It's a very bad thing, in fact. I tiptoe to the urinals to reduce harmful exposure to my shoes. The urinals are the individual kind, which I prefer, but there's no dividing partition, which I don't prefer. Thankfully, the one next to me is unoccupied.

Until Chad arrives to occupy it.

"Barn dog! I thought you'd done a runner. Skipped out on us when it was your round!"

I try to maintain an air of unaffected calm, despite conversing in a public toilet, which I do not find calming. "Nah, mate, of course not. It's just pretty tough to get served out there."

"Yeah, tell me about it. Hey, listen, where'd you disappear to tonight? We really missed you earlier."

This is odd. And uncomfortable at a urinal.

"I just had to see a friend of mine."

"About what?"

"Nothing."

"Where was your friend?"

"Just a block away."

"Then why'd you catch a tram?"

I am so stunned by Chad's question that I break the sacred urinal code of conduct and snap my head to look at him. He holds my gaze. "I came out to find you and when I asked the bouncer if he knew where you were, he pointed to the tram stop."

Book club traitor!

"I watched you get on the tram to Richmond."

If I were a child, I would just close my eyes now and go to my happy place. But because I'm a man, I make a noncommittal "hhrrmmpph" sound, and then go to my happy place. Unfortunately, Chad follows me to my happy place, making it considerably less happy.

"Come on, man, no secrets at Rogerson. We're a team."

I do the "hhrrmmpph" thing again and start to walk away. Chad follows me and does the unthinkable. He reaches out and grabs hold of my shoulder as I try to escape, his hands devastatingly unwashed. This is ranked number two on the list of Worst Possible Things That Can Happen to You in the Men's Toilets (number one involves untied shoelaces). So I'll do anything to get out of there.

"What's going on, Barney? You got a girlfriend?"

"No!"

"I don't believe you." He tightens his grip.

I crumble. "Promise me you won't tell Gloria."

"I won't."

"I'm about to be offered another job."

Chad raises his eyebrows. He's clearly surprised anyone else would also make Rogerson's recruitment error. "Well, congratulations. But why all the secrecy?"

"I don't want to tell Gloria until it's finalized."

"Why not?"

I hesitate.

"Tell me, Barney."

"It's with MacDaddy Communications."

"What? You're kidding me. Why would you want to work for *them*? They're the most unscrupulous crooks in the industry. And they treat their staff like dirt. You have to talk to Gloria about this. She'll tell you what they're like."

I'm not quite sure why Chad thinks I need to defend my career choices to an American who holds me in unadulterated contempt. So I don't. Instead, I throw back a bit of contempt of my own. "Yeah, you're right. They're highly successful, award-winning, and have a client list we could only dream of. Why would I want to work for *them*?"

Chad looks at me like he's my big brother. "Stay away from them, Barney. They're bad news."

"Don't be ridiculous. Jealousy doesn't suit you, Chad."

Chad finally lets go of my shoulder. I retreat out of reach lest he commit another personal hygiene infraction.

"So Gloria knows nothing about it?" he says.

I shake my head. "You won't tell her, right?"

"Of course not. But you have to." He gives his hands a cursory rinse—water, no soap; what does he think that's going to achieve?—and then heads back into the night.

After washing my hands, I return to the bar, get the cheapest two rums on the menu, and find Achal standing alone.

"Chad had to go home. Looks like you've wasted your money."

"You're staying, aren't you?"

"No. I've spent enough time fraternizing in the Valley of the Damned."

"You chose this dump!"

"Did I, Barney? Or did it choose us?"

I'm five beers down, agitated, and surrounded by velour. It is inconceivable that I have any chance of understanding what Achal is talking about.

"C'mon, mate. Let's go," he says.

"I'm not going anywhere. I paid for these rums and I intend to drink them."

Achal steps right up to me so that his face is only a well-timed head butt away. His eyes are terrifying. "Beware of the path you choose, Barney. A man is no more than the sum of the choices he makes. And some choices can never be undone."

This kind of prophetic insight is most unwelcome right now (as always, frankly), so I chase it away with some expertly timed comedy. "I hear you, guru. I chose these drinks and I'll never be able to take them back!" I follow this line up with the visual comedic element of swigging from one of the glasses. This was perhaps not the greatest choice in itself, given that swigging spirits is not *exactly* my forte. I somehow manage to inhale the drink from inside my mouth so that the carbonated alcoholic beverage is sucked up the back of my nasal passages. I'm no doctor, but I'm pretty sure this is *not* what nasal passages are designed for. I have this confirmed by the buzzing assault in my nostrils, momentary blindness, and subsequent sneezing fit. When I recover functional control of my nose, eyes, and throat, Achal has vanished.

I've still got one and a half rums to finish, though, so I move to the corner of the room and try to look *totally* comfortable with being alone and, to be frank, pretty bored with this whole scene. I begin chewing a piece of ice because I think it projects a kind of James Dean–style reckless abandon.

With one glass fully accounted for, I take out my phone and pretend I'm texting someone. I even throw in a simulated chuckle (albeit a contemptuous one) so everyone will know that I'm in the middle of some sort of highly sophisticated *and* devastatingly ironic message exchange. With a supermodel.

Then, miraculously, I actually receive a text message. From Jake.

Jake: *Barney, are you still out?*

Am I ever!

Barney: *Yeah, getting tired of this crowd, though.*

Jake: *Come down to Sugar Ray's on Collins Street. I'll put your name on the door and have a drink ready for you.*

I don't know what everyone's problem is. This bloke is an absolute legend.

Barney: *Sweet as. See you doon.*

Panic!

Barney: *I mean soon!!! See you soon!!!*

I consider an emoticon, but decide against it, still want to play it cool until he offers me a job.

It's unclear whether Sugar Ray's is actually named after somebody called Sugar Ray, but if it is, I think Sugar Ray must be one of the gods. His obvious power and greatness makes the once godlike Archie look like a plastic deity. Sugar Ray's bar is perfection. It's your standard setup of dance floor, booths, and bar area, but what defines Sugar Ray as an immortal is the presence of his angels. Male angels. Female angels. Male angels who look a bit like female angels. And I am standing among them. Me,

Barney Conroy, the guy who never knew these beings existed, let alone ever managed to get into the same bar as them. Sugar Ray is a god indeed, and we are all dancing to the rhythm of his beating heart.

Or is it Avicii?

Jake materializes. "How you holding up there, Barney? You look a little shaky."

"Nah, mate, nah, I'm fine. Just enjoying the beats." In truth, I'm leaning on the bar in the hope I won't fall on the swirling clouds of heaven at my feet. Jake has bought me two drinks since I've been here, which takes my tally for the night to nine, which is one drink above my threshold for hospitalization. But if I die now, believe me, I'll die happy.

Zara walks over to us with a swing of her hips that is most definitely not what I'd expect of a heavenly being. "Having fun, Barney?" She laughs from her throat, draping an arm around my shoulders. Her touch sends a shock wave of pleasure through my nervous system. Her perfume mingles with the heat of her body to produce a combined scent more intoxicating than my nine drinks. The room sways and Zara rocks back and forth before me like a beautiful flower caressed by the warm breath of God.

"Yeah, it's a cool bar," I say.

She smiles at me. Just smiles. And yet it's enough to make me blush.

Jake hands me a shot glass containing some unidentifiable liquid. He gives Zara the same, and then raises his own. "To new friendships," he says, staring into my soul. His eyes are hypnotic and charming again. There's no sign of the acrimony they carried earlier. No sign of any type of danger or threat. Maybe I was imagining it. Maybe I misinterpreted the signals (wouldn't be the first time!). Maybe, just maybe, Jake is as wonderful as I thought, and the haters all around me—primarily Chad—are simply jealous of a man who refuses to be a part of the smallness of their wasted lives.

Or maybe I'm just so drunk it doesn't matter. Nothing matters right now, to be honest. That's what being drunk is all about.

"So, Barney," Zara says, leaning closer in to me so that our bodies are now touching, side by side. "Jake tells me you work with Gloria. How is she?"

"Good, yeah, pretty good." Zara's body is firm, her eyes tantalizing. And I'm really enjoying our dialogue. If I can just hold off on vomiting in her face after that shot Jake gave me, I'll be able to make a much stronger contribution to the conversation.

"We miss her down at MacDaddy. She used to come up with the greatest campaign ideas."

"Yeah, she's good at that."

"You working on anything interesting at the moment?"

Somewhere deep below the surface of the alcoholic deluge that has flooded my mind and body, a tiny modicum of sense still survives. It breathes, exhaling just once, but it's enough to send a tiny bubble of prudence to the surface. It breaks on contact, sending a ripple of caution across my numbed and muted brain.

"Yeah, but I can't tell you about it. You know that." I think about adding "you cheeky little pussycat" and maybe waving my finger in her face, but if I keep my mouth open a moment longer, I'm pretty sure I'll throw up on her. She moves away from me—possibly intuitively—dropping her arm and taking a step to the side. The warmth from her body evaporates and I'm left cold and exposed. I long for her being next to mine.

But I can't tell them the idea.

I just can't.

But I'm so drunk.

And my mind is confused. It's ecstatic. Then desolate. Then exultant. Then pensive. Then blank.

Blank as the unwritten words of my future. So blank that only my heart survives.

And my heart is lonely. So terribly, permanently lonely.

I compromise, which, if you'll revisit the ecstatic/desolate/exultant/pensive/blank exposition of only a moment ago, you'll agree is pretty impressive.

"I can't tell you the idea, Zara. But if you come back here"—I try to beckon her to my side but can't raise my arm past my hips—"I can tell you a very funny story about what happened when Gloria told it to me."

Zara looks at Jake, who nods and hands me another shot. I'm so far past rational thought, I down it in one gulp.

Zara's warmth seeps into me once more. "So Gloria and I had been out to dinner."

Oh, man I'm really struggling now. That shot was not a great idea. I can barely remember my name, let alone the three-act structure of this story.

"And something happened, and then I was asleep and Gloria rang me and I took the call but then I fell asleep, but thankfully I was recording the conversation—which isn't illegal by the way—and when I woke up I said it was a great idea even though I hadn't heard a thing. But I was able to pretend like I'd heard the whole thing because I had it recorded on my phone. Hilarious, right?" I finish the confused monologue a little breathless, and pretty sure I'm about to pass out.

Then Zara twists her body so she's facing me front on. Her warmth is now all-consuming, her perfume rising like vapor from an enchantress's cauldron. She reaches into my dreams and runs her hands down my back. Then she smiles and takes a step away. I lose balance and sway, but don't fall because Jake's strong arm steadies me.

"You mean this phone?" Zara says, holding it in front of my face. She took it out of my pocket without me even knowing. How clever is she!

I start to sing. "Oliver, Oliver. Never before has a boy wanted more!"

Zara looks frightened.

A tidal wave of nausea washes over me. Heaven spins. Its foundations fall away beneath my feet. I make a break for the toilets, too drunk to even care that the lights have revealed multiple breaches of international humanitarian conventions. I splash water on my face. The flood stops rising. I splash some more. The flood begins to subside. I breathe in, and then out. In, and then out. Very. Slowly. My body has gone into reflexive survival mode, knowing that if I have to drop to my knees and vomit in these toilets, my life will surely end tonight.

And so I am preserved.

But I really have to go home to earth.

I make my way back out through the heavens, the angels blissfully unaware of my plight. I find Jake and Zara. She hands me my phone. "Thank you, Zara. I think I need to go home now."

"You all right?" Jake asks.

"Totes. Just want to go for a bike ride in the morning." I don't own a bike. I hate bikes.

"Okay, mate, take care of yourself. We'll be in touch."

We shake hands and then Zara leans in and kisses me on the cheek. She's more alluring than when we met earlier today, and I wonder what it would be like to hold her in my arms. "Bye, Barney." Her fleeting warmth touches me one last time, and then it is extinguished. The memory haunts and consumes me in the same heartbeat.

And then, as she walks away and the room turns into a canvas of indistinct shapes and running colors, I have a revelation. A piercing, shattering, revelation. I realize that here, even here, among the angels of the gods, I am alone. Completely alone. And terribly, terribly afraid.

Barney

Oh, Sugar Ray, please help me. I have to get home to earth.

TWELVE

I don't know exactly how I got home to earth on the night of my visit to Paradise. Whether I was cast down like lightning falling from heaven, or simply driven back to my place in a taxi, I'll never be quite sure. The night is a series of broken memories, unanswered questions, and unspecified regrets, followed by a morning of vomiting with such vigor that I burst a blood vessel in my eye. Not a great look at work on Monday, but easily explained by my participation in a lightning carnival of European handball. (Never happened.)

One thing I do remember about that night is telling Chad that I'm off to a new job. I remember him being a bit weird about it because he's jealous of MacDaddy, but I can't exactly remember why. At any rate, he's been much friendlier toward me since I told him I'll be leaving soon. I guess he's happy

I'm going because he thinks it will give him a free shot at Gloria without all my chemistry getting in the way. Fat chance of that. I know Gloria is too professional for an office romance; otherwise she would have kissed me ages ago. It's one of the many reasons I've decided to accept the job at MacDaddy, once offered, despite my unspecified uneasy feeling from the last time I met with Jake, which was now three weeks ago, which doesn't concern me in the slightest. Not one bit. Why would it? He's busy. I'm busy. He'll call when the time is right.

And, anyway, my mind is occupied now with today's pitch to the Department of Youth. We're all pretty nervous, but trying to keep it together. Gloria is in the boardroom rehearsing her part of the presentation. She's covering the creative concepts today, and I'm outlining the strategy with Chad. He comes and sits down in Gloria's empty chair.

"How are you feeling?" he asks.

"Okay. A bit nervous."

"Yeah, me, too. But we've got a great idea and it's a strong pitch. If we don't win the job, it won't be for lack of hard work."

"Yeah, well that's true." It is. I've never worked so many seven o'clock finishes in my life.

"Listen, Barney. I've been thinking about what you told me the other week. You know, about—"

I cut him off with an urgent whisper. "Yeah, I know what you're talking about." I survey the room to see if anybody is listening, but who am I kidding? Achal is as oblivious as ever, and Diana is in a deep and meaningful conversation with her sister that is now entering its third hour.

"It's okay, I haven't told anyone," Chad says. "I'm not going to pretend we're best buddies, Barney. But I want you to know that I've appreciated your work on this pitch and I'm sorry you won't be seeing it through if we win the job."

Hang on a minute. Have I misjudged this bloke?

"Thanks, Chad. That's very kind."

"Are you sure you're doing the right thing? I mean, I'm not going to tell you how to live your life, but are you sure MacDaddy is the kind of outfit you want to work for?"

I shrug off the lingering doubt. "Yeah, I am."

"You know you're going to have to tell her soon, right?"

"I know. Just not yet. I don't want anything to compromise our chances today."

"Okay. Then there's only one thing left to do." Chad smiles with the perfect mixture of charisma and mischief. Something I have oft attempted but never effected.

"What?"

"Let's knock their socks off. Roger that!"

* * *

"First of all, thank you for giving us this opportunity. We really appreciate the chance to pitch our ideas, especially when you've had so much success with Youth Alive over the past three years." Chad is annihilating them with his exotic accent and obvious pectoral muscles.

My turn to shine. "In fact, coming into the pitch, we had to ask ourselves, what can be done better, when your results are already so strong? This question became both our challenge and our inspiration."

There are five departmental representatives, a group similar in makeup to those who awarded us the Healthy Living job. This bodes well, and their affirming smiles and collegial nods buoy my confidence. Chad and I are tag teaming like Hulk Hogan and Andre the Giant.

Chad again: "We knew we would need something fresh, something relevant, something engaging. And most of all, something that continues to celebrate and encourage the youth of today."

Me now with the tease: "But before Gloria reveals our campaign ideas, we thought it was important to first take you through the strategy that has led us to our creative concept. I know, I can see your disappointment that the strategy guy gets to speak first..."

There are chuckles around the room. Real, genuine, bona fide chuckles. This is the greatest day of my life!

"But at Rogerson, our methodology is one of strategy first, because from strategy comes creativity that delivers results."

Chad: "And we're all about results."

Me: "So let's start with the challenge."

Over the next thirteen minutes, I outline the strategic hurdles and opportunities we have identified for this campaign. The crowd humors me with nods and hums. I'm a little disappointed that I recognize the glances they exchange a few times to suggest that they know all this, we haven't hit on anything new and it's possible the other contenders have presented a similar strategic base. But that's okay, because there are bound to be similarities when we're all working from the same brief. It's our creative proposition that will set us apart.

And that's where Gloria comes in. "Thank you, Barney. And thanks for staying with us while we laid the strategic foundation. Now it's time for the fun stuff." She smiles. I smile. The world smiles with us.

Now for the big reveal. "Ladies and gentlemen. Let me present to you our proposed theme for the next Youth Alive campaign." The excitement builds and Gloria teases it out like a reality TV host. "Are you sure you're ready?"

"Put us out of our misery!" the chair of the department team cries in mock anguish. We all laugh, and I realize, here and now, that I don't want to leave Rogerson at all.

I realize that I have been a fool to think I could find anything better than what Gloria, Chad, Achal, Diana, and Archie have to offer. Yes, even Archie. Rogerson may not be the biggest, best resourced agency. It may not offer the perks of Friday night beers and neck and shoulder massages, but it has something the others don't. It has us. It is ours. And I now feel like part of the team Chad described that has been working so hard to get Rogerson onto the communications map. To build the agency up through hard work, good ideas, and a team that sticks together. Yes, a team that sticks together.

I decide, here and now, that I'm in it for the long haul. And this makes my heart go into overdrive as we wait for Gloria to deliver the idea. I want them to like it. No, I don't. I want them to *love* it. I want them to tell us it's the greatest idea they've ever heard and we're hired on the spot. Then I want to go back to the office and work alongside my team to make Gloria's dream for this campaign a reality.

Here she goes. I hold my breath. "Rogerson communication presents...The Young and the Best-est!"

There's an immediate stir of suppressed activity. Furtive glances, shocked humming, one bloke even drops his pen and groans. None of this, by the way, is what we were going for.

Gloria looks heartbroken. "Is there a problem?" she asks.

The chair responds. "No, not yet, Gloria. Please continue."

She looks at me. I look at Chad. Chad looks at Achal. Achal stares at the wall. None of us knows what is going on. Gloria recovers her composure and battles on. She only makes it through two of our five key campaign pillars before the chair stops her again.

"Gloria, I'm sorry to interrupt, but may I please see a hard copy of this presentation?"

"Of course. I have copies for everybody."

"Just mine will be fine for now."

The room goes silent as the chair looks through our slides. She is considered and measured and, as she turns each page, it sounds like the tearing asunder of Rogerson's hopes and dreams. This is not going to be okay. I don't yet know why, but it is clear that we are not getting out of here with the job.

The chair finishes, takes off her glasses, and looks at Gloria like she's about to put down her pet hamster. "I'm terribly sorry, but we've already heard this idea today. It was pitched to us this morning by another agency."

Chad turns his eyes on me. They are full of unabated fury.

But I don't know why. I haven't done anything wrong...

And then I remember.

It's only a brief memory, but it's a distinct one. There stands Zara, as clear and defined as an angel of light among the armies of darkness. She's handing me my phone, her smile triumphant and assured. And there's me, the village idiot, taking it back from her with adoring eyes, shaking Jake's hand and pretending they think I'm one of them.

I suddenly understand. I suddenly see what I've done. My breath dies in my chest, along with my

hopes, desires, and chances of full-time employment. He betrayed me. The man I trusted with my
career betrayed me.

"I don't understand. How is that possible?" Gloria asks. She's putting on a brave show of professionalism but I can see the devastation in her eyes.

"I have no idea, Gloria. But I think there's little
value in us sitting through the remainder of the
pitch. If you could leave us copies of your proposal,
we will assess it on its merits against the other
competitors, including the identical idea from this
morning."

"All right," Gloria says, her eyes downcast. "If
you have any questions or would like any clarifica-
tion, please don't hesitate to call."

"We'll be sure to."

We are escorted out of the room like eight-
eenth-century convicts headed for the gallows. We
shuffle together, manacled by the chains of our
shame. Nobody looks us in the eye.

The elevator ride is somber. We don't talk because there are departmental staff in there with us.
It's not until we're out of the building that it begins. Chad fronts me. "What did you tell him?" he
yells.

He looks like he's about to clock me, and his
venomous accusation is so loud that passersby

quicken their steps. Gloria looks confused. Achal takes a step closer to us.

"Answer me, Barney! Was that the deal? A new job for our idea? Are you going to work there on the campaign we devised? Is that why you told him?"

"No, that's not what happened. I promise."

Chad scoffs. He lowers his voice but moves right up into my face. It's a frightening experience. "Are you pleased with yourself, Barney? You've gained the world, and all it cost was your soul."

"Chad, what are you talking about?" Gloria asks, grabbing hold of his arm.

Chad continues to stare into my eyes. "Barney gave our idea to another agency in return for a job."

"What? Why? What agency?"

Now Chad's eyes fill with challenge. "You tell her, Barney. Who'd you sell us out to?"

I don't respond. I can't respond. Chad moves in even closer, edging me backward with his chest on my own. I have to take a step back, and then another, until Achal comes between us. "Okay, Chad" is all he says, but it's enough for Chad to stop his advance and move back in line with Gloria. The three of them stand there looking at me. I'm only meters away, but we are worlds apart.

"He gave our idea to MacDaddy," Chad says. "Jake offered him a job in return."

Gloria's mouth drops open. "What? Barney, is that true?"

I don't know what to do. I feel my insides being liquefied by the shame and the guilt and the stupidity that is me. Gloria's shock turns to comprehension. Her voice is soft and broken. "That's why you asked about him at dinner."

"I didn't mean to do it, Gloria. I still don't really know how *he* did it. It wasn't my fault, I swear. They stole my phone." I reach into my pocket, take the offending article out, and start fumbling around with it in the hope of finding some evidence to acquit myself.

Achal takes the phone out of my hand. We stand in silence as his fingers run over the screen. He holds the phone up and we all move closer to see what he's discovered. It's my sent e-mail. And there's a message from me to Jake at 1:38 a.m., on the night we were drinking together. The night he betrayed me. Attached to it is a voice memo entitled *Gloria's campaign pitch.*

I start shaking my head. "I didn't know about this. They stole my phone. It isn't my fault."

Achal hands back the evidence and stands before me with the poise of a righteous king. "Yes,

Barney, it is your fault. Don't disgrace yourself further by trying to eschew responsibility. Bear the consequences of your actions with courage and humility."

I'm silenced.

Gloria is completely still. I want her to be mad. I want her to fly into a rage and start hurling abuse at me right here in the street. I want to face her righteous wrath with courage and humility. But she does something so much worse. She does something I cannot bear. She looks helpless and betrayed.

I start to cry. I know it's not the done thing, but I can't help myself. The tears sting at the back of my eyes as I see her slipping away from me, and I realize what a fool I have been. I want to ask her to stay, to listen to my explanation, to give me a chance.

But even I know it's too late. Even I can see what I have done to her.

They turn as one and walk away.

* * *

I stand there for another ten minutes feeling powerless and afraid. Then I start to get hungry. It's lunchtime, so I decide to lunch. Alone, naturally, but it will give me time to work out how I'm going to get myself out of all this and back into Gloria's good books.

A chicken sandwich and Sunkist later, I still have no idea how I'm going to get myself out of all this and back into Gloria's good books. So I settle on a solid default position.

Blame someone else.

This *is* mostly Chad's fault, after all. He's the one who misrepresented what happened between me and Jake. *He's* the one who made out like I had done a direct trade of our idea for a job. That's a lie. A terrible, Yankee lie. Jake hasn't offered me a job; he may never offer me a job. He didn't tell me he was pitching for this contract and he used Zara's not insignificant wiles to steal my phone. I'm surrounded by thieves and liars—no wonder I've ended up in trouble!

I'm more nervous going back into the office than I was on my first day. I have no idea how to play it, so I'm just going to act like I still work there and it's business as usual. I have no choice. I certainly can't resign, but I won't be surprised when Archie fires me on the spot if Chad has got to him first. Here goes.

I walk through the door and things look pretty normal. It's quiet, and I can sense the pervasive disappointment, but everybody seems to be carrying

on with their everyday tasks, not plotting my untimely death on a whiteboard. Everyone looks up at
me, except Gloria, but Archie is the only one who
speaks.

"Heard it was a tough morning, Barney. You
been collecting your thoughts?"

About what? My next job after you fire me?

"Yes, something like that."

"Well, never mind, son. These things can happen. The trick is to bounce straight back and get on
with the job. We'll have plenty more opportunities."

They haven't told him.

"Thank you, sir." I don't know why I just ad-
dressed Archie as "sir." Perhaps it's because I feel
like a school kid who just got let off a Saturday de-
tention. He appreciates the deference, though,
winks at me, and then gets back to reading the paper.

I sidle in beside Gloria, lean over, and start to
whisper. "Thank you so much for not telling
Archie. I can explain the whole thing. Chad has it
all wrong, I swear."

"Really?"

"Yes?"

"Did you meet with Jake?"

"Yes."

"Did he talk about you working at MacDaddy?"

I don't like where this is going.

"Yes."

"And does he now have a recording of *my* voice on *his* phone giving *you* the campaign idea?"

"Well, yes, but—"

"I've heard enough."

"But that's not the whole story!" The moment I say this I realize I've raised my voice above the whisper needed to keep our conversation covert.

"What's not the whole story?" Archie asks, staring over his paper at me.

"Yes, Barney, tell us, what's not the whole story?" Chad says.

Think quick, Barney.

"*The Bourne Identity*, Archie. We were talking about Jason Bourne and I was telling Gloria, who's only seem the first installment, that she absolutely must watch *The Bourne Supremacy* and *The Bourne Ultimatum* as well. They're essential to understanding the whole story!"

"Get back to work."

"Yes, sir."

I wait a minute for things to calm down before attempting to talk to Gloria again. "Please, Gloria, you have to give me a chance to explain."

"I don't *have* to do anything. What *you* have to do is resign on Tuesday morning."

"What?"

"That's our condition for not telling Archie about your betrayal. Chad wanted to out you straightaway, which I had no problem with, but Achal convinced us to show you some compassion. If you get fired from this job so soon after leaving your last one, it will make it very difficult for you to go anywhere else. Lucky for you Monday's a public holiday so you've got the long weekend to come up with a story."

"But I won't need one. Jake is going to offer me a job."

Gloria scoffs. "Is he?"

"That's what he told me."

"Well, good for you, Barney. Because Jake never lies. Now please leave me alone and let me get on with my work."

"Gloria, it's not what you think. I didn't tell Jake about our idea to get a job—"

Gloria holds up her hand in my face. "Stop talking to me, Barney, or I will walk straight up to Archie and tell him everything."

I consider protesting again when I notice that her hand is shaking. Her cheeks are flushed and there's the tiniest quiver on her bottom lip. I decide to leave her alone.

Until I remember the instant messaging service on our computers.

Barney: *Gloria, I'm sorry. Truly, I am.*

I hit send and hear Gloria's computer chime alongside me to indicate a new conversation has begun.

Bing!

Thankfully, she responds. Unthankfully, she responds likes this:

Gloria: *Please refrain from messaging me, speaking to me, looking at me and anything else that can be classified as interacting with me. I have nothing to say to you. Leave me alone.*

Barney: *Gloria, this is ridiculous. You have to talk to me. We work together!! : -)*

Gloria: *Not for much longer.*

Barney: *But I've decided to stay. I've decided I want to work at Rogerson with you!! :-)*

Gloria: *Stop using ridiculous emoticons and unnecessary exclamation marks.*

Barney: *Okay, I get that you're upset. But can we at least talk about it? Let me buy you dinner.*

Gloria: *Are you delusional or just plain stupid? I never want to see you again, Barney.*

Gloria's on the precipice here so I have to go for something charming to bring her back from the edge.

Barney: *Like, ever?*

Gloria: *[This user is no longer online]*

I look across at Gloria, who's obviously not a Taylor Swift fan, and she has locked her screen and is standing up from her desk. "You ready, Chad?"

"Where are you going?" I ask.

Gloria ignores me.

"We're meeting with the Department of Healthy Living," Chad says. "You won't be required." And then, in a softer voice so that Archie doesn't hear it: "Ever again, you pathetic traitor."

My vision blurs with abject rage and anti-American sentiment. I have to look away as they leave the room together.

* * *

But I'm not beaten yet. I need to get over to Chad's desk to find some hidden secret that will expose him for the would-be girlfriend-stealing shyster that he really is. I can't do that with Archie, Achal, and Diana in the room, though.

It's getting close to four o'clock on a Friday so Archie will be leaving soon. I think I can convince Diana that once Archie leaves we might as well all go home, but Achal is going to be a tougher target.

I'll only need a few minutes, but once he's wired in, he's basically an Indian Zuckerberg.

He has only one weakness that I know of, so I decide to exploit it. I leave the room without any fanfare and ride the lift to the ground floor. There's a convenience store across the road and, like most convenience stores, it has more varieties of soft drink than the human population could possibly need. Most of it is useless to me because my target is a purist; he only drinks lemonade. I grab a bottle and head back upstairs. On return, I find that the universe has finally smiled on me. Archie has already gone, as expected, and Diana is packing her bag.

"Not much point hanging around here," I say.

She stops what she's doing. "What are you up to?"

Am I still so transparent?

"Nothing. I was just going to say enjoy the weekend."

She doesn't look convinced, but also doesn't care. "All right, boys, enjoy the long weekend. See you on Tuesday."

"Bye, Diana."

Achal waves his hand without looking our way. It's time for me to move in. I saunter up to his desk. He ignores me. I sit down next to him. He ignores me. I take the lemonade out of my bag. He looks my way.

"I bought this for you. I wanted to say thanks for convincing Chad and Gloria not to tell Archie about what happened."

Achal takes off his headphones. "So you're going to resign next week?"

"That's the plan."

"It is the honorable thing to do. Thanks for the lemonade." Achal takes the bottle, puts his headphones back on, and returns his attention to his computer. I head back to my desk and watch him, waiting for him to take the cap off and start drinking. He doesn't. This is an unanticipated complication.

I need him to start drinking now if the lemonade is going to get to his bladder in time to force him into the toilets, thus leaving me alone in the room to carry out the rest of my faultless plan. My brain is in overdrive and the ideas are coming thick and fast. I have a packet of chips in my bottom drawer. Nobody eats chips without an accompanying beverage, so I crack them open. It would raise suspicions if I gave him the entire packet, so I shove a handful into my mouth and wander around the room crunching as I go. When I get to Achal's desk, I deploy a kind of *oh, hi, mate, didn't realize you were here* effect and offer him some chips. He dips his hand deep into the packet and rips out a handful, leaving no remaining chip untouched, thus contaminating the entire sample. Achal grunts a thanks and lays the chips down on his desk.

Has this man no understanding of hygienic food handling?

Nauseated, I return to my desk and continue the wait. Ten minutes pass, then twenty. It's after four thirty now and Gloria and Chad will return any minute. My whole career, nay, my whole life, is about to be derailed because Achal is too selfish to drink the lemonade I offered him and go to the toilet! But I won't let it happen. I won't allow his noncompliant bladder to bring me down.

I decide to go a little more direct but not so much that it gives me away. "Hey, Achal, you should drink that before it gets warm!"

"I like my lemonade at room temperature."

"You have got to be kidding me!"

Achal stops typing. "What's it to you, anyway? Do you want it back?"

I sigh. "No, Achal, your lemonade is the last thing I want."

Achal stands up. "Well, what is it that you want, Barney? And before you try to answer, consider that this is a rhetorical question." Achal walks out of the room. Just like that. He doesn't tell me where he's going. Why should he? It's not *actually* a classroom.

I seize my chance. Achal hasn't packed up so he must be off to the toilets—another sign from the universe that I'm in the right. I leap the snake pit Vin Diesel–style and skip over to Chad's desk.

Chad has taken his laptop with him so I start rifling through his drawers. This is the culmination of my plans. This is where I will find the incriminating evidence. I don't know what it will be, but the universe has guaranteed it to me so I keep searching, tossing aside marketing magazines, packets of chewing gum, and tattered notebooks. I'm not sure what I'm hoping to find until I strike...

ABSOLUTE. GOLD.

Fields of gold.

A golden gift. A golden goose.

The gold of Chad Sylvester's passport application.

My heart starts to beat like a Bon Jovi intro. What has got me most excited is not Chad's apparently impending overseas travel, although having the scheming dog out of the country will be to my advantage. What has got me delirious with vindictive joy are the two words written in the *Place of Birth* field.

Los Angeles, California, perhaps? Greenbow, Alabama? No, although that would be cool for obvious reasons.

Melbourne, Australia. The lying, Yankee fraudster is an Australian. Always has been. Always will be, no matter how hard he forces that Zac Efron accent and accompanying smile.

I say a silent apology to the population of the United States of America for the many and varied evil thoughts I have cast toward that country in Chad's name. Then I pick up the passport application and take it to the kitchen/photocopy/stationery room. I read it quickly. Chad's a few years younger than me—fiend—but the most important detail is that he's an Aussie. This is how I'm going to expose him to Gloria. I want her to pity him for his pathetic charade. For living this counterfeit life for so long. This will call into question his credibility as a witness in the case of *Barney v. Rogerson*, in which Barney, the innocent party, stands accused of selling trade secrets to get himself a job elsewhere. Which he most certainly did not do. I'm also hoping, though less positive, that it will drive Gloria into my authentic, unashamedly Australian arms.

The photocopy light is blinding and the normally placid whirr sounds like a jet engine that needs a new muffler. My ears are still ringing when I rush to Chad's drawer and start repacking it. Before I'm done, the door opens and Achal walks in. I'm busted in Chad's drawer. I employ my most effective defensive mechanism.

Act like nothing's happening.

"What are you doing?" Achal asks.

Play it cool.

"Nothing. What are you doing?"

"Returning from the toilet to catch you in the act of thievery."

"That's not a word."

"Yes, it is."

"No, it's not."

"Look it up."

"What's that in your hand?" He gestures to Chad's passport application.

"Yeah, what is that?" echoes a distinctly faux Californian voice.

I stuff it in the drawer, slam it shut, spin around, and see Chad standing in the doorway. He's wearing black pants and a white fitted shirt. With the light from the hallway flooding in behind him, he looks like a superhero. Or a Calvin Klein model. Either way, both of those are a major threat, so I need to go on the offensive. "None of your business."

Superman ignores me and strides into the room. Choosing "flight," I back away and put Achal between the two of us.

"What were you doing in my drawers, Barney?"

I've heard the word "drawers" used as a term for underpants in American sitcoms, so I seize the kryptonite potential of public humiliation. "Don't flatter yourself, mate. Nobody here is interested in your drawers. Did you hear that, Achal? Chad thinks we're fascinated with his underpants!"

Achal: "You make yourself a very difficult man to like, Barney."

Strewth.

Chad opens the drawer and takes out his passport application. "Why are you so interested in this?"

Carpe diem!

"Because it proves that you're a fraud!" I shout, pointing in his face with a triumphant, arm-raised, finger-pointing gesture. Chad looks at me like I'm hard garbage. I flick my eyes to Achal. He is as impassive as the gates of hell. I keep my arm held high.

"What are you talking about?" Chad says. There's a trace of pity in his voice, now, as though I'm some kind of deranged, conspiracy-spouting madman.

I'm not, of course. I'm the triumphant finger-pointer. "You're a fraud, Chad. You come in here every day swanning around like you're God's gift to the public relations universe, banging on and on about new media metrics and conversions and behavior impacts and a whole lot of other pretentious garbage. And do you know why it's garbage, Chad, oh Chaddy Chad Chadster? It's garbage because you're delivering it all in a fake American accent. Which makes you a childish, embarrassing, phony."

My arm is shaking now and the exertion of holding it up with my triumphant finger still pointing at Chad is making me sweat. I can feel it running into my eyes so I need to end this before my vision blurs. I deliver the final, triumphant blow. "And when Gloria finds all this out, she is going to see that it is not me who betrayed her, you scumbag, but you. You, the lying, deceiving, fraudulent American."

My arm drops. A bead of sweat rolls down the side of my face. I have won at last. Chad stares at me for a long moment, trying to work out how he's going to get out of this. How he is going to explain away his lies to Gloria. I wait for his confession. Or perhaps his plea to me to keep quiet, to not give him away. With a life of failures behind me, it is so satisfying to have finally triumphed. To have victory in my hands.

At last, Chad speaks. "Barney, are you all right, man? You seem a little crazy right now."

Why is he quoting Beyoncé? I'm not crazy, I'm triumphant!

I look to Achal for assurance, for support.

"He's not crazy, Chad," Achal says.

Thank you, my brother.

"He's just completely self-absorbed."

You low dog.

Chad again: "Barney, why do you hate me so much, man?"

"Because you've had it in for me from day one! You think you're better than me because you're American. And you're not American so you're not better than me!"

Achal: "Barney, you fool. Chad has an American accent because he lived there from age two to age sixteen. Seriously, man, if you paid attention to anyone's existence other than your own, you could really save yourself a lot of embarrassment."

This is unsettling news, but I'm not beaten yet. "Not the point, Achal! He told me he was an American. That makes him a liar, and Gloria deserves better than a liar."

"Dude, you asked me what part of Canada my accent was from, and I told you it was Californian. Most people follow up with a question about how long I've been in Australia. You walked away and have pretty much ignored me ever since. And, given that you're now so interested, I returned here fourteen years ago. My passport has expired and I need a new one because I'm going back for the first time since I left. I'm kind of excited about seeing my old buddies again, but I guess a selfish jerk like you wouldn't care about that."

The hot sweat of my triumph has begun to cool on my back and it makes me shiver. In a quieter, less triumphant voice, I say: "You still wanted to make me look like a fool in front of Gloria. That's why you told her about my meeting with Jake."

Chad scoffs. "Man, I told Gloria that because it's true. Whether you meant it or not, you gave away our idea and cost us the account. She deserved to know and so did Achal. I'm sorry I got up in your face but I was furious. We're supposed to be a team, man. How do you think it made us feel to find that out?"

"I think we can all agree I don't generally consider other people's feelings."

"A realization at last," Achal says.

"Yeah, well let me tell you, Barney. It made us feel betrayed. Gloria, Achal, and I are the reason Archie has a company and we already felt cheated that some new whiz kid was brought in to secure government accounts. To then have you stab us in the back was too much to handle."

Did he just refer to me as a whiz kid? Maybe I have misjudged this bloke after all.

But one fact still remains. "Maybe so, Chad, but you still sold me out to steal Gloria away from me because you could see that we had something going on together."

Chad narrows his eyes for a moment and then laughs, shaking his head. He takes a step forward and places a comradely hand on my shoulder, General MacArthur–style. "Oh man, Barney. You think I want to get together with Gloria?"

"Of course. I've seen the way you carry on with her."

Chad gives me his most winning, womanizing smile. "Barney, dude," he says, and even I feel hypnotized by his animal magnetism. "I'm getting married next month. Gloria's like my sister, man."

"Getting married? Why didn't anyone tell me?"

There's a thudding sound as Achal smashes his head onto the desk.

* * *

A man needs to know his strengths and weaknesses. Mine are, respectively, few and legion. But one of my strengths is knowing when I'm beat. With much practice comes perfection. And now, on this warm Friday evening, nine weeks after being fired from the public service, I am beat. So beat, that when I skulk out of the Rogerson offices and see Gloria walking toward me, I cross to the other side of the street.

There's really only one thing a grown man can do when he's hit rock bottom the way I have. When he's thrown his career into the bin and driven away the woman he loves. When he's desperate, despondent, and devastated by regrets.

"Hi, Mum."

"Barney, darling, what are you doing here?"

"I just thought I'd drop by and say hello."

Mum is wearing a lavender two-piece tracksuit. She puts her hands on her hips and smiles at me like she's known me since I was born. It makes me feel like a little child again.

I revert to form. "You got anything to eat?"

"Of course I do, honey. Come in."

Mum's home, my family home, is majestic. I follow her through the entrance hall and into the full-sized gourmet kitchen. Saucepans and knives and all sorts of other implements they use on *Master-*

Chef are hanging from the walls like tools in a garage. There are three sinks, an eight-burner stove and, inexplicably, two microwaves.

"I was just fixing some dinner, love. I'll make some for you as well. It's your favorite." Mum moves to the corner of the kitchen, where a toasted sandwich maker is fizzing away. She lifts the lid, scoops out the sandwiches, which are overflowing with sizzling, tinned spaghetti, and lays down another two pieces of bread.

Mum hands me the plate of toasted sandwiches she was preparing for herself. I sit down on a stool at the kitchen bench and eat in silence as she finishes preparing her meal. She pours us both a glass of vintage red wine and sits down beside me. She, too, eats in silence.

"I'm going to lose my job again, Mum."

She finishes her mouthful, takes a sip of wine, and dabs at her lips with a napkin. "I thought it was going well."

"It was. But then I did something really stupid. And now I have to resign."

"Is there no other way?"

I love this about Mum. She won't ask me what I did wrong. She knows that if I want to tell her, I will. Which I don't. I still want her to hold even a microcosm of hope that I'm going to turn into a son she can be proud of one day. For now, she'll just do whatever she can to help.

"Unfortunately not. If I don't resign on Tuesday, I'll end up getting sacked."

Mum reaches out and places her hand over mine. "What can I do?"

"Start a communications company?"

She laughs. Then she picks up my hand and clasps it with both of her own. "You've been doing it tough, Barney. And you're all alone in that apartment of yours. It's not good for you. Why don't you come back and stay here with me for a little while? At least until you find a new flatmate."

"Men over thirty shouldn't live with their mothers. It's bad for their romantic endeavors."

"And how have those romantic endeavors been working out for you while you *haven't* been living with your mother?"

"Not so great."

"So it's settled, then. Let me look after you for a little while, just until you get back onto your feet. And don't worry about money. I'll pay half your mortgage payments until you find a new job."

I hesitate. I love my mum, I really do. But do I want to move back home? The place *is* big enough, I guess. And Mum spends so much time on TV sets and publicity shoots that I'd probably see less of her than I did Lucien. But moving back home would finally cement my status as a complete, unequivocal, 100 percent certified loser. I'm pretty beat, but I haven't lost *all* self-respect.

"You're very kind, Mum. How about I give it some thought?"

She stands up and ruffles my hair. "Don't think too hard about it, Barney. You're still my boy and it's still my job to help you when I can." Mum takes our plates and puts them in the sink. "Right, I bought a tub of gourmet ice cream yesterday and I haven't yet eaten the *whole* thing by myself. You want some?"

"Is it strawberry?"

"Raspberry swirl."

"That'll do."

Mum smiles. "I'll find you some marshmallows as well."

THIRTEEN

It's Saturday morning. I'm alone. The apartment is quiet.

I have no job. No love life. No flatmate.

Today, my only pressing engagement is to decide whether I need to move back in with my mother.

You can probably understand why I haven't yet bothered to get out of bed despite it being after eleven a.m. I'm just lying here staring at the white roof held up by the white walls in this enclosed box that has become my white asylum. I'm struggling to come up with reasons to take the next breath, let alone change out of my pajamas.

I hear a familiar sound, but disregard it. It's the noise of a turning key followed by a door opening, and it must be coming from the apartment next to mine. These white walls are so thin that I once heard my neighbor lose an eyelash in the middle of the night.

But then there's another sound. Footsteps; two sets. One that thuds, one that clacks. My existential crisis is brought to a sudden halt by the very practical realization that somebody is in my apartment. I throw off the shackles of my white sheets, land on the cream-colored carpet, and tiptoe to my bedroom door. Which swings open, smashing me square on the nose.

I'm blinded by the pain and the sensation of being on the threshold of a sneeze so powerful it will blow my head off. I go down swinging, but only manage to punch the door, which is giving a good account of itself because I think I've broken my knuckles.

"Barney, what are you doing, you goose? You're going to hurt yourself."

I don't believe it. There's only one person who could belong to that hypnotically charming voice.

Lucien has returned.

I feel his strong hand underneath my elbow as he lifts me to my feet. As my vision clears, I'm rewarded by his beaming smile. "Are you all right, mate? Do you want me to get you an ice pack?"

I pinch my nose. It doesn't feel broken. "What are you doing here?"

Lucien puts his hand on my shoulder and looks deep into my eyes. "I'm in love."

"With me?"

"No, you clown. With Gisele!" Lucien lets go of my shoulder and backs away from my bedroom door. It is then that I see the celebrated Gisele. And it's probably fair to say that the celebrated Gisele is not at all what I was expecting.

You're not supposed to judge a book by its cover, of course, but if Gisele was a book, I reckon she'd be an illustrated account of the dark side of the spiritual realm. Truly, the thunderous expression on her brow would make the storm god himself look like a childish amateur. She's about five foot, has caramel-colored skin and bright-green eyes, looks like she squats four-wheel-drives as a warm-up, and could probably bench press me eighteen thousand times without breaking a sweat.

Gisele scowls at me as Lucien completes the introductions by asking her to show me her nails. She makes two fists, slowly raises them to shoulder height, and then—bam!—she unleashes her weapons like Wolverine with a migraine. Lightning slaps me across the head as the full wonder of Gisele's multicolored nails is revealed. Like a shiny acrylic rainbow, they fill the room with their glory. And then she draws them in again, lest we be consumed by their power.

"Wow," I say.

"I know, right?" Lucien says. "So, listen, we're moving to Latin America. Gisele's like a goddess over there. They're *really* into nails."

"Awesome."

"Yeah, but we're not leaving for six weeks. We've got a hotel room until Monday, but then we'll need somewhere to stay until we fly out."

This isn't boding well.

"So, since I've still got my key, I wanted to ask if we could move in here. I know it'll be a big imposition on you; you know, with the whole muesli segregation thing."

He's deadly serious. He actually thinks that would be my biggest concern about him moving in here with his Latin American lover.

"But you're the kindest guy I know, Barney. And the only friend I can really rely on."

Snakes alive! I wasn't expecting that.

I deal with Lucien's compliment with some characteristic deflection. "What about your investment properties?"

"I sold them to pay for our villa."

"Of course you did."

"So it's settled, then? You'll help us out?" He actually looks like he'd beg me if I asked him to.

I look past Lucien to Gisele. She's strategizing about how to end me. I don't need to give this a great deal of thought. I'd rather be a pathetic loser who lives with his mother than the third wheel in a relationship between Lucien and Ms. Wolverine.

"Not quite settled, mate. I don't think it's right for me to crowd you here. I'll move back in with my mum to give you some space. You'll need to cover the full rent, though."

"You'll move back in with your mum?" Lucien says, screwing up his face as though he just swallowed a dung beetle.

"Yes."

Lucien shakes his head like they just stopped making his hair wax. "It kills me to have to do this to you, Barney. You deserve more than living with your mother."

"Thanks. That means a lot."

"But, sometimes, mate. True love triumphs over all else." Lucien turns to Gisele. "Welcome home, baby!"

She nods and smiles. A diamond flashes in one of her front teeth.

I go back to bed.

* * *

Mum's in Sydney for the weekend so I decide not to move home straightaway. If I'm going to spend Saturday night alone, I might as well do it in an apartment owned by my bank. So after Gisele and Lucien leave the love nest, I get out of bed and start to plan my strategy for departing Rogerson with dignity and self-respect. After a good six minutes of quiet contemplation, I realize that there's really only one noble way to manage this mess: cowardice and half-truths.

The former comes naturally. The latter will require some thought about how I'm going to turn the debacle I've created into a vaguely plausible reason for leaving full-time employment. So I decide to act on the easier half of my double act first.

There's a reason they don't give medals to cowards, you know. Put simply, there's nothing to warrant recognition. Cowardice, you see, is man's natural inclination. It is the innate response of a frightened heart. That's why courage is so valued. It challenges the easy path. The natural path. The path I'm walking right now. The one that is taking me back to Rogerson because I want to clear out my desk while nobody's there.

My plan formulates on the way to the office. So far, I've decided I won't face Archie in person, but will send him an e-mail instead. It's businesslike, it puts it in writing, it makes my departure official. And it will be easier than standing before him in the flesh. All I have to do now is think of something to write.

When I get to Rogerson, I'm surprised to see a sliver of light beneath the door. Who would be here early on the Saturday evening of a long weekend? Especially after the week we just had. My heart quickens at the possibility that Gloria is behind that closed door, tapping away on the keys. Maybe wearing jeans and a T-shirt. Her hair out, her feet bare, shoes kicked aside because it's a Saturday. This could be my chance to set things straight. To seek redemption. To demonstrate courage. I take a deep breath, think for a moment about walking away, and then grip the door handle tight. I turn it, and push open the door.

My eyes go to Gloria's desk. It's empty. I look up to the far corner of the room and there is Achal staring back at me. He looks like a wild animal startled in its natural environment, frozen in that critical moment of fight-or-flight decision making.

"What do you want?" He's chosen fight, of course.

I choose sarcasm. "You know how much I love it here, Achal. I'm a regular Saturday evening fixture."

"No, you're not."

Man, this guy knows how to push my buttons. "How would you know?"

"I check the previous week's data logs and web activity every Monday morning. You've never been online past 7:46 p.m. And never on a Saturday."

"Are you serious?"

"Yes."

"So you're spying on us."

"It's not spying, mate. It's governance."

"I've come to pack up my desk." This is actually something of an exaggeration. The only item on my desk that isn't property of Rogerson Communications is a USB stick that I take to every new role. It contains ten years of templates, communication planning ideas, and past glories. It's supposed to be the secret weapon that sets me up for success wherever I go. So, yeah, it's pretty useless. But it's mine, not theirs, so I've come to reclaim it.

"What are *you* doing here?"

"Server maintenance. Once a month I have to take the site down for thirty minutes, so I do it on a Saturday evening to minimize disruption to our clients."

"Is that a joke? We don't have enough clients to worry about disrupting."

"It's not a joke, mate. It's best practice."

"Whatever, Achal. If you want to waste your time here, that's your problem. I've got better things to do with my Saturday night."

"Have you?"

"Enough with the prophetic questions! I'm sick of you thinking you're better than me, Achal. You, Chad, Archie, even Gloria. You all think you're better than me and I'm sick of it." I can hear the hysteria in my voice. I know I sound unhinged but I can't help it. I *am* unhinged.

I wait for Achal to fire something meaningful back at me. Some rubbish about finding peace by looking inside myself.

"You should consider professional help, Barney."

"You should consider minding your own business, Achal. Leave me alone."

I'm tired of being the most pathetic person in the room, so I take the USB stick and leave without another word. I'm contemplating going home, but I'm too angry, and sad, and disappointed with my life to enjoy my own company right now. Time to get on the phone. Mike answers my call but he's the father of a toddler, so Saturday night flexibility is a thing of the past. I try a couple of friends from the department, but, at such late notice, they all have plans.

So I decide to face my adversity alone and, when you're Australian, you only have one authentic option available to you to mark a milestone event, low or high.

Get drunk.

Tonight's drinking needs to be an escapist affair. So the velour-decor pub with the stuffed animals is out. So is Sugar Ray's. I'm trying to chase away the pain of my bad decisions, not relive them. I settle on an Irish-themed bar called Leprechaun's Lair, which is sufficiently kitsch to keep the beautiful people away. Its patronage is a mix of broken-down old men and young people so excited to have made it to legal drinking age they don't know any better. There are booths lining the walls, tables in the middle of the pub, and a long bar adorned with Guinness signs. The waitstaff appear to be Japanese backpackers and the barman looks like he lost the will to live at least two decades ago. I order a beer, which is served up on a four-leaf-clover coaster, and then I settle in for an authentic night of Irish/Australian drunkenness.

Here's how my night pans out.

Early on...

Barman: "On your own tonight, mate?"

Me: "Yeah. I've pretty much ruined my life and absolutely driven away the girl I love."

Barman: "Right, well would you mind moving up a stool so these two guys can sit together?"

A bit later...

Me: "Another beer, please, mate. I'm drowning my sorrows tonight."

Barman: "You got anything smaller than a fifty?"

Later still...

Me: "So I guess I just never really felt like I could be myself, you know. I never really knew who I was or what I wanted to be. It's hard, man, 'cause I reckon I've got something special inside me. Something that the world should see. I've just got to find a way to bring it out. And Gloria, man. Gloria brings it out in me. She is my light in the darkest hours."

Random bloke: "That's beautiful, man. You keep searching inside yourself. You'll find it, man. You'll find what it is you were put on this earth to do. And when Gloria sees that, she'll realize just how special you are."

Me: "Thanks, man. You're like a brother to me, you know that."

Random bloke: "I think I'm going to vomit."

Really, really late...

Unspecified large male: "Time to wrap it up, lads. We're closing in ten minutes."

Me: "This has been the best night of my life. Ev-er. Best ever. I love you, mate."

Random bloke: "Arrrrrooooooooooo!"

Unspecified large male: "All right, that'll do. Time to go. You driving them home?"

Achal: "How could I possibly drive them home, mate? I don't own a car."

Unspecified male (aggressively): "How am I sup-posed to know that, sunshine?"

Me: "Hey, easy, mate. We don't cop racism in this country anymore."

Unspecified large male: "Get out of here before I call the cops."

Random bloke: "Arrrrrooooooooooo!"

FOURTEEN

Wait a minute. What was Achal doing there? Did I dream that bit?

Sometimes when I drink too much, I find it difficult to distinguish the real parts of the night from the parts that followed me home into my nightmares. Speaking of which, how did I get home? Once again, I have no idea, and yet, despite all the drinking and the memory loss, I have no trace of a hangover, whatsoever. I put this miracle down to the electrolyte icy pole and four multivitamins I consumed before going to bed.

I must have had a decent sleep, too, because I feel pretty rested. I turn my head to my clock radio to check the time.

And my world tips on its axis.

The bed swings around the room as the numbers dance like maniacal devils before my eyes:

11:36, 11:36, 11:36, 11:36. The numbers spin like pin-wheels and when I close my eyes they come hurtling toward me like rocks tumbling down the crumbling mountain of my life.

I have a sudden and desperate need to rehydrate but I am trapped in my bed until I can stop it lurching on the ocean of this alcohol-induced storm. I start sweating—I'm always sweating!—and I pin my arms on the mattress beside me like I'm riding on a giant, spinning disc. Eventually, it starts to slow. I raise myself up out of bed and try to duck around the heavyweight champion who has entered my room and begun pummeling the side of my skull with a series of proficient, businesslike blows. I make it to the bathroom as he lands one final punch on the back of my head. It throws my brain forward, causing it to collide with the inside of my forehead. This triggers a chain reaction, which brings the entire contents of my stomach up through my mouth, mostly, and my nose, some-whatly.

Aussie, Aussie, Aussie!

By 11:45, I am spent. A ball of disgrace in the corner of the bathroom. I try to move and the heavyweight boxer pummels me again. I feel my life slipping away. Perhaps literally as well as meta-phorically. If you can die from being too Australian,

I can't be that far off. The apartment buzzer rings. As intrigued as I am to know who is visiting me unannounced on a Sunday, I can't move.

Then it buzzes again. I respond with a dry retching spasm. My eyes start watering and there's snot running down my nose and into my mouth. The buzzer again, only this time it doesn't stop. It just does this: buzzzzzzzzzzzzzzzzzzzzzzzzzzzzzzzzzzzzzzz. Which is so annoying that it galvanizes me.

I lift my arm to the toilet roll holder and use it to raise myself off the ground. For a moment, this works, until my weight rips it off the wall. I fall down, cracking my head against the toilet bowl on the way through. Oddly, this doesn't hurt; clearly my pain capacity has reached its threshold and I wouldn't even feel the usually excruciating torn hangnail right now. But there *is* blood, which I distinguish from the snot and tears already adorning my face by its sickly warmth. The possibility of a fatal infection from a toilet bowl–inflicted wound is enough to get me back onto my feet

I tear off a handful of toilet paper from the murdered roll holder and run it over my face. The collection of bodily fluids makes me gag, but I keep my stomach down and head to the intercom to shut off that infernal buzzing. There's nobody in the camera shot, so I deduce that the wretched thing has malfunctioned, right at the time I most need it to just shut up. I lift the receiver in the vain hope the noise will end.

Miraculously, it does.

Even more miraculously, I hear a voice.

"Barney?"

A familiar voice.

"Barney, let me in, you worthless fool."

A friendly voice.

"Is that you, Achal? Why can't I see you?"

"How many other Indians do you know, mate? Stop wasting time with moronic questions and let me in." My instinct is to be offended at Achal's suggestion that I wouldn't have a multicultural circle of friends, but given that he is dead right, I decide to let the insult pass.

I buzz him in.

"No way I'm going to stand in front of that surveillance camera, mate," Achal says as I open the door. "I'm very protective of my recorded image. Never know where it could end up."

My skull cracks. "What?"

"Good, you're dressed."

I look down at myself and realize, for the first time since regaining consciousness, that I am indeed dressed. Fully dressed, in fact, right down to my shoes. Same chinos and shirt I was wearing yesterday.

"We've got fifteen minutes to get to the train station. Let's go."

"I can't go anywhere like this. And why would I want to go to a train station?"

Achal looks me over. "You look like a cadaver, and you're bleeding from a wound on your head, but you have to be there. You have to fight for what you love."

"What are you talking about?"

Achal ignores me, walks into my apartment, fossicks around for a good ten seconds, and returns with a surfwear mesh cap I bought after attending a twentieth-anniversary screening of *Point Break*. Achal jams it down on my head, and it stems the bleeding.

"Please, Achal, I don't know what's going on. I just want to go back to bed."

"Didn't you get my messages?"

"What messages?"

"I called you sixteen times this morning and left sixteen messages telling you I'd be here by twelve o'clock to take you to the train station."

I find my phone, still in my pocket. It's on silent and there are, as Achal has testified, sixteen missed calls and sixteen new voice-mail messages.

I'm so confused. And tired. And ashamed. "Please, Achal, I don't know what this is all about. I'm sorry, but I need to go back to bed."

"Barney, I didn't follow you to that odious bar, watch you drink yourself into oblivion, and then spend sixty dollars in cab fares getting you home so that you could go back to sleep."

"You followed me to the bar?"

"I followed you to the bar."

"Why?"

"Because a man with a broken heart is a dangerous beast. Mostly to himself. And I wanted to make sure you would be all right."

"Why didn't you come and talk to me?"

"You're an obnoxious drunk."

A solid ball of emotion forms in the base of my throat. "And you brought me home?" I ask with a croak.

"And I brought you home."

My eyes sting. "Why?"

"Because you're my friend."

This is too much for me. I wrap Achal up in a fierce hug of mateship and thanks. He responds by going absolutely rigid, arms by his sides. "Thanks, Achal. I really appreciate it."

"You're hurting me and you smell foul."

I let him go and wipe away a stray tear. I'm a bit tired and emotional and Achal's compassion has broken down my usually stoic and immovable defenses. "What should I do now?"

"You've got thirty seconds to get whatever you need for a three-hour journey."

I don't think. I just do. Wallet. House keys. Sunnies. Lip balm. And we're out the front door.

There's a brand-new hatchback sitting outside my apartment block, shining bright red like a jewel from the subcontinent. Standing beside the car is a mesmerizing Indian lady. Her clothes, red and purple silks, are as bright as the ones they hold up at the end of washing powder commercials. I think the dress thing she is wearing is called a sari, which is traditional Indian attire. Her black hair is tied back and she has a gold nose ring and a red dot right in the middle of her forehead. I don't think I've ever been in the presence of such an exotic person in my life, including Beth.

"This is my wife, Mahima," Achal says.

"Pleased to meet you, Barney," she says with the kind of lilting accent that first made me fall in love with the subcontinent.

When I express surprise that Achal has a wife, he suggests that if I ever thought about anyone other than myself, I might have bothered to ask, and he would happily have told me about her. This is the second time I've been schooled by Achal about taking an interest in other people. What he doesn't know is that it's been a lifelong approach to relationship building; I think it might be time to revise the strategy.

I change the subject. "I thought you didn't have a car."

"It belongs to Mahima's cousin. He's fastidious about it, so don't bleed on anything."

I settle into the passenger seat and close my eyes.

"I think we should start with the electrolytes," Achal says.

"What?"

"Quiet. I'm not talking to you."

I open my eyes, which takes some considerable effort, to see a bottle of grape-flavored electrolyte solution being passed into the front seat. At even more considerable effort, I turn the flaming bowling ball of my head to see Mahima smiling at me.

"Drink up, Barney. It will make you feel better."

"Thank you," I whisper, and she's right. Its effects are almost instantaneous. "This stuff is amazing."

"Cologne, please, my dear," Achal says. Mahima hands me a bottle of unidentifiable cologne.

"What do I do with this?"

"Spray it all over your clothes...and in your hair."

"Are you serious?"

"Are you, Barney? You're wearing last night's clothes, your breath carries the putrid essence of vomit, and your hair reeks more than a Bombay gutter after a storm. Start spraying."

I do, and the effect is to make me smell like Achal, wearing far too much cologne. Though I've never smelled a Bombay gutter before *or* after a storm, I presume this is an improvement.

As Achal drives on, Mahima works through the rest of the recovery kit, which includes three dry biscuits, traveler's toothbrush and toothpaste, breath freshener, paracetamol, and hand cream, a bizarre but welcome item.

By the end of the kit, I feel like a lukewarm corpse; a major improvement. "Thank you," I say to my saviors. "But how did you know I would need all this?"

"Cultural assimilation," Achal says, negotiating backstreets and alleyways that may or may not be open to vehicular traffic. He does his best to run over about half a dozen innocent pedestrians on the way through, but they all escape unharmed. I can't work out where we are or what direction we're headed, partly because of my hangover but mostly because we are driving down streets I didn't know existed. And I've lived here all my life. Achal has only been here a few years but has managed to bring us out only meters away from Southern Cross train station. Which begs the question of what exactly I'm doing at Southern Cross train station.

"Get out," Achal says.

"What are we doing, Achal?"

"I'm not doing anything, but you're about to get on a train to Bendigo, which has a connecting bus to Bungleton West. The joining instructions, your ticket, and your lunch are in here." Achal hands me a plastic bag as we all get out of the car.

"Bungleton West," I say. "Gloria."

"You need to find her. When you do, drop the mask. Drop everything you think she wants you to be and be the man you really are. Be the reason I like you. Go and win her over, my friend."

"Why are you doing this, Achal?"

Achal puts his arm around Mahima. "Because we believe in love, Barney."

I stare at the two of them standing there. Mahima in her exotic clothing, Achal in his black tracksuit pants and yellow hoodie. "Thank you. This is the kindest thing anyone has ever done for me."

"It was lovely to meet you, Barney," Mahima says. "Achal has spoken about you a great deal. Despite your obvious shortcomings, he is very fond of you."

"Thank you."

They turn to get back in the car. But before Achal drops into the driver's seat, there is one more thing I have to know. "Achal!" I call over the nonstandard, optional sunroof. He stops and stares at me. "What did you do all night at the bar while you were waiting to take me home?"

A toothless smile forms on his lips. "Drank warm lemonade, mate. And plenty of it. Now get to platform four. Your train leaves in three minutes."

* * *

I need a speech. Actually, no I don't. I need *the* speech. The greatest speech ever written. The speech that plumbs the depths of my heart, ascends the heights of my love, and crosses the great breadth of my remorse. So far I've come up with *Hi, Gloria.* I've got plenty of time to work on it, though. Between the train ride to Bendigo and the bus trip to Bungleton West, there are about four hours of travel ahead of me. It's not the ideal way to manage a hangover, of course, but thanks to the cure proffered by my teetotaling Indian friends, I think I can do it. I certainly feel better than I would if I were outside, given that it's about nine thousand degrees today.

So I rest in the air-conditioned comfort of my train carriage, waiting for My Inspiration to arrive. But she's a fickle friend, My Inspiration, and no match today for the slow, gentle rocking of the train and the singsong rhythm of the wheels over the tracks. I begin to fall into a delicious sleep.

And then she visits me.

My Inspiration; she comes to me behind closed eyes.

And this is what she tells me to say.

Gloria, I have no right to be here. Not in your life, not in your town, certainly not in this room with you. I have no right because I betrayed you. It wasn't deliberate, it wasn't calculated, but it happened. And it happened because I was thinking only of myself. My whole life, Gloria, I have been thinking only of myself.

Until I met you.

You showed me truth, integrity, beauty, and grace, all in a smile. You made me hope in myself, made me believe in us.

Us. It sounds ridiculous, I know. How could there possibly be an us? But there is, Gloria, and there has been from the moment I first saw you. It hasn't been as obvious to you, perhaps. But for me, us has overtaken my heart.

Barney

I never want us to end, Gloria. I'm kidding myself, I know. It's a fool's dream to think we could be together. But I'd rather die a hopeless fool than a lonely sage. I'd rather meet my end still hoping, still believing that in another time and another place, in a world where I could have seen more clearly how to cope with the wonder and the radiance that is you, in that world, there may have been a chance of us. One thing I know for sure is that a life wasted hoping in us would be more fruitful than a thousand destinies of triumph and success without you.

There's a sharp repeating pain just above my right collarbone as My Inspiration takes on an officious, manly tone. "Excuse me, sir. Can I see your ticket, please?"

I remember where I am and reach up to wipe the drool off the side of my face. I dig into my plastic bag and produce my ticket, much to the inspector's surprise. He examines it and then smiles, shrugging his shoulders. "Sorry, sir, I thought you might have been homeless and riding without a valid ticket, what with the smell and the dried blood and the plastic bag and all."

"You're right on one count, dear chap. My heart wanders without a home, but my ticket is valid indeed." He backs away. I get out my phone and, while My Inspiration is still clearly manifesting herself, I type in the speech she just gave me, word for every majestic word.

I have *the* speech. Now I just have to deliver.

* * *

We pull into Bendigo train station, and under a blazing hot sun I make my way to the bus transfer terminal, rolling my sleeves up in a futile attempt to stem the inevitable sweating.

The bus driver greets my presentation of a valid ticket with the same level of surprise as the inspector on the train. I find a seat near the back and settle in, imagining my reunion with Gloria. She'll be hostile and resistant at first, of course, but with the speech provided by My Inspiration, I calculate the threat of physical injury as medium/low.

After an hour of staring at endless rows of colorless paddocks and disinterested cows, I'm in such a crippling, waking stupor that it takes me hearing it three times to realize the bus driver is yelling at me. I snap out of my low power state and into high processing mode. The bus is empty. The bus has stopped. The bus driver is getting agitated.

"End of the line, mate. You need to get out."

I look through the window. I wouldn't say I'm intimately acquainted with the local sights and cultural markers of Bungleton West, but absolutely nothing looks familiar from my last visit. This place looks like an actual town, rather than a pub in the middle of the bush.

"Hang on, mate. Where are we?" I ask, heading down the aisle to the front of the bus.

"Bungleton."

"Bungleton West?"

"No, Bungleton. Bungleton West is seven kilometers that way."

"You're joking me."

"I joke you not."

He points away from town toward a desolate region that looks precisely like the wasteland of Gloria's hometown.

"But my ticket's for Bungleton West."

"No, it isn't."

"Yes, it is," I say, as I pull it out of my pocket. It's crumpled and torn, but it is most definitely for...

"Achal," I hiss.

"I beg your pardon?"

"My friend Achal bought me this ticket but he's obviously got confused between Bungleton and Bungleton West. Probably because he's Indian."

"Sir?"

"Yes?"

"Get off the bus, please."

"But how am I going to get to Bungleton West?"

"There's no further transport this late on a Sunday."

"It's only five o'clock! Buses run all night in the city."

"I'm terribly sorry, Mr. Gekko, but we don't have need of all night buses out here in the badlands."

Am I getting lip from the bus driver? Is there nobody who finds me above contempt?

"What am I going to do?"

"Walk. It's not that far."

"Can you drive me?"

"No."

"Please."

"Get off the bus."

I can see this hard nut will never crack so I follow his instructions and step down. As I'm walking away he calls out to me.

"Sir!"

Hope surges through my tired legs. He's changed his mind after all!

"Perhaps instead of blaming your Indian friend, you could have checked your own ticket and the giant sign on the top of the bus that says 'Bungleton.' Life's a lot more rewarding when you take charge of your own destiny, you know."

Schooled.

Again.

Barney

Socrates the Bus Driver closes the door and rumbles away. I spend a moment formulating my plan. It's pretty simple really. Just start walking.

* * *

I really should have given this plan a bit more time to formulate before moving straight to execution. I've been walking for fifty-five minutes and I'm now forced to come to terms with my certain, impending death. My impulsive decision to *just start walking* is set to cost me my life. A more rounded human being would probably have gone and bought some water, or food, or even a can of lemonade. Anything to sustain them on a day that is so hot I have run out of sweat.

The road to Bungleton West is a single strip of bitumen with dirt shoulders on either side. I can't walk on the bitumen because it's so hot my feet are sticking to it with every step and it feels like one never-ending piece of black chewing gum. Which sounds disgusting, but given that Achal's care package ran out a couple of hundred kilometers ago, I'd take the black chewy right now to save my life. I'm wearing shoes, by the way, that were not designed for this kind of off-road adventure. They're fashionable, not functional, and I put them on sometime early yesterday afternoon. It's now approaching six o'clock a day later and I'm destined to die in them.

So I'm walking on the dirt shoulder, trying not to slip with each step as I grow weaker and weaker. I need to do something to ensure my survival. I'm not giving up easily, so I think back to all the living in the wild–style programs I have watched over many, many years of television consumption. Surely all that time flicking channels must have embedded in my brain a technique that could now save my life. All that comes to mind is that scene from *National Lampoon's Vacation* when Clark W. Griswold, played by Chevy Chase, wanders lost through the desert. He ties his jacket around his head, bedouin-style, to protect himself from the sun. I don't have a jacket, just a shirt, but it seems like a good idea to me, so I take off my shirt and do the very same, wrapping it around my cap so that it falls from the back of my head and over my shoulders like a cape.

Having no shirt on would normally be a source of near-fatal embarrassment for me, but given that I'm so close to death, all my usual cares have flown away. I feel an immediate improvement in my condition as my core temperature drops a fraction, but enough to keep me alive.

I keep walking.

And I keep walking.

And I keep walking.

Cows low at me. Sheep bleat. A donkey makes that ridiculous donkey sound. And yet no car passes my way. No terrifying, bearded kindergarten teachers are traveling this road tonight.

Why not? Where is everybody? Surely at least one person needs to get from Bungleton to Bungleton West before nightfall?

I keep walking.

I am that one person.

I keep walking.

I am so wretched and debased that horses whinny and rear backward as I pass, flaring their nostrils and rolling their eyes as though I'm here to recruit them for the apocalypse. The earth turns into a giant marshmallow as my legs sink into its fluffy, sugary depths. I want to lie down and taste one last sweet mouthful before I die.

Oh, sweet Gandalf, I'm hallucinating. I'm not going to make it. I'm done for!

And then I see it. A shining beacon of life among the black hole of lifelong boredom all around—the Bungleton West pub. I feel like a wayward mountaineer as he descends from the great peaks to the waiting media throng below, a little bruised and battered, but alive enough to draw a great cheer and flash of cameras as he raises his arms in defiance of death.

This is the vibe I go for when I walk into the pub. It doesn't matter that I'm shirtless and putrid. That I have caked blood in my hair and dust on my designer chinos. What matters is that I'm alive. They can call off the search party. Tell the reporters Barney is alive.

And then, like so many times before, I rather wish I were dead.

The pub is full. They eat early in the country and the scene I encounter is very much like every Western I have ever seen. This is the part when everyone goes silent, stops whatever they're doing, and looks my way.

I reach for my gun.

Then I remember I don't have a gun. So I stand and survey the crowd, looking first across the bar, and then into the dining room beyond.

I find her, and she's looking at me like I'm some kind of heavenly apparition. At least that's how I interpret it. What is abundantly clear is that she cannot believe that I just walked in the door. This is good. It's the shock I was hoping for.

I'm a little giddy now that I've stopped walking, and the pain of the past twenty-four hours has finally caught up with me. But I have to remember

Socrates the Bus Driver's words. Take control of your own destiny, or something like that; I can't recall it exactly. Whatever he said, Socrates would be happy to see what I'm about to do next.

Then I see Socrates at a table next to Gloria's and I get distracted. That lying villain said he couldn't bring me here. I glare at him. He gives me the thumbs-up. "Murderer," I mouth.

I try to swallow but it feels like that time I poured an entire can of chocolate milk powder into my mouth, though less delicious. But I have to speak. My speech is ready. I begin.

"Gloria." It comes out as a croak, but it sends a ripple of whispering through the crowd.

"He's a friend of Gloria's."

"He's obviously from the city."

"Why doesn't he have any stomach muscles?"

Gloria doesn't move from her table. She's not going to make this easy for me. And neither should she.

I cast my mind back to *the* speech, but can't remember the next line, so I take my phone out of my pocket. "Gloria, I have no right to be here. Not in your life, not in your town, certainly not in this room with you."

And then I stop reading.

Because I didn't come all this way to recite a scripted speech.

I came here to be the man Achal likes, the one Beth and Mike once knew, and the man I hope Gloria will one day love.

The crowd is still silent, all staring, all waiting for my next words. Stamper is sitting with Gloria's family. I catch his eye and he gives me a nod. I put my phone in my pocket, take a deep breath, and then project my voice across the room. "I'm not very good at life."

Nobody moves.

"I find the simplest things very challenging. Dressing myself, for example." I hold my arms out at my sides so they can get a good look at my filthy, shirtless torso. There's a ripple of laughter.

My head throbs.

Come on, Barney. Keep going.

"Social interactions are fraught with danger. When I'm introduced to somebody, I never know whether to go for the kiss or the handshake." I look at Stamper again and chance my arm. I have to take some risks if this is going to work. "Thankfully, Stamper doesn't mind a peck on the cheek."

People laugh. A man hoots. Stamper inclines his head and winks to let me know we're all good.

My confidence builds.

My limbs ache.

"I'm from the city..."

"We can tell by your waxed chest, Fabio!" It's the orange-haired waitress who threatened to have me cut by a left-hander.

"Don't be fooled," I say to the crowd. "This hairless bust is a natural phenomenon." I lock eyes with the waitress and smile. "It's lovely to see you, again, by the way. I can't wait for another lukewarm serving of your signature food poisoning tonight." I turn back to the crowd. "Seriously, when I got home after eating here, they had to read me my last rites five days in a row."

Another round of laughter. Louder this time.

My stomach cramps.

"Anyway, as I was saying, I'm from the city. And you'd expect a bloke from the city to know how to catch a bus, right? Well, I tried to catch a bus to Bungleton West, and ended up in Bungleton. I would have been here a lot earlier, but instead of offering me a ride, your friendly bus driver"—I point to Socrates—"decided he'd try to kill me instead. Has anyone actually been outside today? Would you have made me walk seven kilometers in my chinos if you wanted me to live?"

Socrates shrugs his shoulders. "You didn't have a valid ticket. What did you want me to do?"

Somebody directs a good-natured boo at him and the crowd joins in. People are booing and it's not because of me.

This is my most successful routine in years!

Socrates raises his arms in surrender, but he's smiling along. "Hey, I don't make the rules. I just follow them."

More booing.

The people are turning. They're on my side. Now is my chance.

"You're probably wondering what I'm doing here."

"It's not for your good looks!"

Work with it, Barney.

"Fair call. I could use a wash. And a checked shirt. But I'm not here to do a stand-up routine, either. I'm here because although I'm not very good at life and I find most things pretty difficult, there's one thing that comes as naturally to me as breathing."

I look at Gloria. Her face is neutral. I hold her gaze.

"And that's loving Gloria Bell. It's the easiest, smartest, and most accomplished thing I'll ever do."

Still, Gloria gives me nothing. The crowd has gone silent again. I plead for her forgiveness with my eyes. I try, with that one, silent stare, to tell her how sorry I am.

It feels like nobody is breathing. Like everybody is waiting for Gloria to make her decision. It feels like they're on my side.

Yet, still, she gives me nothing.

I'm having trouble focusing now and my hands are shaking.

"Gloria," I say, but there's nothing more. My physical ordeal has overcome me and all I have left is a mind full of useless information and crippling regrets. Lines from songs and movies and television commercials. That's all I've got.

The room begins to spin. The pain is approaching childbirth level. I have to speak before it's too late.

Find something, Barney. Find something in there that tells her what she means to you.

"Gloria," I say again, possibly for the last time. "You had me at hello."

And then I fall into the strong, immovable arms of death.

* * *

Turns out they were actually Stamper's arms. At least I assume they were, because he's the one who's now carrying me up a flight of stairs. He's like a forklift with me lying across those prong things at the front, except that he's supporting my head in the crook of his elbow like I'm a baby. Who'd have known a man with such a perfectly geometric jaw could be capable of such tenderness?

We enter a bedroom and he lays me onto a firm single bed. My final resting place. He puts a bottle of water to my lips. Though I want to tell him it's wasted on a dying man, I sip at it nonetheless. No point dying thirsty. Another man enters the room. I close my eyes as he prods, pokes, asks me to breathe, and takes my temperature, all in vain, of course, but he is bound by the Hippocratic oath.

"Thank you, doctor," I whisper, because it's important to show gratitude to those who have tried to save you.

"I'm not a doctor," he says. "I'm a vet."

This is an unwelcome development. I don't mind dying in a foreign place beside a checked-shirt cowboy, but to have my final physical examination performed by a veterinarian is an insult I don't want to take with me into the afterlife.

It galvanizes me to sit up, which I do with Stamper's assistance.

"You'll be all right," the vet says, though I'm not sure why you he thinks I should take his diagnosis seriously. "You're suffering from heat exhaustion and dehydration. Plenty of water and rest over the next twenty-four hours will get you back on track."

"Thanks, Reg," Stamper says.

"Pleasure."

Reg the vet leaves the room and Stamper pulls up a chair beside my bed. "How you feeling, mate?"

"Like a lame dog."

He laughs. "Why are you wearing your shirt around your head?"

"To protect it from the sun."

"But you're wearing a hat."

"So was Chevy Chase."

Stamper grips my arm, as if to steady me from falling into complete delirium.

"You don't smell great."

"I could do with a wash."

He lets go of my arm. "I think that might be a bit beyond me."

"Not by you!" We sit in awkward silence, and if he's imagining what I'm imagining, the awkwardness is well deserved.

"Where's Gloria?" I ask.

"Downstairs with her family."

"Is she going to come up and see me?"

"Her exact words were something like 'let him rot in the eternal fire pits of hell.'"

I blanch. I've never blanched before, but now seems like an appropriate time to add it to my repertoire.

Stamper laughs and slaps his knee. "I'm only joking, mate! She's not that cold-hearted."

Country people. They're hilarious.

"Yeah, of course. I know that. I was just playing along. Gloria would never talk about rotting in a fire. It's an internally inconsistent metaphor."

"Listen, Barney. I've known Gloria my whole life. I don't know what you did but she's pretty angry with you right now." He leans in close. "You didn't hurt her, did you?"

"No! Never! I'd never hurt her."

"Good, because if you did, I'd be compelled to kill you."

I try to laugh away my very genuine concerns that he isn't joking.

"What did you do?"

"I betrayed her for my own gain at work. But that's why I'm here, Stamper. To tell her how sorry I am."

"Hmmm. Well, it's a good start, I guess. I'll go downstairs and see if I can get her to come up and talk to you."

"Thanks, mate."

Stamper stands up and heads to the door.

"Stamper, wait."

He turns in the doorway.

"Do you think she'll forgive me?"

He gives me an appraising stare and rubs his beautiful chin. "Hard to say, Barney. But there's one thing I know for sure...she's worth the fight."

* * *

As far as ebbs go, I think it's fair to say I'm at my lowest. I'm sitting propped up in the bed of a stranger with unknown personal hygiene standards while still wearing my shirt around my head.

I'm shirtless and covered in a thick layer of sweat-caked dust that can't hide the fact my core muscles have been neglected for the past two decades. I continue to reek of a man who hasn't showered in more than twenty-four hours but who has done a significant amount of sweating in that time, with his only counter measure being the application of far too much of a cologne favored by unnecessarily aggressive Indian males. My head feels like it's in a tightening vise, my legs ache like the plague, and my stomach is in two minds about whether to just give it all away and cast itself out through my throat.

And I'm pretty sure Gloria is about to tell me she never wants to see me again.

In short, low ebb. Seriously low ebb.

I close my eyes to try to ward off the throbbing pain encircling my head. Then the door opens, creaking to announce an arrival. I breathe in. And breathe out. This is it.

I don't need to open my eyes to know it's her, but when I do, I am rewarded with a vision of the woman I love looking at me like I'm roadkill. She is backlit by the shaft of light that floods into the otherwise dim room. Her hair is out and falling around her face as she leans forward to examine me. She is dressed in jeans and a light blue, short-sleeved shirt. Something about the way she is looking at me tells me there may still be a chance. I don't know what it is exactly, but I wait in hope for her next words. Words of redemption and rebirth.

"Are you going to vomit?"

I hadn't planned that far ahead, but since Gloria has mentioned it, my body now seems to think it's a pretty good idea. I lean over the side of the bed to find a bucket left there by the vet; not such an amateur, after all. I vomit with sufficient gusto to bring on a bout of sweating that cuts rivulets through the dust on my body. My head pounds in time with my convulsing chest, I have a heavy snot discharge and I think the heaving may have reopened the cut on my head because I can now feel something warm and sticky running into my ear.

"Well, you sure are a catch. Which lucky girl is your date for the night?"

Despite the pain that now owns my body, I take hope and courage in the absence of an immediate, outright berating. I try to be funny *and* contemporary. "Do you fancy your chances in a rose ceremony downstairs?"

"Do you really think this is the time for a vacuous pop-culture reference?"

Okay, that's it, I'm done. It's time to fall on my sword. "That's just the problem, Gloria. I will always say stupid things like that because it's in my DNA. Instead of saying 'don't be vacuous', you might as well say 'don't be Barney.' I am who I am, and I'll never be good enough for you."

"What a load of sad sack, self-pitying drivel," Gloria says, sitting down in the chair beside the bed. "I can't figure you out, Barney. You show glimpses of being a great man..."

Hang on a minute. Sudden ebb increase!

"...then you demonstrate that you're so weak and spineless and completely lacking in any kind of self-confidence or self-belief."

Ebb decrease.

"And then you do this." She waves her hand over me, *Exhibit A.* "I'm not even really sure what this is, or how you've ended up here, shirtless and doing a second-rate Bear Grylls impersonation."

"Clark W. Griswold."

Gloria laughs. "Okay, so sometimes your vacuous pop culture references do work." She sighs and shakes her head. "I can see that you've done this for me, Barney. And as angry and disappointed with you as I am, I can't help but be just a little bit impressed."

"I was going for a lot impressed."

"Don't push your luck. You used it all up in your routine. That was a risky strategy you employed out there. Mocking the locals could have got you into some serious trouble."

"Calculated risk. Since they're all closet comedians, I figured they'd be able to laugh at themselves. I'm not as dumb as I look, remember."

"Okay, slightly more impressed now."

"You're the only one that matters, Gloria. And I know you're a Chevy Chase fan, so this..." I spread my arms "...is all for your benefit."

Gloria smiles. "You see, Barney, this is what it should be like. This is what it *could* be like with you all the time. Natural. Unforced. No weirdness. But just when I start to think you're actually a pretty good guy, you go and betray me. And not just betray me, but betray me to Jake MacIntyre of all people."

I don't even start to defend myself. Because what I did was indefensible. It's time for me to stop believing my own lies. Of course I knew MacIntyre was bad news. Of course I knew something wasn't right and there was no way he was interested in recruiting me based on word-of-mouth about my work with the department. I still don't know exactly what his motivation was, but it certainly included duping me into coughing up our campaign idea so he could steal Rogerson's account. And, worst of all, I knew that he had done something to hurt Gloria.

But I ignored all that because I was selfish and foolish and reckless, and the only good to come from this debacle is that, for the first time I can remember, I'm being honest with myself. I can see myself clearly. And I don't like what I see. At least not all of it, anyway.

I want to do something about it. I want to be better, but I'm not convinced I can repair the broken parts alone. For that, I will need an *us*. "Gloria, can I show you something?"

"Haven't you already shown me enough?" She inclines her head at my dirt- and sweat-caked body.

An idiotic, self-deprecating joke comes immediately to mind.

And I let it go unsaid.

For once, I let it go unsaid.

I reach into my pocket and take out my phone. I hand her *the* speech. "This says it all."

Gloria reads in silence. I'm hoping for some sort of clue in her facial expression to what she's thinking. Her mouth is neutral, her eyes are clear, and her breathing is steady. She hands me back the phone. "Did you write this?"

"Yes."

"Do you mean it?"

"More than anything."

"You still have to resign."

"I know."

She goes quiet and I see her retreat within herself, as though she's having a conversation behind closed doors. I watch her, but she doesn't meet my eyes. Hers are seeing something I cannot, until the moment she resurfaces and her gaze locks on mine, steady and strong.

"The last time you were here, you asked me to marry you."

"And you've had a change of heart?"

"I'm not marrying you, Barney. But I've decided not to completely rule you out of my life, either."

"Sounds fair." Actually, it sounds like the greatest thing that's ever happened to me.

Gloria takes my hand. It is the contact I have so longed for, and it is as wondrous as I had hoped. I'm not yet capable of moving, but even if I was, I would rather lie here forever in this stranger's bed than have her take her hand away.

"I want you to promise me something, Barney."

"I promise. Whatever it is, I promise."

"I'm serious."

"So am I."

"I want you to promise me that you'll stop trying to be somebody else. Stop trying to be what you think everyone wants you to be. Stop trying to be what you think I want you to be. Just be yourself."

Mum, Achal, Gloria...I'm sensing a thread.

Gloria squeezes my hand and smiles like she can't help it. "Be the guy who just *owned* that room of closet comedians downstairs. You know they all want to buy you a bourbon now, right?"

"That's a terrifying prospect." I squeeze her hand back. "But what's even more terrifying is that you might not like me when I'm myself."

"Then it's not meant to be, Barney. But I'd rather try, and fail with someone genuine than spend the whole time I'm with you wondering who's really there behind the facade."

I take a deep breath. "Okay, Gloria. I promise."

She squeezes my hand tight. "Good. For now, though, you need to shower, and eat, and sleep. We'll take you back to our place, but don't get ahead of yourself. You've got a long way to go before you're off the hook completely."

I close my eyes and the pain in my head begins to subside. In this darkness, the touch of Gloria's hand is magnified on my skin. I'm battered, bruised, and filthy. I'm lying topless in a stranger's bed. But with Gloria's hand in my own, I don't need to get ahead of myself. I'm exactly where I belong.

FIFTEEN

It's two days after my return from Gloria's farm and I'm officially unemployed. Archie waived my notice period because he thought I was having some kind of nervous breakdown. "What do you mean you don't have a job to go to?" he asked.

"I'm just going to take some time out to see what it is I really want to do with my life."

He recoiled and made the sign of the cross.

"All right, well you can finish today. I'll pay you to the end of the week."

"Thank you, but that's not necessary."

He raised his hand to silence me. "Enough! Rogerson Communications looks after its own. In the good times, and in personal, mental crisis. Roger that!"

I've come back to Lucien and Gisele's apartment to use the wireless Internet—Mum's a little slow when it comes to modern technology—and, thankfully, the happy couple is not around. I've got my laptop set up and I'm scouring job sites for inspiration. I think I still want to stay in communications—there's nothing else I can really do—but I need to find the right employer. A private sector firm with a public sector attitude would be perfect, although mythical.

The buzzer rings. I stand up and walk to the video intercom, wondering if it's Achal hiding again so that the CIA can't get his image. But it's not Achal, and this man is not afraid of being on camera.

"Hello, Jake."

"Barney, mate, sorry to ambush you like this but I really need to talk to you."

"The last time I talked to you, you stole our idea and cost me my job. I think we're done talking."

He looks remorseful, at least as much as he can through the grainy fish-eye lens. "Listen, that's one of the things I want to talk to you about. I didn't mean for that to happen. Not the way it did, I swear. It just kind of spiraled out of my control. Let me come up and talk about it. I brought muffins."

Muffins? Is this guy for real?

I don't respond.

"Please, Barney. Just hear me out. I think you'll like what I've got to say."

I hesitate. What would Old Barney have done? Run down to greet him like an excited lapdog? Probably, especially since he has muffins. What does New Barney, Real Barney, want to do? Well, frankly, I want to hear what this is all about. If I turn him away, I'll never know why he's back when there's nothing more I can do for him now.

"All right. But not for long. I'm very busy."

I curse my decision to wear tracksuit pants instead of jeans today. Levi boot cuts would have done a much better job of *not* giving the impression I've given up all hope the way tracksuit pants do. When I open the door to Jake, he looks and smells as incredible as I remember. My instinct is to bow before him, but New Barney doesn't bow. He plays it cool.

"S'up?"

"Can I come in?"

"Yep."

We sit down opposite each other at the kitchen table. I don't offer him a drink, but I do take one of his muffins. Nothing wrong with that. New Barney can take hospitality if he wants to.

"How did you know where I live?" I ask, forgetting for a moment that I no longer live here.

"I know people." Jake smiles winningly and I try very hard not to be won. Very hard. But it's an extremely winning smile!

I keep it together. "Right. So why are you here?"

"To explain."

"There's nothing to explain. You tricked me, used me, and betrayed me. You played me for a complete fool, and now I have no job and very slim prospects of getting another one."

"Come and work at MacDaddy."

I drop my muffin.

"I know that sounds unexpected, but let me explain. When we took your idea, we weren't pitching for that job, I swear it. It was just out of curiosity to see what kind of work Gloria was producing. We were asked to pitch at late notice after the department realized they hadn't met their procurement requirements."

"I find that hard to believe. Nothing gets past the procurement officers."

"Not usually, but they made a mistake because the procurement team thought the incumbent agency was pitching for the job. They weren't."

"Which meant they needed another one to comply with departmental policy," I say.

"I'm not pretending I didn't do anything wrong," Jake says. "I shouldn't have used your concept.

But..." He spreads his arms, raises his hands, and shrugs his shoulders. "My competitive instincts got the better of me. And it was such an amazing idea!"

"Yeah, but it was *our* amazing idea. You had no right to pitch it as your own."

"I know, and for that I'm sorry. But it's done. I want this campaign to be a success. And I want you leading it, Barney."

Jake leans down and opens the leather satchel beside his chair. He takes out a document and lays it on the table, pushing it my way. I drag it toward me with one finger and scan my eyes over the front page, maintaining a pre–Daniel Craig, James Bond kind of cool.

Until I see the salary. "That's nearly twice what they're paying me now!"

Jake laughs. "You probably should keep that to yourself, Barney. It's not a great negotiation technique."

You failed me, Brosnan!

"But why do you want to pay me so much?"

"Because I'm taking a backseat, and I want you to be the Operations Manager. As well as leading this campaign, you'll also need your finger in every other MacDaddy pie. You'll be working hard, but I'll be paying you well."

"What will you be doing?"

"Concentrating on my real estate portfolio."

Of course.

I pretend I'm reading the contract to buy myself some time. My instincts are at war. The integrity instinct is telling me to tear the contract up in his face. The mortgage instinct is telling me to sign it before he withdraws the offer. I think about Gloria. How would she react to this? I mean, I wouldn't be betraying her. I never said I wouldn't go to Mac-Daddy, although that's only because we never anticipated me actually being offered a job. But Jake won't be there anyway, so what difference does it make whether I'm working there or at any other firm? Who am I kidding, though? No other firm is going to give me this opportunity. It's the classic once-in-a-lifetime offer.

The best offer I will ever receive.

"Jake, this is a great offer. I'd be crazy not to take it."

Jake claps his hands together. "Good man! You're going to absolutely tear it up at MacDaddy, Barney. I know people, and I know you're going to be a superstar."

"You don't know people that well, Jake." His hands are still clasped in a clap, but his smile fades. "I'm saying no."

Jake flinches. It's the first time I've ever seen him caught off guard. His smile disappears completely. He cocks his head as though he's misheard me. "Are you serious?"

"Yes. One hundred percent."

He looks like I just told him I turned down front row tickets to Adele. "But why?"

"Because there's more to life than gainful employment, Jake. There's more to life than being defined by your job."

"Of course, yeah, I get that. Work-life balance and all that stuff, right? If you're worried about the hours, you shouldn't be. We work hard but we play hard, too."

"It's not the hours."

"So it's something else."

"Yes."

"It's someone else."

This is about to get very awkward, but New Barney doesn't run from awkwardness if that's what it takes to be true to himself. Old Barney would have faked a heart attack right now. But not New Barney. New Barney is facing this front on, which may give him a genuine heart attack anyway.

"It is someone else, Jake, but I think we've talked enough. Thank you for your very generous offer, but I'm going to let it pass."

"Barney, I want you to think about what you're saying. Take another look at that salary. Nobody is every going to offer you that kind of money again."

"Money's not everything, Jake."

Jake's tone takes on a nasty edge. "Seriously, Barney, did you write the book on how to be the world's biggest loser? Can you hear yourself right now?"

"I think you should leave, Jake."

"I think you should start listening to me." He stands up, places his hands on the table, and leans forward so his face is close enough that I can see the crow's-feet around his eyes. For the first time, I notice that he looks tired in the natural light. His eyes are bloodshot and his skin tone is more orange than brown. His teeth are so impossibly white, they betray his ridiculous vanity. "Before you go throwing away the greatest opportunity of your life, there's something you need to know about Gloria, mate. You need to know about the game she's playing."

"What are you talking about?"

"Oh, come on. Don't tell me you haven't noticed." He bears his teeth as he talks. "She's all cozy and friendly when she wants something from you, and then when you ask for a little bit you're entitled to in return, she suddenly becomes Little Miss

Purity." He sneers at me. "Or haven't you asked for a piece, yet?"

"A piece of what?"

He scoffs. "Oh man, Barney, you really are as stupid as you look. No wonder you spent so long in the public service. A hack like you would never make it in the real world."

This is really confusing. And pretty insulting as well, just quietly. "Then why did you just offer me a job?"

"To destroy Gloria!" Jake slams his fist down on the table and I jump up from my chair. "It's obvious she needs you to win these government accounts, and I don't want her getting close to *anything* that looks like success. Not her and not anybody who supports her."

"Why? Why do you hate her so much?"

Jake stands up tall and draws his lips back in a fiendish, joyless smile. "Because you don't say no to Jake MacIntyre."

They don't give medals to cowards, you know. Because cowardice, you see, is man's natural inclination. It is the innate response of a frightened heart. That's why courage is so valued. It challenges the easy path. The natural path. The path I'm *refusing* to walk right now.

I stand up to my full height, puff out what exists of my chest, and put on my best Russell Crowe as Maximus voice. "Well, Gloria said no to you. And I'm saying no to you. So I don't think that whole 'you don't say no to Jake MacIntyre' thing is working out so well for you."

Jake curls his top lip as he appraises me. Then he rounds the table. I hold my ground. Jake fronts right up to me, his chest less than a hand's length away, his nose almost touching mine. Even though he's about to pulverize me, he still smells great.

I swallow.

Jake reaches up and takes my T-shirt in both his fists.

He pushes me back against the wall.

I brace myself.

The front door opens and two people tumble in, laughing and intertwined.

They see us and freeze.

Nobody moves.

Until Lucien speaks. "Get your hands off my mate, pretty boy, or I'll ask Gisele here to scratch your eyes out. And she's a fingernail model, so you really don't want that to happen." Gisele sidesteps Lucien, places her feet shoulder-width apart, raises her fists, and does her Ms. Wolverine.

Jake lets go of my T-shirt but doesn't step back. "You're pathetic, Conroy. And you'll never be anything in this industry. I'll personally see to that. You *and* Gloria are finished."

"Party's over, Goldilocks," Lucien says. He grabs Jake by the shoulders, spins him around, and, in one deft and awesomely powerful move, throws him out the door. Gisele picks up Jake's bag, chucks it in his face, and then she and Lucien slam the door together.

I look at the two of them. They look at me.

We all burst out laughing.

EPILOGUE

If this was a fictional story, the author of my life would probably, by now, have given me a ton of amazing job offers to make up for the one I turned down. To demonstrate to the reader that the path of integrity leads to reward. That good guys can finish on top.

But this isn't a fictional story. This is my life. My messy, chaotic, magnificent life. So I have not had a single job offer, and not even an interview for a permanent role. I've managed to score myself a short-term contract, though, and I'm running a campaign for the launch of a sustainable, organic dog food. I'm really excited about being back in the game, and I think there's a lot I can do with socialization and cross-channel pollination on this one.

Chad, Gloria, Diana, and Achal are all still working at Rogerson. Chad and I aren't best mates, exactly, but we do have a good time whenever I meet them for Friday night drinks.

Achal and I have started playing tennis against each other on Tuesday nights. He's very good, and very competitive. He abuses the ball a lot, and me even more. It's terrific fun.

Our tennis matches are part of my new program of personal improvement that includes physical exercise and not periodically drinking myself into mind-warping oblivion. I actually feel pretty good, and even took part in this amazing, multichannel engagement campaign called Track Your Attack.

I've given myself four weeks to write a new stand-up comedy routine and make my triumphant return to the Richmond Tavern open-mic night. I'll run some focus testing this time. Achal might be my best bet. He's brutal, and has no regard for my feelings, but he was the only reason I got a laugh that first, auspicious night.

Mike and Beth have another baby on the way. I know, can you believe it? Some people, right? I'm secretly hoping it will be a girl and I'm secretly *very* excited about holding her in my arms.

Lucien and Gisele have moved to Latin America. He sends me, on average, four selfies a day from his villa overlooking the ocean. They're getting married at the end of the year and I think I might just make my international flight debut to be at the wedding.

Before that, though, I'm accompanying Mum to this year's TV industry Logie Awards. She's being inducted into the Hall of Fame, and I can't wait to walk the red carpet with her, proud to be her son.

As for my romantic adventures, well, Gloria and I are taking it slowly. We don't want to rush, and are more focused on getting to know each other better before we commit to joint back accounts. This is important given that I only recently met New Barney myself and need to get to know him a little better as well.

After I turned down Jake's job offer, Gloria told me the whole story about what happened to her at MacDaddy. It was her dream job working in such a high-profile agency with someone as visionary as Jake. He asked her out for a drink one night to celebrate a campaign win. She thought it would be a career-limiting move to turn down an invite from the agency owner. A drink turned into dinner and, as she described it, there was a misunderstanding about how she was going to express her gratitude for the meal. The rumors about her started two days later. Vile, baseless lies that attacked her character and virtue. She couldn't stay on in that environment, and that's when she went back home. I asked her why she didn't file a complaint and she told me I'd know the answer to that question if I were a woman. The inferno of injustice that burns inside me when I think about it must be like the tiniest spark compared to Gloria's own outrage. But she doesn't dwell on it and she's told me not to, either. So we're both reducing Jake to a distasteful memory that has no bearing on our future together.

A future, I might add, that's looking pretty bright, considering Gloria and I have now been out to dinner five times. It is my great hope that a day will come when I never have to eat dinner without her again. But that's probably a little ambitious for now.

For now, I'm just happy with what I've got.

And you know what? You're not supposed to get fired from the public service.

But I'm glad they fired me.

CAN I ASK A FAVOR?

See that picture there?

That's me being REALLY happy whenever somebody leaves a review of my book online. You don't have to say much and it only takes a few minutes.

If you can spare a moment to share your thoughts, I'd be extremely grateful. Every review is so important!

Thanks! Guy

ACKNOWLEDGEMENTS

It took me four years to write and publish *Barney* and there are many people I'd like to thank.

Mum, Dad, Matt, Dave and Emma who have supported and believed in me the whole way through.

My friends who read and commented on various drafts as the story developed—Jon, Rob, Shane and Scott (who also helped me realize that writing is artistic, publishing is commercial).

Kiele Raymond, my editor, for making this an immeasurably better novel, and for understanding Barney and sharing my passion to tell his story. It was like you knew him better than I did!

Lyn Tranter, for her advocacy and support, and whose belief that I had written something worth reading convinced me to find a way. Kit Foster, my designer, for sharing his talent to create a cover that could not have better captured the story's spirit and purpose. David Coen, my copyeditor, whose keen eye eliminated mistakes I didn't even know I was capable of making.

The Wattpad community, who so generously supported my short stories about Barney, and the

Wattpad staff who featured and then awarded my collection *The Chronicles of Barnia*; your encouragement helped me to put this book into the world.

My children, Abigail, Beatrix and Leo, who inspire me and who tell me such wonderful stories of their own. You are more creative than I will ever be!

Finally, I could not have written this book without the love, support and guidance of my wife, Anna, to whom it is dedicated. Early on, she told me the story had lost its way, and that's what helped me to put it back on track. Thank you, my love, for being my fiercest and most dedicated critic.

ABOUT THE AUTHOR

Guy Sigley lives in Melbourne, Australia. A father of three young children, Guy is a stay-at-home dad. In easier times, he worked in marketing communications in the public service.

After writing many manuscripts over many years that nobody particularly wanted to read, Guy decided it was time to try his hand at comedy.

He brings you *Barney: A novel (about a guy called Barney)* in the hope it will make you laugh, maybe cry, and certainly see a little bit of Barney in yourself.

www.guysigley.com